There is an irreverent and joking air about Pazzi's writing. But his proposition is not simply aggressive and sacrilegious. . . . In reality Pazzi's game is serious. Behind his irreverent sense of invention there is a readily apparent measure of sympathy, a religiousness, and a tenderness in confronting the fragility of the world that is the conclave; at its belonging to another time, at its obstinant resistance to the vortex of contemporary globalization. . . . The sarcastic sneer becomes a smile. From the series of comic events ultimately emerges a conciliatory solution between the past and the present, between Rome and the world, between the ancient Occidental culture and new peoples. Between reality and fantasy, between games and the truth.

— *L'Unità*

A captivating, surreal novel. Irreverent, yet not cynical. . . . From these pages transpire ideals now obsolete in today's times, like hope for a world that is more just in its treatment of the vanquished. This though, comes between the lines. The lines themselves are literally diabolical, for it is the Devil who leads the dance between the walls of the antiquated, sacred Palace, where the aging princes of the Church have gathered to deliberate who among them is the most deserving of the papal throne. Not even Fellini, with his Rome populated by silent monsignors dancing on rollerskates, dared such a bold undertaking. . . . Refreshing, and uncannily of our times.

— *La Rebublica*

Pazzi is meticulous in recreating the ambience of that high-ranking prison, with all its rituals, hidden maneuvers, its secret obligations of daily life. . . . As much as the author is faithful to the realities of this historic event, he abandons himself to his imagination as the story unfolds. . . . The narrative proceeds along a razor's edge where fantasy risks descending into the grotesque; indeed the distance from the sublime to the ridiculous at times seems precariously narrow. But fortunately the author has calculated well, and keeps the novel on firm footing.

— *La Stampa*

Conclave

Conclave

A NOVEL

Roberto Pazzi

TRANSLATED BY OONAGH STRANSKY

STEERFORTH ITALIA

AN IMPRINT OF STEERFORTH PRESS · SOUTH ROYALTON, VERMONT

Conclave
by Roberto Pazzi

First published in Italian by Edizioni Frassinelli, Milan, 2001

Printed in Canada

Conclave is winner of the 2001 Zerilli-Marimò Prize for Italian Fiction, spon-
sored by New York University and the Fondazione Maria and Goffredo Bel-
lonci. Funding is made possible by Baroness Zerilli-Marimò, as well as through
contributions from Casa della Letterature in Italy. The publishers would like to
thank Baroness Zerilli-Marimò for her support of this publication.

The translator and the publisher would like to acknowledge Teresa Lust for her
editorial contributions to this translation, and to thank her for her expertise,
help, and guidance.

For information about permission to reproduce
selections from this book, write to:
Steerforth Press L.C., P.O. Box 70,
South Royalton, Vermont 05068

Library of Congress Cataloging-in-Publication Data

Pazzi, Roberto, 1946–
[Conclave. English]
Conclave / Roberto Pazzi ; translated by Oonagh Stransky.
p. cm.
ISBN 1-58642-066-6 (alk. paper)
I. Stransky, Oonagh. II. Title.
PQ4876.A98C6613 2003
853'.914–dc21

2002154517

FIRST EDITION

At times, only the eye of Madness can behold the sun.
RITA MAZZINI

T

I

*I*T IS HARD TO tell what time it is, because all night long it seemed like dawn was breaking, due perhaps to the light that had been left on in the room facing his. Upon rising he was able to make out indistinct figures in motion behind the dark yellow glass of the opaque window. The movements of the apparitions had been accompanied by the sound of a dog howling, more a call than a lament, as if the animal were trying to capture the attention of whomever was awake on the uppermost floor — either he himself, or the unknown guests in the room behind the yellow window. The courtyard was so dark and narrow that he could not see the dog, if indeed it was down there at all.

The bells begin to ring from all corners of Rome, heralding the arrival of the morning light and drowning out the dog's mournful baying. Morning Masses are being announced, and it is not unlikely that the prayers of the priests and the thoughts of the faithful during those services will focus on the events that will be taking place in that very building where he is trying so hard to fall back to sleep.

Not all of his companions in this adventure, the illustrious guests in that wing of the Apostolic Palace, suffer from insomnia. One morning they had been joined in the Sistine Chapel after a noticeable delay by one of their youngest members, His Eminence of Ireland, who had only recently been elevated to the rank of cardinal. Immediately, one of the electors most inclined to believe in presentiments predicted that the young cardinal would be the one elected, and on that very day. His prediction was subsequently proved wrong not just once, but in both rounds of voting. His had not been a sleep visited by the Holy Spirit, but simply delayed by a weakness of the flesh.

One of the oldest cardinals, Oviedo of Madrid, who was also having difficulty closing his eyes at night, remembered the silence that had reigned throughout those high-ceilinged rooms during the last conclave — only two surviving electors were there now to remember it. The events had unfolded in very little time, but Rome was a different city then; to begin with, the sound of its traffic could not yet be detected rising up into their rooms in the palace.

"If you buy yourself some good wax earplugs, like the ones I have, your problem will be as good as solved," Celso Rabuiti, the cardinal of Palermo, had suggested to his Spanish colleague in his usual ironic way.

Who could be sleeping behind those yellow glass windows? He can't figure it out, although that part of the palace, on the third floor, does seem to be occupied primarily by Italian cardinals.

The Italians are the most active faction, meeting on a daily basis during the break between the morning and afternoon rounds of voting in hopes of reaching an agreement as to who should receive their vote. The loss of the papacy weighs heavily on the Italian people, and it is rumored that a top political figure has even put pressure on an Italian member of the Sacred College: "It doesn't matter if he's from the south, or even if he's old, but please, Your Eminence, elect an Italian. The nation does not enjoy the position in the European Union that it so rightly deserves; we have such strong hopes. Make sure an Italian gets elected. . . ." Such rumors evoke ghosts of the past, such as

Puzyna, the bishop of Krakow, who presented the veto of the Austrian emperor during the conclave in which Sarto would ultimately become Pius X. These days manipulation is much less direct, much less obvious. He didn't think an Italian politician would ever act like that now.

Those restless shadows, their forms indistinct yet lively during the night, seem like some kind of silent theater or a Chinese shadow play, mimicking life and alluding to its essentials: power, intimacy, anger, seduction, words accentuated by silence and gesture, secrecy, conspiracy, prayer.

It might not be the only room where shadows lurk at such a late hour, but he is not aware of any others. He can only think about them. Just like the millions of people who at that very moment, in one part of the world, are sleeping and dreaming, while in the other part they are running around like crazed ants, only to have their roles reversed later on. He has always been amazed at just how hard it is to imagine those who are far away, especially those who are dearest to him, as they move about in his absence. Thinking about them never made them seem any more alive; instead, it only made him feel lonelier. That is why he loves photographs and telephone calls, even though they only serve to intensify his nostalgia.

Still, those shadows provoke a number of questions, sparking his curiosity as to what will happen when they disappear and the figures emerge from the room in the flesh. They also convince him that he will not succeed in returning to sleep, although he does not yet want to wake up Contarini. From the absolute silence in the adjoining room he can tell that his chaplain and personal secretary is still sleeping. He looks over at the telephone. Should he call his sister, Clara, in Bologna? No, it's too early. He wonders if Francesco, his nephew, took his engineering exam. It would have been his second attempt, and he had even asked his uncle to say a prayer for him.

There he is, together with his mother, in the silver-framed photo that the archbishop brings with him wherever he goes. The older Francesco gets, the less he looks like his father. He certainly doesn't look like me, the cardinal thinks. No, more like his grandmother, or his poor uncle, Carlo — his nose, or his mouth when he laughs. Uncles and aunts are quite valuable when studying resemblances, but at the risk of finding all sorts of mysteries in kinship.

He tries to lie down again, forcing himself to stay in bed a little bit longer. It is only five o'clock in the morning. He can't say Mass with Contarini until seven. Instead of speculating on the shadows across from him, or on his nephew's family traits, he should pray. So many people have asked him to remember them in his prayers, and almost all of them have confided in him — a sorrow, a worry, a fault, a secret.

He looks at the gilded prie-dieu with its scarlet cushion, set up beneath the crucifix, a furnishing that must be present in the cell of each of the 127 cardinals in the conclave. He thinks of everyone praying in the same pose, with the same gestures, all of them dressed in red and black. An assembly line of prayer. He wouldn't be part of it. He can pray lying down in bed while looking at the frescoes on the vaulted ceiling, the molding on the gilded doors, the ornamental details on the armoire that opens up onto a small altar where he celebrates Mass.

He picks up his rosary and begins to recite his prayers for the members of his congregation who are most in need. A woman whose twenty-year-old son is dying of cancer. A man whose two daughters are heroin addicts who had disappeared for a year, but are now in a rehabilitation center. An elderly widow with no family. Two men — a mayor and the president of a large company — who lacked the courage to confess why they needed spiritual assistance, but simply said that they did. Maybe it was the sense of guilt that the powerful sometimes have, or maybe they were involved in some kind of scandal.

He begins to pray, and from the images of his devout rises a vague and confused fetor of weakness, vice, turpitude, and egoism: the primary matter from which all humans are made, including himself and the shadows in motion across the way. But there is also a strange capacity for giving oneself over to something, for expending oneself fully for a person one loves. Truly, he thinks, the only power capable of releasing people from egoism is still love. And the miracle of loving another person more than oneself still occurs. He looks at the crucifix hanging on the wall. It is twisted and dark, the work of an eighteenth-century sculptor who wanted to give his creation an expressionistic touch, a Flemish accent, something northern. The ribs are splayed, the bones exposed, the body arched and tense, its countenance furrowed with suffering. The loincloth swathes the body loosely, as if a strong wind were tearing it away. He has seen similar crucifixes in a museum in Stockholm, a part of Europe that existed on the margins of classicism.

He looks away. He cannot willingly pray in front of that crucifix. He puts his rosary on the bedside table and feels the need to close his eyes. Maybe reciting the Ave Maria has made him drowsy, or maybe he feels the need to return to sleep to postpone getting up, saying Mass, leaving his room. He often finds refuge in sleep when seeking to avoid things he does not like.

Monsignor Contarini has started to move about in the adjacent room, getting up and opening a door. There's his first cough. And there is the sound of his first cigarette, which he lights and smokes in secret. Soon the window will be opened to let the smoke escape. In all his years of service, Contarini must have attempted to quit twenty times.

There's no use trying to go back to sleep now.

The truth is that he just doesn't know how to pray anymore. His thoughts stray as he moves his lips, and the stories of other people's lives play out like a film in front of him. This forced vacation, this state of suspension that is the conclave, has intensified an odd and relatively new habit of his: that of stepping outside himself and imagining the lives of others while forgetting about himself. People say he is an excellent confessor. Unfortunately, his official functions as cardinal and archbishop of a large industrial city in northern Italy don't permit him to practice that ministry except on rare occasions.

Once, during a pastoral visit to a remote town, he had spent almost the entire day at the confessional. The young people of the town, those few who had come to the church to kneel before him, had particularly enchanted him. They seemed not to want to sever the bond that had sprung up between them, and relentlessly pressed him with their questions, especially personal ones. Their confessions had little to do with faith, rather, they were motivated by a strange combination of a hunger for love and the desire to use that unusual outlet as a means of revealing their own lives without shame, timidity, or embarrassment. Through the grate of the confessional he saw them, their eyes fixed on his, their heads meticulously shaved, a gold earring glistening in an earlobe or a diamond stud in the nose.

He began to feel uneasy when one of them asked if he would be coming back soon.

"Why do you ask?"

"Because I want to come with you."

"With me? Why?"

"Because no one listens to me here. I have to pretend with everyone."

"What are you hiding? Why do you have to pretend?"

"I have to hide everything: that I don't want to work, that I'd like to travel, that I'd like to be rich. I want to drive a Ferrari and not my father's Fiat. I like my best friend's girlfriend. I want to live in the city."

"In the city?"

"Yes, that's why I want to go to Turin with you. Do you need a driver? Or a cook? I know how to drive. I can also make crepes that are out of this world, and pizza, and at least three kinds of pasta sauce."

"But I don't eat a lot: a little pasta, salad, sometimes meat."

"Even better. That kind of stuff is easy to make."

"I'm an archbishop; it would be a boring life for you. By the way, how old are you?"

"Nineteen."

"It would be very boring for you to live with a sixty-three-year-old man."

"I've always liked older people better. They're more interesting. And besides, you're someone, not just anyone. I wouldn't be bored."

"Before becoming this interesting old man, though, I was young myself. Every age has its advantages. Live your youth as if it were a gift, because soon it will disappear. Don't be in a hurry to end it."

"That's all talk. No one cares about young people; young people are nothing."

"Nothing is what the Almighty likes best. Remember what the Scriptures say about children: 'If you are not like these children, you shall not enter the kingdom of Heaven.'"

Upon hearing this quote from the Bible, the boy stopped talking. It wasn't that he didn't believe the words; on the contrary. Perhaps by merely mentioning the Scriptures the cardinal had distanced him. The confession had simply been a pretext for getting close to a celebrity, to someone who emanated the magic aura of success.

In a small town a cardinal is like an actor, a tycoon, almost as important as a soccer player or a pop singer. Even some of the youth in his own seminary occasionally expressed the dream of an ecclesiastical career.

A career in the Church.

Here he was at the apex, in the conclave. Yet he had given himself over to nostalgia for those at the lowest level, for his students in his seminary in Bologna.

He decides to get up. He hears Contarini's movements growing more and more frequent, his discrete way of indicating that it is time to prepare for Mass. The archbishop makes his way to the window to look outside, now that there is more daylight. The yellow window across the way is less distinct now, and the silhouetted figures have gone, although he can still hear the dog barking.

He looks up and notices that the sky in Rome is a different shade of blue than in his own city. More of a lapis lazuli — the African influence, no doubt — and there is never any early morning fog, as there is in the north. It's nicer waking up here.

He goes into the bathroom and looks at the lion-footed tub and the small oval window. There are 127 bathrooms just like this one in the palace, he thinks. And at this very minute they are all being used by the same number of elderly cardinals. He looks at his reflection in the mirror. He ought to shave; he didn't shave yesterday, and he has grown stubble.

Five days have already passed since the cardinals sequestered themselves in conclave, after the proclamation of the *extra omnes* by the chamberlain of the Sacred College. The doors of the Apostolic Palace have been sealed; all communication with the outside is forbidden unless approved by the chamberlain's secretary. Everyone had been asked to turn off his cellphone, but someone must have broken the rules, because yesterday all the cellphones were confiscated for the duration of the conclave. He knows that some of the Americans had left theirs on; he walked in on them once while they were using them. And many others might have done the same.

He nicks his left earlobe while shaving with his straight razor. His right arm aches, sometimes making all movement difficult; one of many arthritic pains that bother him at that time of year. He even feels the twinge of pain when he gives the solemn benediction in his cathedral, from the altar next to the Chapel of the Holy Shroud.

He suddenly envisions the benediction of *urbi et orbi* from the balcony of Saint Peter's. He stops, looking at himself squarely in the mirror, his razor in midair. What if he is chosen? What if he had to do it?

He braces himself with his left hand on the side of the sink and looks down. He has no chance of seeing himself in that position. His name has never been mentioned, neither by the Roman Curia nor any other group. He doesn't represent any specific political faction, and he has no connections in the upper ministries of the Church. Actually, as a recently named cardinal he is still under observation from the Vatican. He knows they consider him more of a pastor than a scholar or a politician. And from the names that have emerged as possible candidates, pastoral skills do

not seem to be high on the list. After a pope like the one who just
passed away, it would be difficult to elect anyone who lives in the
shadows, as he does, among the Italian people. Yet he cannot
forget that he owes his elevation to the rank of cardinal to that un-
forgettable man.

"If divine Providence had wanted things to be different, and if
I had remained in my diocese, I would have lived a life like
yours," the pope once told him during a luncheon, only a few
years before the consistory in which he was named cardinal. "I
hear that in your area the birthrate has gone down and the divorce
rate is up," he then added.

"Yes, it's the result of a misguided sense of well-being, without
any spiritual values whatsoever. But there have to be other reasons
for the changes, I just don't know what they are. But I try —" the
archbishop interrupted himself, putting his silver fork down on
the Limoges plate. He didn't want to tell the pope that he was
looking for the answer within himself. But that was exactly what
the pope went on to say.

"You're trying . . . to find it within yourself."

He nodded and looked at the fragile old man. How had he
known?

Throughout the entire meal that memorable day, the atten-
tive but not benevolent manner in which he had been studied by
one of the most influential men in the Curia, Vladimiro
Veronelli, the chamberlain of the Holy Roman Church, had not
escaped his notice.

Instinctively, he had perceived mistrust, reserve, more antipathy than esteem, as if evidence of his inability to govern the
Church had emerged in that fragment of conversation, as well as
proof that his open nature would surely be problematic. The
supreme vertices of the Church must represent certainty, for only
certainties can satisfy the needs of the weak and confused millions. These seemed to be the thoughts of the man who had
studied him so intently that morning, responding to his comments with so few words.

And today Veronelli is the chamberlain who, together with

Dean Antonio Leporati, has readied to the last detail the complex machinery of the conclave, a mechanism that is destined to find a successor to the pontiff who left such a tangible mark on history. He is the man who must converse in Latin but also prohibit the use of cellphones in order to stop information from being leaked to the media. He is the man who must seal the doors to the outside world, as has been done for centuries, with the escutcheon of the crossed keys of Saint Peter surmounted by the Pavilion of the Vacant Throne, but he must also prevent the cardinals and their chaplains from connecting to the Internet to gather news from the outside world.

No, the archbishop of Turin stands no chance at all of proclaiming the benediction of *urbi et orbi* from the balcony of Saint Peter's.

2

WHILE HE IS celebrating Mass with his chaplain, Monsignor Giorgio Contarini, a ray of sunlight makes its way through the hinges of the cabinet doors and falls directly onto the white cloth and golden chalice on the altar. A ray as warm as a caress, but strong, illuminating the altar and the consecrated host. He feels the sunbeam on his aching right arm. It alleviates the pain. Gentle and affectionate, it feels like the hand of a loved one resting on his arm. His thoughts go to the people who are dear to him: his sister, her husband, their son, his dead brother's widow, Contarini, his friends from the seminary who got married and had children, and whose children have since had children. Then he thinks about the people who have died. They far outnumber the living. There are so many he can't even remember all their names. He sees a sea of faces, their names swept away by the wind.

He surprises himself during the blessing of the host by pronouncing the canon in Latin, and even Contarini makes a gesture of amazement, tilting his head to the side, as if to make certain he is hearing correctly: *"Hoc est enim corpus meum."*

Why did he say those words in Latin? It is the language in which he first heard Mass when he was a child, not understanding the significance of the words, but participating as if in a mysterious magical ritual.

He stares at the communion wafer in his hands. He seems resigned to believing in the miracle of the transformation of the bread into flesh. How many times in his life has he held the host this way, feeling tired, inadequate, uncertain, and distracted by the sounds of life churning around him? Feeling stupid, mechanical, extraneous. And with that wafer in his hands he has felt burdened by the banalities of daily life, almost defeated by its absurdity, and by a sense of futility in this replication of the sacrifice at Calvary.

Now it is his secretary's coughing that distracts him, and the blaring of a car horn in the distance, and now the smell of the floor wax, and the sound of footsteps in the hallway: someone who is hurriedly opening and closing the doors in the Sacred Palace, on this, the sixth day of the conclave. His stomach begins to growl, drowning out all the other noises because it comes from within, from an uneasy and disobedient body, a body that is perhaps indifferent to the miracle that is now taking place in that room.

In his own ancient cathedral, his inability to concentrate on the host can be blamed on the uncomfortable vestments, on the slowness of the rituals, or on the burgeoning crowds. He can also find excuses for not answering the question, "Do you believe? Do you believe that I am your God?" Here, however, the space is intimate, comfortable, and discrete, and no one expects theatrics from him. Except for Contarini, who stands behind him, he is alone with the host.

So why can't he be completely present? Why can't he answer that question? Can a man such as he even relate to those who must elect the pope? Worse still, can he relate to whomever might be elected?

He kneels, as he has always done, before the host. The ray of sun has shifted; when he stands up for the benediction of the wine in the chalice, it no longer shines on his arm. The rest of the

Mass flows by in a river of words that memory transmits to his lips, as dead as the nameless faces of people whom he had loved and who are no longer with him. He follows a formula of precise words, this time all in Italian, according to the reform of the Second Vatican Council. And as though complicit in that silent race toward the end of the rite, Contarini is no longer bothered by his cough.

Once the Mass is over, his secretary serves breakfast. On the table next to his napkin and his cup is the mail, which always arrives a day late, already opened. The rules of the conclave are strictly enforced.

The sounds of morning activity can now be heard throughout the Apostolic Palace.

"Your Eminence, the elections are scheduled for ten o'clock. That's in one and a half hours. I'll prepare your cassock and your papers. I have to meet with the Prefect of the Pontifical House; I believe they have new instructions for us."

"Something's bound to change. The rules are outdated, like the way the mail is censored."

"There's a message from Cardinal Rabuiti, of Palermo. I believe it didn't escape the censor's office, either."

"That couldn't be. Correspondences between ourselves, inside the conclave, can pass freely; they wouldn't do that to us."

"I wouldn't be so sure."

He opens the missive and reads the miniscule handwriting:

> Dear Ettore,
> We must have a meeting this morning before the
> general elections — you, Genoa, Naples, Milan,
> Florence, Bologna, and Venice. Please try and
> make it. It's important. We'll meet in my study.

What could be so important? Piecing together a scheme against the cardinals of Eastern Europe, who were so strongly favored by the public? Or against the black cardinals — the sons of Africa — who were the real future of the Church, according to many others.

What about Asia? And the Chinese problem? A Chinese pontiff to avenge the heirs of Matteo Ricci, the mathematician-missionary, would gain a tremendous following, issuing a challenge where the Church is still illegal and clandestine, its members still the objects of persecution.

He goes over the list again: Genoa, Naples, Milan, Florence, Bologna, Venice, and himself, Turin. The cardinals from the Sacred College were notably absent.

"Where are Rabuiti's rooms?"

"In the wing directly across from ours. I know the way, but we'll have to hurry, so that I can accompany you and still be on time for my meeting."

"I'll get ready immediately." He quickly puts on his black cassock with the scarlet buttons and trim and dons his scarlet zucchetto, then places his mail inside his dossier so he can read it later. "Let's go, Contarini."

He locks the door after they leave the room and hands the key over to his secretary. It is cold and dark in the long hallway, where the sun never enters, and an odor of mildew prevails, the scent of the mold growing in the walls where the plaster is blistering and peeling. He sees a nun turn quickly down a hallway in front of them. A nun? How could that be? Women aren't allowed in the conclave.

"Was that a nun?"

"No, Your Eminence, that was a Benedictine monk."

How could he have made that mistake? In their universe there is no room for women. Indeed, until a few conclaves ago, the elected pontiff had to undergo an examination to verify his manhood.

He watches Contarini walk up the corridor with the brisk pace he no longer tries to match. The familiar scent of his secretary's cologne lingers in the air. Contarini looks as impeccable as ever: his clergyman's suit neatly pressed and a perfect fit, his shoes with their satin buckles freshly polished, his hands manicured, not a hair out of place. Contarini is definitely the archbishop's best assistant, yet also the most mysterious. The glimmer in his eyes when the archbishop mistook the monk for a nun had not gone unnoticed.

Contarini was young, just over forty. The sealed letters of rec-
ommendation that the archbishop received before taking him
into his service told the story of a tragic marriage that had ended
with his wife's suicide. After her death he chose to enter the priesthood. No one had ever succeeded in prying the details of that
devastating event from him, yet something of the husband still
resonated in his elegant secretary's manner. Giorgio Contarini
still wanted to please, as if some fragment from his married life
still reverberated in his new life as the inseparable guardian angel
of his archbishop.

He did not like the extent to which Contarini groomed himself,
or the meticulous attention he paid to his wardrobe; the archbishop
was often criticized by his secretary for his own modest choices in
clothing and shoes, in furnishings and linens. But he never ob-
jected, and was won over by his secretary's acute eye for color, his
knack for combining foods, by his taste in perfumes and the flowers
that adorned the altar, by his capacity for selecting gifts for the
many people who circulated around the archbishop's Curia.

Once, when Francesco had come to Turin for his uncle's
birthday, a single comment had unveiled his jealousy for Contarini: "We could have gone out on your birthday, rather than
staying here with your secret agent."

"But it's more intimate here," Malvezzi had replied when his
secretary had gone to answer the phone.

"Not really, not with him around. Besides, he smokes so
much! Far more than I do."

His nephew had touched on Contarini's weak spot. In everything else he was close to perfect.

"No, Your Eminence, this way. We can take the spiral staircase
as a shortcut." Contarini's voice brings him back to the present.
He had been about to turn to the right, down the hallway where
the monk had disappeared.

That is another thing about his secretary. He never loses his
sense of direction, not even in the most chaotic Roman traffic
when their car, despite the guidon on the hood that gives them
the right-of-way, gets lost in a sea of cars and buses. He is always

ready to exchange words with taxi drivers and parking attendants. But he somehow manages to stay calm, never losing the subtle air of superiority that, unless it enrages his opponents, usually gets him his way. When this happens, the archbishop sinks into the back seat and hides behind the drapes in the car, embarrassed by the tone of voice that Contarini employs, but lacking the courage to scold him because of the positive results he obtains. He knows that Contarini not only detects his unease, he takes a certain pleasure in it, enjoying his superior's dependence on him, and perhaps even relishing the opportunity to try his patience.

The cardinal descends the spiral staircase, raising his cassock with his right hand so as not to trip. The ancient wooden staircase creaks with every step, and light barely filters down from a skylight above them. Still, Contarini sees well even in that penumbra as he moves ahead with his light, swift step, even picking up the pace a little bit.

On one of the landings a sliver of light comes from under one of the closed doors. Behind it they hear muffled voices engaged in a heated discussion that immediately breaks off once the speakers are alerted to the presence of someone on the stairs.

Contarini stops and looks at him. He seems to be waiting for orders, but he has an odd smile on his face.

"Let's go, Contarini, there's no time to waste."

He realizes only after the fact that his words were uttered in a whisper that could be misleading, as if he were trying to remain undetected, hoping not to interrupt whatever is being discussed behind those doors. Rather than appearing embarrassed, his secretary seems to be enjoying himself, and the archbishop is not surprised when he replies in a loud voice, "Of course, Your Eminence. Right away!"

Contarini knows who those people are; he probably even knows their names. The archbishop and his assistant are two or three flights farther down when they hear the door open, and Contarini immediately stops to look up, trying to determine who it is.

"Contarini, let's go! We're already late." His voice is raised now, too, in irritation. It is not the first time that his secretary has challenged him, revealing a headstrong character at odds with the submissiveness warranted by his position.

Contarini hurries down the stairs. Finally they reach the spacious landing above the central staircase that opens onto the wing where the other Italians are residing. They walk through a doorway emblazoned with the insignia of Pius X, and are greeted by a voice.

"Come, Your Eminence, what an honor. All the other cardinals are gathered in the archbishop of Palermo's rooms. They've been waiting for you." It is a prelate in the service of Cardinal Rabuiti. He kneels to kiss the archbishop of Turin's ring, while Contarini departs for his meeting.

"Please, Your Eminence, follow me," the prelate says.

And so begins a new series of labyrinthine peregrinations, but this time all on the same floor, through hallways decorated with the coats of arms of recent popes and portraits of secretaries of state: Merry del Val, Maglione, Gasparri, Tardini. They turn a corner and cross a long loggia leading to the courtyard of Saint Damasus, which is crowded with lemon trees in terra-cotta vases, and then enter yet another hallway, lined with windows and flooded with daylight. Finally the prelate stops next to a small, well-concealed door that is cut into the plaster of the wall. He opens it without knocking and stands aside to let the cardinal of Turin pass through.

In the doorway stands Rabuiti, the archbishop of Palermo, short and stocky, his face radiant and cheerful. He is about to break into a smile, an expression that comes readily to him, even when discussing serious and private matters, as they will soon be required to do.

"I'm so glad you could join us. How very kind of you. I told our friends that you'd be here; I said, 'Ettore will come, you'll see, he wouldn't miss our breakfast meeting!'" Gently taking Malvezzi's arm, he guides him through another door. "Look who's here — look, it's Ettore!"

There they are, all of them gathered around a table, enjoying a breakfast far more abundant than the austere meal that Malvezzi had just shared with his secretary, prepared for them by the nuns in the main kitchen. A gigantic wooden crucifix in a classical Do-natellian style — nothing at all like the gothic cross that had so unsettled Malvezzi as he knelt praying in his room — hangs on the wall above them. Everyone is dressed exactly as he is, because in just under an hour they will proceed to the Sistine Chapel to cast their votes.

He studies their faces one by one, faces that have appeared along with his in the press and on television during the pope's journeys throughout Italy, always welcoming the pontiff to their Sees, climbing into the limousine behind him, fending off the crowds with an ever-present smile; the polished smile that Rabuiti had perfected. He remembers their comments to the journalists as they crossed the threshold into the sacred grounds, responding to questions about the possibility of emerging from the conclave as the next pope. They trembled at the mere thought, or said it was a bitter chalice from which they did not wish to drink. Or they knew themselves to be the last person to deserve the honor, or else they did not even want to talk about it, so unworthy did they feel. Following an age-old script, superstition demanded that every prince of the Church deny himself the hope of any possi-bility of being elected. Everyone knew that "he who enters the conclave a pope, comes out a cardinal." But not a word had been said to Malvezzi, or to the patriarch of Venice.

The table has been set with large silver coffeepots full of hot chocolate; the same drink that has often been prepared for popes after Mass to restore their strength after their night of fasting. The baroque silver service shines brightly under a Murano lamp, which has been turned on in full daylight to underscore the luster of all the accoutrements on the table. He sees Rabuiti ap-proaching him with a chair. "Come and sit down. We'll talk after you have something to eat. The hot chocolate is still warm; let me pour you a cup."

3

*I*T'S TRUE; HE WAS unique. No other pope has been able to open himself to the world as he did, interpreting the anxieties of all of humanity. Still, we must nominate a successor. But just as important, and even more difficult, as we have already seen, we must first find one." The lively Sicilian archbishop turns to the issue of the day, and immediately continues, "That is why we must ask ourselves what we want, and we must prepare ourselves before heading to the elections, instead of gambling on the results of a majority vote. We must find someone who will convey our deepest convictions. A majoritarian decision shouldn't be an end in itself, as it seems to have been over the past few days. In fact, I blame myself for not having met with all of you earlier."

"These days haven't been in vain, Celso," says the bishop of Genoa, Silvio Marussi. "The first few days of other conclaves have always been somewhat theatrical, but they're necessary for understanding where the Holy Spirit will lay his hand."

"But the Holy Spirit could use some help. I agree with Rabuiti," interjects Alfonso Cerini, the archbishop of Milan, his voice serious and calculated. The others have all been waiting to hear his thoughts before pronouncing their own opinions.

"That's right. We can't simply leave this to fate, and we must act quickly," agrees Aldo Miceli, the patriarch of Venice.

"As the oldest one here," interrupts the bishop of Florence, Nicola Gistri, "I can't let you forget that even when Pius XII died it seemed impossible that we would find a replacement for him. It was the same for Pius XI and for Benedict XV, not to mention Pius X, who orphaned us on the eve of the war and whom today we venerate on the high altar —"

"Right. We mustn't get discouraged. It won't help us at all as we struggle to make our choice," interrupts the cardinal of Bologna, Siro Ferrazzi, bringing his hand to his chest, only to realize that he has left his pectoral cross in his room.

"Besides," says Salvatore Carapelle, archbishop of Naples, looking directly into Cerini's eyes, "the heroic virtues of our venerated pontiff, once proved, will only serve to add another pope to the rank of saint."

"Indeed, once they're proved. . . ." says the archbishop of Milan. And with those words, thinks Malvezzi, a second gravestone has just been placed over the body of the deceased pope. He also realizes they are waiting for him to add his own comments to their list of pronouncements.

And so, at the risk of his career, he pulls down the mask for all to see. "We're here because we want to elect an Italian, not because we want to decide on the most deserving candidate, isn't that right?"

"Why Ettore, what do you mean? An Italian and the most deserving, if possible." The correction comes from Rabuiti, whose smile does not lose its veneer, even in the face of a pronouncement so lacking in tact. Nonetheless the cardinal of Palermo is grateful to Malvezzi for exposing the heart of the matter.

"Not an Italian at all costs," Carapelle says, "However, we do want to explore all our options." But as he listens to Cerini, he immediately regrets his words.

"An Italian, at all costs," Cerini says. "Absolutely at all costs."

A profound silence falls over the group. The successor of Saint

Ambrose has just nominated himself, and no one can pretend to ignore him. His candidacy has been pronounced with all the prestige of his position and of his city. Only the cardinals from the Roman Curia are missing, notes Malvezzi, as they had not been invited to the meeting. Presumably they are already on Cerini's side; he would have seen to that. Or maybe it is only a political maneuver: convince the diocesan pastors first, and then the Vatican politicians.

"Ettore, your hot chocolate is getting cold," Rabuiti says attentively. Malvezzi hasn't even had time to take a sip, so struck has he been by the urgent speed of this game of agreement, this initial attempt at discerning their opinions before firing any shots. Why be surprised? Millions of faithful all over the world are waiting to hear the name of the representative of Christ on earth. It is only normal to expect the ancient machinery of the conclave to pick up steam in order to generate a result. For the conclave is also this: a game conducted behind the scenes, burdened by pressures and defeats, victories and compromises, until the new figure in white emerges — a figure on whom the world can project its need for a father, for an intermediary between God and man; a figure whom the vast majority of humanity would never renounce.

The Dalai Lama responds to this need, as do the Imam of the Ismaelites, the patriarchs of Moscow and Constantinople, and all the Muslim ayatollahs. Each one does his part to reassure man that he is not alone, and that his suffering, his unhappiness, his aging, and ultimately his death have a definite purpose as part of God's design. Not for one moment does God abandon his creatures. Every second is counted and weighed; nothing is done without a reason. Man has needed this belief since the dawn of history, ever since he first feared thunder and lightning, imagining them to be the shadow of his father, Zeus. And so it is even now, in this age of the Internet and the Concorde, the atom and the antibiotic. There is a need to belong to a religion, to one of those powerful societies of mutual aid, united in taking pity upon man, who never grows up, who has yet to learn how to confront the Void from which he is made.

Malvezzi sips his hot chocolate slowly, reveling in the uncomfortable silence following Cerini's speech. He is resolved not to interrupt it, in spite of Rabuiti's imploring smile.

Carapelle's feeble voice assumes a nervous falsetto as he begins to speak, picking up where no one else would. "Alright, Alfonso, we'll vote for you. And I'm sure many other countries will do so, too. After all, they're only seven of us here."

"We have a lot of work to do to convince the others," the Venetian patriarch says.

"Italy must regain its supremacy over the Roman Catholic Church. A pope of Italian blood will reinvigorate the strength of our race, the pride in our universal vocation, the magnitude and scope of our intelligence and our Latin sensibility; all that has disappeared from the heart of the Church because of the commingling of cultures too near their barbarian roots."

Who could hope to deny the successor of Saint Ambrose after such an overwhelming show of support? His famous speeches have enchanted universities, cultural foundations, and exclusive philosophical circles; no one remains immune to his allure.

Just then, however, a prelate enters the room to inform Their Eminences that the process of identifying the electors in the Sistine Chapel has begun. Not only is it time to go, but a possible delay on account of the entire group might make people suspicious.

No one is surprised by Alfonso Cerini's self-candidature. Only Gistri, the cardinal of Florence, could possibly compete with him, if he weren't so old. He is practically excluded from the vote by passive consent, as are all the other diocesan cardinals over seventy-five, who have reached the mandatory age of retirement and are no longer considered valid candidates for the papacy, as opposed to their colleagues in the Roman Curia, who are allowed to continue their duties beyond that age.

So the cardinals disband without further comments, taking pains to reach the Sistine Chapel in "random order," as Rabuiti suggests.

While Malvezzi ascends the spiral staircase that Contarini had accompanied him down earlier, he reflects on the advanced ages of his colleagues; what an assembly of geriatrics. Suddenly he hears the same voices that had caught his attention before — young voices, impetuous and ironic, caustic and mocking when offended, lively and uncontainable when bursting into laughter, and capable of rising and falling in a way that the aged cardinals' voices no longer can.

Who could they be? Personal assistants, chaplains in service to the cardinals, secret clergymen, acolytes, candle-bearers, chaplains of honor? Maybe they are members of the Swiss Guard, that troop of men who do little except instigate passion and rivalry, occasionally even with tragic outcome, as in the triple homicide committed years ago by one of their youngest members. Everything had been covered up by the only judge who could arbitrarily decide what had happened and then quickly archive the case. But Malvezzi knew what had befallen those three — the commander, his wife, and a young soldier — as he had been acquainted with the young Swiss Guard. The man was the nephew of one of his oldest friends from the seminary.

While contemplating the particulars of the chilling incident, which had been recounted by his friend one evening at a conference on theological studies, he reaches the opened doors to the Sistine Chapel, where a crowd of domestic prelates, Swiss Guards, chaplains, and cardinals is gathered. One by one, the cardinals are announced, and they walk in to take their places on their thrones, under their baldachins. One hundred and twenty-six thrones with baldachins line both sides of the room. The throne belonging to the chamberlain, the 127th member of the conclave, stands apart from the others, close to the altar.

Only one of the baldachins will remain raised upon the proclamation of the new pope. The others will be lowered in homage to the pontiff, and the *Tu es Petrus* will be sung as the chamberlain and the dean hurry through the maze of rooms that connects the Vatican Palace to the Basilica of Saint Peter's. There, from the balcony, the news will be announced to Rome and to the rest of the world with the proclamation of *Habemus Papam*.

Malvezzi observes the Asian cardinals — a group of Japanese, Vietnamese, Indian, and Filipino men who always remain together while waiting to be called to the elections. They continuously express their awe at Michelangelo's artwork, turning their heads in unison to admire the walls and ceiling, the sibyls and prophets, then directing their collective gaze up the shortest wall to the scenes of the *Last Judgment*.

Malvezzi can't imagine how the signs and symbols of Michelangelo's universe must appear to men from those cultures. Of course they had all been educated in Catholic seminaries and universities, but their minds had been raised on the figural universe of Brahma, Vishnu, and Shiva, on the struggles between Good and Evil. Malvezzi had seen the beautiful artwork portraying the gigantomachy between those two princely forces during his travels to Bali, Bangkok, Lhasa, and Calcutta. Michelangelo was nurtured on the Athenian and Roman vision of Man, and his virile nudes resonate with classical harmony, influenced by the works of Pheidias, Praxiteles, Scopa, and Lysippus, his inexhaustible fonts of inspiration.

Thanks to the cultural mediation of Catholicism, bridges have been erected between the Orient and the Occident, between Hellenism and Judaism, and between the Roman and German worlds. This was exemplified even in that realistic crucifix looming above his prie-dieu, a product of a Gothic vision that evoked the gloom of Lutheran predestination. Everything came together in the fresco in a singular theatrical representation. The separate parts worked in harmony, no piece more important than another, each one faithful to its own raison d'être, each one following a script that had yet to be completed, with the forthcoming pages containing the unforeseeable conclusion to the drama, still far from the final catharsis.

Malvezzi realizes that he, too, has been lost in contemplation of the *Last Judgment* for several minutes, just like the Asian cardinals, oblivious to the crowd around him.

"Excuse me, Your Eminence; we need to check your identification," a prelate's mellifluous voice calls him to the entryway.

He notices Cerini standing next to him in silence, his expression inscrutable. Who knows what he is thinking as he enters the hall on what could be a most auspicious occasion.

Suddenly all of the lights in the Sistine Chapel come on and the words of the *Veni Creator Spiritus* rise from the gallery of the papal choir. The last cardinals quickly take their seats.

When the singing fades Chamberlain Vladimiro Veronelli orders the guards to close the chapel doors and the marble railing that surrounds it.

Extra omnes.

Everyone must leave. Only the 127 electors and the assistant prelates can remain. But something makes the chamberlain furrow his brow. He reads a note from the pontifical physician, Prince Aldobrandini: four eminences are ill and cannot leave their rooms. The chamberlain shakes his head, visibly annoyed, and decides to delay the roll call in order to appeal to those who are absent.

Voices swell through the great hall. The unexpected delay triggers conjectures and comments, causing the reflective atmosphere created by the singing of the *Veni Creator* to disappear completely.

4

*H*ALF AN HOUR later, the Maronite patriarch Abdullah Joseph Selim solemnly appears at the marble railing, leaning on his crosier and waving away all offers of assistance from a domestic prelate.

The chamberlain's invocation has had an effect on only one of the absent electors.

As for the other three — the cardinals of Rio de Janeiro, Santiago del Chile, and Sydney — nothing can be done. Monsignor Attavanti, secretary of the College of Cardinals, whispers this unfortunate news into the chamberlain's ear, emphasizing the fact that everything has been tried. "The cardinal of Sydney was in terrible pain; at one point he no longer wanted to listen to me, and simply pulled the sheet up over his head. The archbishop of Rio de Janeiro didn't let me finish talking either. He told me to leave and let him die in peace."

"What about Santiago del Chili?" the displeased chamberlain asks, ringing his bell to bring order to the chapel.

"Your Eminence, he was . . . in the bathroom, and I was too embarrassed to speak to him from the antechamber. His secretary let him know I was there. The archbishop assured me, though, that his incontinence will preclude him from participating in today's elections."

The image of a cardinal sitting on a toilet eases the tension to a certain extent. Veronelli will have to be content with Selim, who is now advancing slowly toward him, and seems to be threatening him with his raised staff. His pale face, and his spirited eyes peering from behind the black strips of veil that descend from his round hat, in sharp contrast to his long, white beard, give him a majestic appearance that attracts everyone's attention and silences the crowd.

"If I don't leave the conclave alive, Your Eminence, it will weigh heavily on your conscience. I don't know what difference it makes" — a sudden coughing attack interrupts the Lebanese cardinal, impeding him momentarily from continuing — "if I participate in today's round of voting or not. It's too early to decide anything; conclaves need time. Your hurry is bad counsel."

"Several days have passed, dear brother, and time is not what it once was during the last conclave. It passes twice as quickly now."

"But we are not held to observe it. Even illness is a chance for reflection. We must not imitate the race against time that goes on outside. Caution of the spirit can often be disguised as frailness of the flesh!"

Cardinal Veronelli does not reply. The assembly seems torn by opposing reactions, but everyone seems to have paid close attention to the confrontation. The Maronite has charisma, and his indubitable physical suffering has only increased the pathos of his words.

Veronelli watches contentedly as the ill man exercises the virtue of obedience and slowly takes his seat next to the archbishop of Turin.

In a hurry to conclude? He, who is single-handedly responsible for the most difficult conclave of the last centuries, under pressure from the governments of half the world? He is the one who must respond to the phone calls from the Italian and French presidents, from the head of the United Nations, from the leader of Ukraine, from the Nobel Peace Prize committee, with their endless urgings to elect a black pope in homage to all who had been persecuted. Not to mention the Jews. What did the Lebanese patriarch know about the pressures the Jews had placed on Veronelli regarding the cardinal of Sarajevo, who was an ardent opponent of Islam, or their insistence on an unqualified guarantee that a Palestinian would not be elected, as many religious organizations in the Middle East had been proposing.

There is the Palestinian cardinal now, seated to his left on his throne near the railing, quiet as a lamb, intent on reading his breviary, or so it seems. He doesn't take part in the discussion or exchange comments with his neighbors. Judging from his appearance, he could be the most meek and seraphic prince in the Church, but in truth, he is capable of hiding a collection of Uzis and machine guns in the trunk of his diplomatic car, destined for his flock in Jerusalem.

But now it is time to read the roll call and open the floor to discussion before the voting. It is already 11:30, and it is not wise to lose control of that uncooperative assembly for more than a few minutes.

Cardinal Dean Antonio Leporati reads off the list of most eminent and reverend cardinals in alphabetical order, including the names of their titular churches in the city of Rome. The silence is now almost absolute. When the roll call is finished the chamberlain announces that the floor is open, should one of Their Eminences wish to express himself before the voting commences.

For several minutes they mumble in small groups, as if many of them were holding back, speaking among themselves in order not to address the assembly as a whole. No one wants to assume the responsibility of determining the course for a conclave still on the open sea. The names on the ballots incinerated during previous elections were now merely imaginary sightings, mirages, and deceptions. The news that the votes of the Italians, and possibly even the French and the Spanish, will converge on the cardinal of Milan has not yet circulated throughout the entire assembly, although most of the members, much to their irritation, learned of the rumor during the exchange between the Maronite patriarch and the chamberlain.

"History has taught the Italians nothing," the archbishop of Havana said. "They're trying again."

Ettore Malvezzi looks around him, studying the faces of the people closest to him: the Lebanese patriarch, the cardinals of Palermo, Bologna, Paris, Vienna, Cologne, Bordeaux, Madrid, and Toledo. Farther on are the people who make up the "armies of Eastern Europe," as Rabuiti occasionally calls them, with both antipathy and irony: the Uniate cardinal from Lviv and the Latin one too, the cardinals of Riga, Budapest, Zagreb, Warsaw, Krakow, Minsk, Kaunas, Prague, Fagaras, Alba Iulia, Nitra, and Sarajevo.

Where will the hostilities begin? Who will make the first move against the most defenseless and yet the oldest and most universal power in Europe? Malvezzi hears a noise from his left, next to Cerini. Someone is trying to attract the attention of his neighbor, the archbishop of Palermo. He intercepts a message from an agitated Marussi, the bishop of Genoa. "You should nominate our candidate."

But Rabuiti doesn't answer. He seems frozen in thought, absorbed in contemplation of the prophets and sibyls on the ceiling, and deaf to all entreaties. The chamberlain's secretaries begin to prepare the trays of ballots, which they will distribute throughout the Sistine Chapel. The persistent silence convinces the members of the Sacred College that Selim's call for reflection was not in vain. It is still too early to speed up the machinery of the conclave. From the altar the chamberlain gives the order for the ballots to be distributed without further delay. It is past noon; the bells of Saint Peter's have just struck the hour.

The cardinals lean over their tables. Some search for their glasses, or pore over the list of candidates one more time. Some of them busily unscrew the caps of their fountain pens, or quickly write in a name, or whisper to their neighbors, while others, like Malvezzi, sit immobile with their ballots in front of them, staring at the white paper and the insignia of the Vacant Throne.

He watches as the Uniate cardinal from Lviv summons one of the secretaries to return his ballot, and Stalin's ironic question comes to his mind: "The pope? How many troops does he have?" He is tempted to write in the Uniate's name, but he has already given his word to his Italian colleagues. He can't do it. Someone might check the ballots. He doesn't know how, since the ballots will be incinerated, but it's possible someone could find out.

He leans over and slowly writes in the name of Alfonso Cerini, archbishop of Milan.

Half of them have already placed their ballots on the silver tray that will be emptied into a large golden chalice on the altar, as Malvezzi shakes himself from a reverie that has momentarily distracted him from the events underway in the chapel.

He had been captivated by the scene of the awakening of the dead in Michelangelo's fresco; in particular by the expressions of uncertainty, surprise, confusion, and wonder on the figures' faces as they are called back to life by the trumpeting angels. What was the name of the contemporary writer who had evoked the life of Lazarus, exiled from death, and forced for the second time to breathe the air and the unhappiness of the living, always longing for sleep? Was it an Italian poet? Corrado Govoni? Or Rilke?

"Your ballot, please," a prelate says, forcing him to open his half-shut eyes, the name of the author still evading him.

"Did you fall asleep?" asks his neighbor Selim. "I'm tired, too. They must have woken you up, too, in the middle of the night, in order to convince you . . ." Malvezzi smiles without replying. But the Maronite, who evidently likes him, doesn't give up. "I voted for you."

The cardinal of Turin feels the blood rush to his head. "You did what? Are you joking?"

"No. I think you're worthy."

"Don't ever do it again. Please. It's a wasted vote. I could never . . ." Malvezzi can't complete his sentence, overcome by a sudden fear, as if something were preventing him from continuing, from revealing how he had felt earlier that morning as he celebrated Mass with the sacramental host in his hands, unable to reply to the question, "Do you believe? Do you believe that I am your God?"

"Who are you to say that you could never? What do you know about the capabilities of God?" the imposing man asks, raising himself up on his staff and glaring at Malvezzi. For a moment this penetrating look reminds Malvezzi of the tragic light in the single exposed eye of the Condemned Soul in Michelangelo's fresco — the figure is covering his other eye with the palm of his hand in response to the sentence of eternal damnation. It was the figure that had struck him most when he first saw the fresco as a child.

The patriarch's secretary has already appeared to assist the elderly man down the steps and out of the chapel for a rest while the votes are being tallied. He needs to drink, as his rising fever has made him feel dehydrated. The chamberlain allows him to retire to his cell before the results of the election come in; the eleventh round since the conclave began.

Malvezzi looks at the empty throne next to his, and the memory of that man's piercing gaze still lingers. Everything happened so quickly, and then he was gone, without a doubt the only member of the Sacred College who voted for him. He looks around to make sure no one, especially Rabuiti, overheard their conversation. But the ailing man's voice had been so weak, and Rabuiti seems caught up in an intense conversation in French with one of the cardinals from Eastern Europe.

"Your Eminences are kindly asked to be seated," Veronelli announces, standing before them. He is assisted by the two cardinal scrutineers as he reads from a register held by Monsignor Attavanti.

"The following are the results for the eleventh round of elections for the Supreme Pontiff of the Universal Church and Bishop of Rome. Out of 127 possible cardinals, 124 are present to vote. The following votes were cast. . . ." The monotonous and psalmodic tone in the chamberlain's voice informs everyone that, once again, a majority has not been reached. This time, in fact, the votes are even more scattered. The archbishop of Milan got twelve votes, but at this point it is a dangerous showing, one that could compromise his candidacy in the future.

When Malvezzi hears his name called with the single vote cast in his favor, he is struck with fear once again. Rabuiti turns to look at him, and his sarcastic smile indicates that he thinks Malvezzi voted for himself.

"As we have not reached the quorum of a simple majority that has been sufficient since the fifth round of voting, we will adjourn until later this afternoon, at five o'clock, when we will proceed with the twelfth election. The punctuality of Your Eminences would be most appreciated." Veronelli's voice interrupts Malvezzi's thoughts, reminding him that he must now leave the chapel and return to his cell, where Contarini has prepared a meal for him.

There is a crowd at the doorway again. The cardinals are in no rush to leave the hall as they comment in their various languages on the situation, which is proving increasingly difficult to resolve. The name of the archbishop of Milan is in the air; some of them go up to him to express their regret for the lack of consensus, promising their continued support. The candidate listens with his usual impeccable reserve, shaking their hands and thanking them. Only when Rabuiti comes to greet him does he express his innermost thoughts. "They don't want me, dear Celso. And it couldn't have been presented in a worse way."

"It was too early to announce your candidacy. We risked losing it altogether. But we can still make up for it. I'm meeting with the Germans now, and with London and Dublin later on. I'll talk them out of other possibilities. I'm sure the French and the Spanish will be with us — but let's go somewhere else to talk."

"Yes, absolutely. Let's also talk to the Maronite; he was right."

Cerini, or "La Signora" as his enemies call him, is always so extravagant, Rabuiti thinks. Here he is, ready to build a bridge with his enemies, ready to become their friend and cash in on a truly superior open-mindedness. Now he will call himself *laudator temporis acti*, claiming to be nostalgic for the slow pace of ancient times, to be enamored of contemplation. Meanwhile, here we are, swiping our identification cards through a computerized system in order to leave the premises. Still, for the votes, it might be a good idea to talk to the Maronite; he did make a rather theatrical exit. But first, Malvezzi should be made to account for himself. Who would have thought he'd vote for himself?

The remaining cardinals crowding the doorway step aside to make room for the three prelates, who are walking up the aisle with the box of 124 ballots to be burned in the chapel stove. The ancient tradition of burning the ballots had been restored, announcing the results of the election, either negative or positive, with black or white smoke. The archbishop of Bogotá lets everyone know in Spanish that the smoke signals are ridiculous, not to mention arduous. Frequently, the indistinct color of the smoke leads to confusion. And who knows how to light a wood-stove these days, anyway? The Cuban cardinal agrees with him, adding in a loud voice that if he were chamberlain, he would proceed directly to another vote, and they would continue on into the night until a decision was reached, even if people were sick!

"Did you hear? They've given Contardi the last rites," says the Mexican cardinal, Ezcuderos.

The news that the seventy-nine-year-old cardinal of Rio de Janeiro is gravely ill silences everyone, turning their thoughts away from that regimented and contrived meeting confined only to men — that epitome of symbolism, ritual, and tradition that is the conclave — to the temporal and unpredictable realities of death. Their minds race to their countries, their cities and homes: places the ill man will never see again. And they suddenly become aware of an insurmountable obstacle impeding their freedom of choice, which underscores, amid their pain and anxiety, the reality of an event suffered by many in the past: it would not be the first time that someone had died during the conclave.

"Today, Your Eminences, let us pray for our brother Emanuele," the chamberlain says, his voice carrying across the chapel to the crowd gathered already at the exit.

5

*T*HE DEATH OF Emanuele Contardi during the night reduces the members of the Sacred College in the conclave to 126.

The chamberlain, who is well aware of the negative repercussions of this mournful event on the progress of the conclave, directs his anger toward the pontifical physician Aldobrandini for admitting a moribund cardinal. He never should have allowed it, for the good of the Church. This new obstacle will further slow the movements of a motor that is already struggling to gain speed. Under the guidance of the prince assistants to the throne, Orsini and Colonna, the funeral will be held, with only the cardinals in attendance. It will steal precious time from the elections, but above all it will expend energy, casting a dark shadow over each one of those old men that may complicate matters. The chamberlain understands the psychology that governs those powerful cardinals, and he sees their growing intolerance of the sequestering imposed on them by tradition, forcing them to adapt to rhythms reminiscent of a medieval brotherhood.

Not many of the cardinals look kindly on the regular clergy, as the priests are called who have chosen monastic orders, the most

prestigious of which are still cloistered. One of the few cardinals elevated to the purple from such a monastery is the Estonian Matis
Paide, who was required by his oath of allegiance to renounce his
contemplative life in accepting his scarlet hat, and to direct his spirituality to one of the vacant Vatican ministries. He was assigned a position in the Ministry of the Congregation for the Evangelization of
the People, which he accepted as if it were a punishment, and a
trace of that resigned obedience characterized his style of governing,
stifling his joy in the promulgation of the truth as revealed by Christ.

In the case of the conclave, the opposite dynamic is taking
place. The ex-Trappist monk is better prepared than anyone else
for that escape from the world. He is generous with his advice and
quick to make himself available to the chamberlain and his officials, as if his experiences in the cloister made him uniquely of
service to those now in need.

On the evening of the funeral for the Brazilian cardinal, Paide,
who is from the Estonian island of Sarema, finds himself alone
with the chamberlain in his rooms.

"I'm worried, Paide, very worried, about how things are going,"
Veronelli says, collapsing into his armchair.

"You shouldn't be. It seems like everything is going the way it
should, as it has so many other times," says the former monk, who
had lived at the Tre Fontane cloister in Rome for almost twenty
years.

"But we no longer live in the past. This is an unprecedented
situation, pressed by irrefutable contingencies, constrained by the
legacy of a pope who has grown larger than life. How can anyone
live up to him? Do you see how everyone disagrees? Sometimes I
think they don't want to find a successor, but then the idea of an
extended stay here fills them with terror."

"You're exaggerating, Vladimiro. We've only voted a few times
now. Some conclaves have gone on for several months."

"A week has gone by already."

"That's only seven days."

"God created the world in seven days."

"We've only just begun to understand the blessings of this

cloistered experience. It's still too early to appreciate it entirely."

"The blessings of this cloistered experience? Do you really think they could think of it like that?"

"They ought to stay here for a year! Then they would truly have a sense of rebirth upon coming out."

"And who would govern the Church in the meantime?"

"It would govern itself. And the faithful would rediscover the value of their pastors, in the absence of their sins."

"You're thinking like a Trappist now, and not like a cardinal. When you accepted the zucchetto from the pope you took on that responsibility, too."

"I'm trying to help you, but you don't want to understand what I'm saying. You're thinking in mundane terms, too much like the terms of the powerful."

"Why, we cardinals aren't powerful? Doesn't the precarious stability of several governments rest on the shoulders of the men lodging here? Aren't they influential in deciding the outcome of a thousand political alliances, of countless regimes and economic forces? Even in Italy they've come to appreciate our powers of mediation after our success at negotiating labor strikes in the cities."

"You shouldn't use those words within these walls: parties, unions, coalitions, economy, industry. The world dies under the burden of those words. If you employ them here, this conclave will be reduced to the ridiculous, as is the world for those who want to write with a feather pen instead of a computer. Let the impure language of the world cease — at least here!"

"But I have to mediate between the two worlds that you want to keep separate! You know who called me a little while ago under the pretense of sending his condolences for Contardi? The President of the Italian Congress! You should have heard him questioning me, insisting on learning the names of the frontrunners. Then he went on to talk about fairness in the schools at a time like this, trying to influence me!"

"Let him talk, let them all say what they will, confuse them with chatter, and always say yes. The lies you utter will be holy lies, in the service of truth."

"So you align yourself with my way of doing things?"

"Did anyone ever declare war on you? When did I ever fail to perform my duty? I've been in charge of the ministry that the Holy Father imposed on me for almost ten years now. God knows how difficult it was for me to leave my cell at the Tre Fontane. There, I only had God above me. I was already dead to the world! But then that venerable man burdened me once again with the load I had cast off."

"Don't you think that it takes something out of me to police the Sacred College, and to attend solely to the practical and political problems of this event?"

Paide doesn't answer. He would rather not hurt his friend by saying that, given his nature, he is the right man for the job. He decides to change the subject, and does so in an extreme and surprising way. "Actually, cloistered life can be a joy, but those who have never experienced it often need help to see it that way. The body needs to be conditioned to appreciate it, and the senses, too. Look at us northerners, who live in constant isolation in our semi-deserted countries. I had to walk thirty miles before meeting another person. Other than my sister, Karin, I never saw or played with any other children when I was growing up, and the only adults I knew were my parents and my grandparents."

"So what do you think I should do to mitigate the rigors of this retreat?"

For the second time, Paide chooses not to say what he is thinking. Veronelli, who reduces everything to its most practical dimension, won't understand. He must advance slowly, so as not to overwhelm him. "You know, in our solitude many of the taboos that exist in crowded societies were eliminated. We sought each other out because there were so few of us."

"Well, we're quite numerous here. Besides the 126 cardinals there are 110 service people at various levels, 20 domestic prelates, a troop of 100 Swiss Guards, and each cardinal's personal secretary, and that's not counting the nuns in the kitchen, who aren't allowed into the conclave itself."

"The feeling of solitude is the same. Up there, on my island of

Sarema, we were surrounded by nature. Here we stand before God. As a child I could only perceive of God through the sea, the grass, the stars, and in the light of the aurora borealis. Then my eyes looked within and I could see."

This is difficult philosophical terrain for Veronelli to tread.

Paide is filled with compassion for him. He doesn't want to make him feel inadequate, nor does he want to humiliate him. He has the old Vatican ways about him; he can't absorb things that are foreign to his way of thinking. It is the destiny of most men — to be dead before they die, in their inability to accept the new and diverse.

Given the chamberlain's limitations, Paide sees how useless it is to circumvent the argument. Better to proceed directly to the heart of the matter. "Do you know what the greatest joy was for me, as a child, on my island? Taking a sauna with my parents, as naked as God made us, on the edge of the lake behind our house. We had everything: furnaces and tubs, even birch trees right outside the door. We'd use the branches for lashing each other's backs."

"Once, when I was in Helsinki, the Lutheran bishop who was hosting me took me to a hotel for a sauna; I got a terrible cold."

"They probably didn't teach you how to do it properly. There is an art to taking a sauna. Maybe it would be worth trying again. I could teach you how."

"Where? I don't think I'll be going back to Helsinki any time soon."

"Not in Helsinki. Here."

"Here?"

"Yes, in the conclave."

The chamberlain of the Holy Roman Church, Cardinal Vladimiro Veronelli, Titulary of the Church of San Carlo di Catinari, looked directly at the former Trappist monk who had been elevated to the purple expressly for the fame of his spirituality and doctrinal policies.

"Don't be shocked. All the cardinals from Eastern Europe would be happy to have access to this relaxing treatment, alternating dry heat and steam, just as they do in their own countries, and the way I did when I lived with my parents. There's nothing wrong with the nudity of the body; the experience helps eliminate all sorts of barriers between us. Think of the people shut inside here: age and power have made them rot inside, amid barriers higher than the Great Wall of China."

"You're not joking, are you? You really believe in this . . . what should I call it? This madness, this nonsense, this transgression. No, I'm sorry, but I have respect for the cassock that we wear."

"I'm not being clear, am I? A retreat should be a joy, a rebirth after being dead to the world, albeit a rebirth somewhere else, in a different way. . . . But it needs help. The body is a gift from God, not a sin that we need to be pardoned for."

"When you were in the monastery at the Tre Fontane did you have a sauna?"

"No, it was a Catholic convent, and in Rome, so I had to respect the rules. No, I'm talking about a different monastery. The one on my island, in Estonia. But now we need to think about this conclave, which you rightfully see as unique in all of history. You're afraid that it will last a long time, too long for these elderly men who have never experienced the joys of solitude. Most of the cardinals here haven't been suffocated by the trappings of their vestments, but by their power, by their roles and their privileges. They're like actors who have grown weary of their scripts. They've forgotten about nudity without sin, without malice, they can no longer recall the innocence of the nudity of a newborn child."

"Do you really believe we can take saunas in the conclave?"

"Look at the crucifix on the wall behind you. Except for the loincloth, it is naked, as naked as each one of us was made. Our brothers pray in front of the very same crucifix each night before they go to sleep."

"I hope you're not comparing Christ on a cross with a naked cardinal!"

"You're the one who injects malice into that comparison, with your Roman, counter-reformist culture that denies holiness of the flesh. To think that one of the most beautiful promises of our religion is the resurrection of the flesh with the glorious body that we had when we were young, at the height of our youthful vigor."

"How can you ignore the fact that some of our guests might not be able to look at naked flesh with innocent intentions?"

"I don't pretend to ignore it. I only think that some of them wouldn't feel that inclination if they had been accustomed to being naked as children. Assuming that such an inclination is truly a sin, and not simply a perception that differs from that of the majority . . . No, don't look at me like that; I don't have the same thoughts as my brethren with the carnal gaze, you can rest reassured."

"Do you know what would happen if the world were to find out that the cardinals were taking saunas during the conclave, instead of reading, sleeping, conversing, and praying?"

"The world? What is the world? What we have in our heads? The past that I was describing no longer exists, you said so yourself. The world is constantly in flux. That's why you worry so much about governing this conclave, because none of your previous experiences can help you now. You have no handbook to refer to. The world is made by us, by our courage to make it a better place for the love of man."

"Perhaps I'm just too old to follow you. All I know is that I am, and will remain, a cardinal of the Holy Roman Catholic and Apostolic Church."

"The sequester should be experienced like a Mount Carmel of delights, not a Thebaid of diabolical temptations, or a desert of thorns. The joy of the senses also brings us to God, and it is an ineffable joy. Think of Saint Bonaventure rather than Thomas Aquinas."

"But your proposal is unacceptable. The other cardinals wouldn't tolerate it either."

"It's only one of the initiatives that would help us to better endure this experience, but there are others. Personally, I don't think it would create too much opposition. You're forgetting that half of the cardinals have cultural traditions that relate directly to the body, to physicality. In the Middle East, Turkish baths are common meeting places. Indians give great spiritual meaning to the pleasures of the body. And how can we forget that all across the Mediterranean, both Greeks and Romans considered the thermal baths a cultural and political meeting place, not simply a place for pleasure? Remember the human experience that preceded Christianity; it still runs through our veins."

"What do you expect me to do? Transform the Apostolic Palace into a luxury hotel with beauty parlors, massages therapists, two kinds of restaurants, a bar, and a gym?"

"Now that you mention it, the conclave does need to be updated. But it's late now, Vladimiro; I don't want to take advantage of your kindness. Sleep on it."

"All I will be able to think about is the desecration that would occur between these walls."

"There, too, I'm forced to disagree with you. The sacred is not only renunciation, penitence, hair shirts, and darkness, but also expansion, happiness, beauty, and light. Goodnight. See you tomorrow."

They say goodbye without shaking hands. The chamberlain is greatly unsettled by his conversation with "the Monk," as Paide is called by those same people in the Vatican who call the archbishop of Milan "La Signora." Paide, meanwhile, leaves with conflicting feelings. He is full of regret at having disillusioned the chamberlain, who only expected some simple advice on how to speed things along, and he is surprised at how he let himself go, bringing up such topics.

Paide walks down the long hallway that leads to the staircase. At the corner of the narrow passageway he hears a pendulum clock strike the hour. It is two o'clock in the morning. He feels a strong draft coming from a large open window that faces south, toward the city of Rome. The distant lights of the city pulse with vitality, even in the middle of the night, when the hours devoted to rest can also accommodate the other necessities of the flesh; pleasure above all, and love, in whatever form it takes.

In that hour stolen from sleep and dedicated to conversation, he had undergone a strange test, aimed more at himself than at the chamberlain. There, in the heart of the Catholic tradition,

where everything was filtered by ceremony and nothing was improvised or left to chance, he had dared to speak of carnal
pleasure, of the joy of living, of a conception of the sacred that saw
both beauty and victory in Christ.

What had given him the courage to speak like that? In days
gone by he would have been barred from carrying out his duties.
He would have been taken to the Holy Offices and put on trial.
Were his ideas a form of heresy? Was the Devil at work in his en-
flamed defense of nature and the senses? What did he really know
about love and pleasure, after all, he who had sublimated his pas-
sions into his faith for so long. At the age of twenty he had been
enchanted by a most beguiling light, there in the desolation of his
island, but he came to realize that this passion for his sister Karin
could never be legitimized.

Upon the manifestation of that love, the first and only of his
life, he felt obliged to abandon his island forever, and without
leaving a trace. He used to worry that Karin would come after
him. Five years after he left, when he was a student of theology at
Marburg, he received news of her premature death. He didn't
even have the courage to return to his parents to mourn with
them. And yet, from then on he felt the desire to love her, and to
live out the burning flame of their passion through prayer.

Now, at the age of sixty-six, that memory lived on inside him,
intact. It was as if almost fifty years hadn't passed at all. Oddly
enough, he had learned to be grateful to destiny for having let
him experience the fever of love for a woman.

Naturally, women were forbidden from the conclave, just as
they had been excluded from the sacerdotal life of all those aged
men. Half the world is missing from that echelon of people who
must understand the world and minister to its ills. They must
temper its violence, accompany it through its follies, and pardon
its weaknesses. The marvelous scandal of reason is that it supports
universal love in the renouncing of love. This was the path he
took after the incident with his sister, long before he could realize
that it was the first step. Now he sees that it had been the biggest
blessing of his life.

But maybe he is wrong about his old confreres, who lie in their beds now, paying off the debt to their bodies through sleep. Perhaps many of them retain in their hearts the secret of a love that was forbidden or impossible or denied by the very ethics that they now represent. And perhaps from this repression they, too, summoned the strength to love God.

6

THE TABLE IN Ettore Malvezzi's studio where the Italian cardinals have reconvened is cluttered with newspapers printed in several languages. The cardinal of Palermo selects the most malicious headlines and reads them aloud.

"'Still no agreement on the tenth day of conclave'; 'A battle of factions in the most difficult conclave in centuries'; 'Do the Italians stand a chance? Black smoke after the seventeenth round of voting'; 'Cerini burned on the first round.' Can you believe it!" Rabuiti exclaims, noticing the pun on Cerini's name, which means matches. "'Eastern cardinals are favored, but a French curate is in the running.' Did you hear that Jean? This one's about you." He turns to show the headlines of *Le Monde* to the former pontiff's secretary of state. "But wait, listen to the Chinese; I've already got the translation: 'How much does the Roman conclave cost per day? The so-called representatives of a God of poverty laze around in comfort and luxury at the expense of the Italian State, with no intention of leaving. Our government did well to deny a travel permit to the Chinese cardinal in Hong Kong.' Things never change with China, though the Russians are a bit more moderate in their aversion to orthodoxy: 'The cardinals of Rome take their time; who knows what goes on inside that center of power?' Catholicism hasn't been so visible in Russia since the times of Dostoyevsky."

"Even back then, they didn't really understand what was going on," says Nicola Gistri, the archbishop of Florence, who knows Russian well and had translated the newspaper articles. "During the reign of Peter the Great, they held a weeklong revelry in which they parodied the court of Rome and elected their own pope."

Gistri had been the one to suggest a meeting of the Italians in Malvezzi's chambers. They all suspected the archbishop of Turin had voted for himself, and wanted him to feel the burden of his untrustworthiness. Malvezzi agreed to the meeting without hesitation, accepting their suspicion in silence. Nothing could make him reveal the name of the person who had voted for him — how could he possibly explain his conversation with the Lebanese cardinal? It would only have magnified a truth that continued to frighten him, especially in light of the recent elections, and the increasingly tempestuous climate created by the Eastern European and American cardinals, who seemed intent on resurrecting ghosts from the Cold War. And the single vote in his favor would still remain.

Over the past several nights sleep had not come easily to him; his senses were tuned to the many sounds coming from the various wings of the ancient palace, whose hidden secrets he was slowly beginning to pry forth, revealing hidden life teeming behind the closed doors.

A few mornings earlier he could no longer bear to lie in bed awake, so at five-thirty he put on his cassock, moving stealthily so as not to arouse Monsignor Contarini in the other room. He strolled up and down the corridors on his floor of the Apostolic Palace, gazing at the frescoes of Alessandro Mantovani, who in the times of Leo XIII had been heralded as the new Raphael. He was surprised to discover that hardly anyone was still sleeping at that hour. He encountered prelates and waiters hurrying to reply to calls from his colleagues. He saw personal secretaries going up and down the stairs toward the kitchen, the trays in their hands either full of food or laden with medicine bottles, carafes of water, and drinking glasses. He even saw doctors rushing back and forth: one carrying a blood pressure cuff, another a box of syringes. The fundamental cause for all of this pre-dawn movement, the unfortunate impetus, was that his colleagues in this adventure, though advanced in age, had not yet attained the eighty years that would end their right and obligation to participate in the conclave.

The following night Malvezzi traveled beyond the atrium on his floor to the loggia that opens onto the courtyard of San Damasus, in search of some fresh air. Passing in front of a doorway, he heard the cardinal of Sydney cry out in pain, soothed only with the help of morphine. So desperately had the cardinal wanted to participate in the conclave that he asked his doctor not to reveal the advanced state of his cancer. Apparently, the quantities of morphine permitted by the Vatican physicians were quite generous. Someone, it might have been Rabuiti, said that the archbishop of Rio de Janeiro owed his demise to abuse of the same substance during his final crisis in his battle with leukemia.

At dawn that morning, Malvezzi returned to his room and called the operator, asking to be connected with his sister in Bologna. He knew that Clara woke up early.

"Is that you Ettore? How are you?"

"I'm fine, just a bit worried."

"Why? What's going on?"

"Nothing; everything's at a standstill. You've probably read the papers. But let's talk about something else. How's Francesco? Did you buy him a car? Is he going to America this summer?"

"Of course we bought him a car. We had to. It's safer than going around on the scooter. So we've gone from living in a state of constant fear to one of light apprehension. You can imagine. Anyway, we had to get it for him; all his friends have one."

"What about America?"

"We haven't decided yet, but I don't think so."

"You made him study English ever since he was a child and yet you expect him to spend his summers in Rimini or Rapallo?"

"I think there's a girl behind it. That's the real reason he wants to go."

"A girl? Already?"

"He's twenty years old, Ettore!"

"Who is it? Do you know anything about her?"

"Of course! She's two years older than he is, and she's going to America to work as an au pair. She's from a good family, as we used to say."

"We still say it. Have you seen her?"

"Several times, without him knowing; you have no idea how it feels to see him with his arm around that little blond. Yesterday he finally introduced her to us."

"Now don't be jealous!"

"I'd like to see you in my place."

"You're right. But maybe you shouldn't let him go to America. I think he's too young."

"Not really, Ettore. Several of his friends have already traveled extensively."

And while his sister continued talking, responding to all of his questions, Ettore Malvezzi felt the oppressive atmosphere of his rooms begin to lift, and his thoughts were transported to distant realms of memory, to the image of his nephew in front of him the last time he had seen him — already taller than he was. Francesco was always energetic, always on the go, always calling someone or receiving a phone call. He would talk to several people at once — his uncle, his mother, his friend on the phone — always while eating, his shirt unbuttoned, an earring in his left lobe.

In the middle of his conversation with Clara, Malvezzi was pulled back to the realities of his current situation, and the bright image of youth that had been entertaining his thoughts was abruptly erased. Near the wall a few feet away from him, two large rats were scuffling over something. It must have been some kind of food, maybe the remainder of the cheese sandwich he had left on the tray the night before. For some reason, Contarini hadn't picked it up before he left. They were hideous looking rats: black, long, and skinny, with pointed faces, long whiskers, and bright white eyes.

He shivered. These were not the gentle country mice that he was accustomed to in his house in the hills of the Langhe. And they weren't like the water rats that live in the canals of Venice either. These animals had a sinister way of moving; they were very bold, rushing toward the tray to grab a piece of cheese, even though he was standing right there.

"Ettore are you still there? Can you hear me?"

"Yes, I'm here. Sorry. I got distracted."

"Are you all right? How's your arthritis?"

"It's fine. I got distracted by a pair of rats, two incredibly big ones."

"What! Call someone and tell them to disinfest the Vatican," Clara exclaimed. She never had much sympathy for the clergy.

"It's not that easy," Malvezzi said, and as he and his sister were exchanging farewells, the two rats, just a few feet from him, launched into a battle over a piece of provolone, with a singular display of impertinence. It was a bitter duel, full of advances, retreats, bites, and ferocious battle squeaks. "I have to go now; these rats are really going at it."

"I forgot to ask you something. It's nothing important, but it made me wonder, and it made Francesco laugh. A friend of mine from Vicenza called to say that she had read in the paper that they were going to start up a Turkish bath in the conclave. Is it true?"

"Turkish bath? How did they come up with that one?"

"I don't know, Ettore, but all the same, they should liven the conclave up a bit."

After he hung up, Malvezzi rolled up a newspaper to chase away the rats, but they ran to the other side of the spacious room, toward the doorway that opened into Contarini's quarters. Just then, the secretary appeared. Upon seeing the rats he lost all sense of composure and began to scream.

"Contarini, what are you doing? Go get a broom! Tell someone they need to disinfest the rooms. Go!"

Contarini, who was never one to repress his need to smoke, not even in front of a cardinal, pulled a cigarette from his pocket and quickly lit it as he prepared to leave.

"Not in my room!"

But the chaplain's slender figure had already disappeared, although certainly he wouldn't be bold enough to smoke in the hallway. Likewise, Malvezzi's nephew Francesco used to drive his mother crazy over all the cigarettes he snuck into her house.

Malvezzi can't keep his thoughts from returning to his nephew, even as the meeting with the Italian cardinals heats up over the headlines in the newspapers that are spread across his desk. Suddenly, the door swings open and a young Swiss Guard appears. He wavers unsteadily on his feet, his uniform in disarray, and he holds his helmet in his hand.

None of the cardinals dares say a word. A drunken guard? Someone could raise a fuss about this, causing endless problems for the chamberlain and his court.

The young man evidently opened the wrong door, and Malvezzi suspects he knows where the man was headed. He recognizes the soldier's strikingly handsome face, his blue eyes, and the rebellious shock of blond hair protruding from his helmet, and knows him to be one of Contarini's most frequent companions.

"How dare you disturb us?" the archbishop of Milan says, expressing the affront, and perhaps the inkling of fear, that his colleagues are feeling. "And what a state you're in! Tell me your name. Tomorrow I'm going to report you to your commanding officer." But the biggest surprise is yet to come. The young man turns around quickly and runs out of the room, disappearing into the labyrinth of hallways.

"Ah, blissful youth. Let him go; in truth, it must be tedious to be a twenty-year-old, guarding such old men." The words just tumble out of Malvezzi's mouth, almost before he realizes it. He was speaking more to himself than to his colleagues, but he had been thinking about Francesco, and how the blessed irrationality of youth can restore a sense of humanity even to the conclave.

But "La Signora" seems to think otherwise. "I'm surprised at you, Ettore: defending a young ruffian who has betrayed his orders. Why, he offended and ignored us," Cerini says.

Dean Leporati, the only cardinal to rush from the room in an effort to call the soldier back, returns, struggling to catch his breath. "He disappeared. If I were a few years younger I would have caught him. Tomorrow I'll have the commander find him; they'll be able to recognize him."

"No, let him be. He's probably so scared he'll never try any-thing like that again," Malvezzi insists, not at all intimidated by Cerini and his comments. He tries to change the subject, hoping to draw their thoughts to more urgent matters, such as how the conclave is being portrayed in the press. "I think we should screen all the news that leaves here; it might even be necessary to block the phone calls. Or just tap them."

"That will be hard to do, Ettore, and besides, it would only in-crease the number of clandestine calls," the archbishop of Flo-rence says, accepting the invitation to ignore the young soldier's rashness. "You can forget about that diabolical Internet, too."

"I've noticed something, and it surprises me that no one has mentioned it yet," says the archbishop of Milan. True to form, his preamble promises a polemical argument. Everyone becomes silent, eyes fixed on Cerini at his dark corner of the table. "Listen, are we in charge of the conclave, or is it being run by the men who own those tabloids full of lies? To panic about not moving quickly enough is to admit that we must adjust our position ac-cording to the image that we are generating, thanks to the media and all their falsehoods. We've known the owners of these papers for quite some time. We know whom they fear, whom they serve, who runs them, and what they've paid in order to get where they are today. We might have even used their influence in our favor once or twice, to present certain facts in a more appealing light. This is what I have to say: let's not read the papers anymore. We must have the dignity and courage worthy of the task to which we've been called!"

"You're right, Alfonso," Malvezzi says, surprised that Cerini reasoned in ideal terms rather than political ones, "we're chasing our own images in order to catch them. It's as if our shadow had become more powerful than our body, and the body was nothing more than a slave."

"If the Church falls into the trap of looking for a consensus, then we're in trouble," the Florentine prelate says, looking around the room through his thick glasses to see who else would be willing to ignore the clamor of the media over such a closely followed event.

"Let's not exaggerate now," Rabuiti replies, piqued that his colleague from Milan has opted for such an antiquated position. "Television has always been good to us. Even the opening of the conclave earned us millions of spectators." He then takes the opportunity to abandon the thorny argument by calling the cardinals back to the priorities on their agenda. "Excuse me, but didn't we come here to prepare for the next round of voting? Shouldn't we be talking about what we've learned from sounding out the others?"

The conversation instantly returns to the elections, and to the maneuverings of some of the nations most recently come to the fore.

7

CHAMBERLAIN VERONELLI doesn't even have time to finish his dinner. He has to rush off to Saint John's Tower with the chief engineer of Vatican City, Count Nasalli Rocca. Two nights before he had been able to linger in peace over the meal prepared exclusively for him by the nuns in the kitchen: saffron risotto, artichokes *alla giudea*, fruit salad with maraschino liqueur, and a white wine from Locorotondo.

Actually, he had been forced to savor each mouthful of the meal prepared for him by the nuns, because he was still unaccustomed to his new dental implant, which rendered his gums extremely sensitive and did not allow him to chew with his usual speed. To think he had once been such a fast eater. As a boy, he was often scolded for hurrying through his meals, unlike his brothers, who always provided a better example. He hadn't heard from his brothers in a long time, nor from his sisters-in-law, nor his nephews or nieces, who were all married now, with children of their own. An enormous family, they weren't in the habit of asking favors from their eminent uncle, who secretly favored one of his nieces, a novice in a convent in Naples. Of course, they had given him their fair share of headaches, and occasionally he had even spoiled them. But they never gave him as many headaches as the brothers who surround him now. Every day he has to contend with their enterprises and schemes, their attempts to violate the rules, their spiteful acts and rivalries, their alliances and sudden annulments, and the oddities of a mosaic so intricately composed of diverse races and traditions that it simply wore him down.

As he was considering the paradoxical results of the meeting he had held with the cardinals from Eastern Europe, he mused over the recent strange occurrences.

First, there had been the invasion of rats. They weren't sewer rats, or river rats, or field mice; they were monstrous things with ferocious faces and beady eyes. In a matter of days they had divided up the terrain like troops from Hell, bent on taking over Paradise. They scurried between the cardinals' feet in the Sistine Chapel, even while the *Veni Creator Spiritus* was being sung. When the Cardinal of Tokyo felt himself being bitten as one of them gnawed on the sole of his shoe, he let out a scream, enriching the chromatic scale of that sacred hymn with a truly dramatic, albeit somewhat comical, high note. That same afternoon the elections showed the first semblance of a majority — it was the most consistent election since the beginning of the conclave — and the focus was on one of the most debated cardinals: the Palestinian, Nabil Youssef. However, Veronelli thought, as he slowly sipped his wine, it had been a cruel joke to simulate an agreement on him, almost a trick of the Devil rather than the inspiration of the Holy Ghost. After his name was read out, the rivalries and debates exploded as never before. The archbishop of Boston even got to his feet and walked toward the Palestinian's throne, exclaiming in English, "Don't get your hopes up; your career ends here!"

The problem of how to deal with the rats had not yet been solved. Extermination crews weren't allowed to enter the conclave, even though new reports on the alarming situation were reaching the chamberlain on a daily basis.

The most worrisome complaint came from the Vatican Museum. The horrid animals had begun to gnaw away at altars, icons, drapes, and veneer tables. They chewed on paintings of every imaginable kind, although it seemed as though they had a preference for the sacred ones, which were most prevalent in that collection, unique in all the world. It was horrible to see them gnawing on the saints' haloes and bishops' miters; they left teeth marks on the wheel of Saint Catherine, on Saint Lucy's eyes, and on Saint Agatha's breasts, on the aureoles of cherubs, on the Madonna's cloak as she fled to Egypt, and on Christ's red robe as the Roman legionnaires were casting lots. And when the rats returned, only emboldened by the attempts to chase them away, they chewed through the mane of the lion resting at the feet of Saint Jerome in his study, through the oars of Saint Paul's boat, which had shipwrecked at Malta, its sails torn by the wind on the Sea of Galilee, just before Heaven calmed the storm.

The phenomenon became especially disturbing after someone noticed that the indefatigable teeth of the blasphemous creatures had not even grazed the holy figures of Christ or his venerated mother. Even the poor, lost chamberlain (as two cardinals from the Curia, Rafanelli and Rondoni, had taken to calling him) had deduced that God was protecting the palace where for centuries he had been continually served and betrayed.

How long would this go on? It seemed to depend on them, on the gifts the Holy Father had bestowed upon them, illuminating their choices. And not just choices about voting in a conclave that had reached its twenty-second day, but those that arose daily out of the communal life these strangers were living, and from the diverse customs they held dear. One of the most unpleasant choices had been made just a few hours earlier, during the chamberlain's meeting with the cardinals from Eastern Europe in the quarters of "the Monk," Cardinal Matis Paide.

Everyone had agreed with Paide when, with a detached air, he repeated his request for a sauna and Turkish bath. Polite in his actions, he asked simply and spontaneously, as if he had been requesting only the favor of an extra blanket for those old men who were so quick to take chill. Veronelli suspected that he owed to Paide the indiscreet leak to the newspapers that the cardinals in the Vatican might profit from the therapeutic vapors of such structures. Who else could it have been?

Again, it seemed like the image created by the media had dictated their behavior, and not vice versa. The chamberlain knew that this point had recently been discussed in one of the Italians' most explosive meetings. He had been forced to give in, although he couldn't quite believe it would actually happen. He gave orders to the construction crews to work day and night to renovate Saint John's Tower in a distant wing of the palace and erect the structure within two days. In exchange, however, the chamberlain made the Eastern Europeans agree that if the votes once again seemed to be centering on the Palestinian, they wouldn't dispute it. Who knows, Veronelli thought to himself, maybe the Palestinian will be elected pope before the Turkish baths are ready.

But that is not what happened. The elections, both in the morning and the afternoon, brought a renewed dispersion of votes. Meanwhile, two days after the chamberlain's slow and painful dinner, Count Paolo Nasalli Rocca, the chief engineer of Vatican City, informed His Eminence that Saint John's Tower was ready. If His Eminence would kindly come with him, he would gladly show him the new structures at work.

"At work? Already? Since when?"

"This afternoon. The archbishops of Prague and Warsaw and their secretaries decided to inaugurate it," says Nasalli Rocca, marveling that Veronelli hasn't been told.

So, immediately following his dinner, consumed much more hurriedly this time and reduced to only a few mouthfuls on account of his denture problem, the chamberlain agrees to follow the architect of that abominable service to Saint John's Tower. The chamberlain walks slowly, carrying a bag hastily prepared for him by his personal assistant. He has no desire to know what clothes are inside the bag; he simply doesn't want to think about how one should present oneself in such a place. Consequently, he left the choice of what he should wear to Monsignor Squarzoni, who for twenty years has been in charge of his wardrobe, together with Sister Maria Rosaria, who is waiting for him outside the conclave.

As they pass from one dimly lit room to another, he realizes that the closer they come to Saint John's Tower, the more his apprehension grows at asking the engineer the question he did not have the courage to ask his secretary: how does one dress in a Turkish bath? He is on the verge of opening his mouth to pose this embarrassing question when a wave of rats rushes out from a room, stopping the men in their tracks. There are too many to count, far more than have been seen altogether in all the various wings of the Apostolic Palace. And yet, the place had been inspected from floor to ceiling by an emergency squadron of would-be exterminators — members of the papal choir, armed with rat venom and summoned to take on a new trade in light of the infestation. Because of their isolation from the outside world during those days that had been passing ever more slowly, resourcefulness was essential.

"Not here, too! Not here! I have no one else to send. They're all helping out with the artwork in the museums. What will the world say when they find out that Leonardo da Vinci's *Saint Jerome* has been eaten by rats?"

"Be careful, Your Eminence, they're dangerous. They might bite. Since we've started locking up all the food, they're ravenous."

"Please go first, Nasalli Rocca, you who have fewer winters weighing over your shoulders and can better withstand the danger."

But it is not easy walking down the long hallway that leads to Saint John's Tower. Why so many rats should be drawn to that one room, they do not understand. The chamberlain motions to Nasalli Rocca to stop for a moment. He wants to look inside the room. He retraces his steps and throws the door wide open.

And then he understands. It is a repository for paintings — the official portraits of the cardinals, waiting for restoration. Their likenesses have all but disappeared, with only vague outlines remaining: their lineaments, their scarlet capes, and their hands resting on the Gospel. The room swarms with the monstrous destroyers, who are bent on erasing faces, names, and titles from memory. The jumble of canvases and frames has become an immense, quaking mass, crumbling and collapsing before being devoured by the ravenous beasts.

When the door opens, the rats seem to recognize a threat. The larger ones leap down in bunches and scurry for the exit.

Nasalli Rocca barely succeeds in pulling the chamberlain from the room to safety, and then struggles to close the door.

"How absolutely hideous!"

"Tomorrow morning I'll call the Municipality of Rome, Your Eminence. They have specialists they can send in."

"But we can't, you know."

"As you decide, Your Eminence, but the situation calls for an exception to the rules of the conclave."

"Why, because of rats? Those aren't such great pieces of art-work. And maybe some of us ought not to be remembered, anyway."

"What about the artwork in the Vatican Museums? And the canvases in the chapels of the Vatican Palace?"

"Those I'm concerned about, but the choristers can manage for now."

"Those mild-mannered men? They have wonderful voices, but forgive me, Your Eminence, they certainly don't know how to handle an extinguisher or a water gun, not to mention a gas mask. They're hopeless!"

The chamberlain calms himself and stares straight ahead. He lets the discussion drop. It had to happen during his conclave, when all he wanted to do was retire and move to Arcetri, in the hills of his beloved Tuscany. Why did this have to happen to him?

And now? What does one do in a Turkish bath? How does one behave among so many nude men? Because there, inside the baths, the naked cardinals will no longer have anything that distinguishes them from other men. He takes a deep breath and asks his question. "Nasalli Rocca, why don't you come with me into the Turkish baths?"

His tone is so weak and imploring that it embarrasses the engineer. What on earth should he say to that trembling old man? But Nasalli Rocca, who is fifty-two years old, six-feet-two, handsome, in good health, and well-versed in human nature, recovers his composure and says nonchalantly, "Of course, Your Eminence. But you'll have to lend me a towel because I didn't bring one with me."

"Towel? Why? Does one wear towels in there?"

"Well, yes, either a towel or a robe. But I see your bag is well equipped."

"I have no idea what's in it. Monsignor Squarzoni prepared it for me. I haven't got the slightest idea as to how one behaves in such a place. That's why I'd like you to come in; you know how these things work."

The head engineer smiles at the cardinal's ingenuousness and inexperience.

They are almost at the entrance to the tower. The engineer explains that the sauna and Turkish bath lie just beyond a new glass door, but before they reach their destination he musters up the courage to make a suggestion to Veronelli. He too had been afraid of saying something.

"Excuse me, Your Eminence, but about the invasion of rats: there is one way of remedying the situation. It's old-fashioned, but it's much more efficient than disinfestations, though it might be slightly inappropriate."

"Why, do you think a sauna is appropriate? At this point, nothing surprises me."

"Cats, Your Eminence. Cats have been the surest way of dealing with rats since God created the universe."

"Cats! It's true! They would end the problem. We have them in Arcetri, too."

"Rome is full of cats. Some neighborhoods are overrun with them. And they couldn't ask for a nicer meal than our rats."

"You're right. My nephew in Trastevere feeds at least ten of them. Why didn't we think of it before? Find out how we can go about capturing a good number of them. We'd be doing a good service to the neighborhoods. If necessary, we can even pay for them. Or if their owners lend them to us, we can promise to return them. We can guarantee them the animals will be well-fed. If they're pious people they'll have the added indulgence of assisting the Church."

"And if they're not pious, maybe they like art. Don't forget the museums, Your Eminence."

"You'll have to act with discretion, at any rate. We can't just ask the government for help like that."

"Of course, I'll equip our most adept seminarians for the hunt. I just hope the choristers will have better luck catching cats than they did snaring rats."

"Let's hope so, Count, let's hope so. Just do it soon, please."

When the chamberlain crosses the threshold into the sauna it is past 11:30 at night. He feels so relieved by the thought of the cats that he even finds the strength to smile at the two monsignors in purple terry cloth robes who kneel down to kiss his ring.

"This way, Your Eminence. We'll show you to your changing room."

"The head engineer will need one, too; he wants to see how his work of art is functioning," Veronelli calls out, following the two monsignors with a light step.

8

Only the cardinals of Prague and Warsaw? No, the engineer must have heard wrong. We've been working all afternoon trying to serve everyone who . . ." the tired face of the older monsignor reveals he is telling the truth. "It's been practically a parade, only . . ." he interrupts himself, thinking it improper to make such a comparison.

"Indeed, a true parade," says the chamberlain, his confidence growing. "Isn't human nature strange? I was so sure that I'd be criticized for this blessed structure. Now that I think of it, I should bless it, I suppose."

"The vessel of holy water is already here for the asperges. Here is your changing room; the engineer's is over there."

"Hand me my bag. Let's open it together. I have to lend something to the engineer, though I'm not sure precisely what. He forgot his bag at home," the chamberlain says nonchalantly, preferring not to show the two assistants that he doesn't know what the bag contains.

Out of his bag come a pair of woolen thermal underwear with suspenders, two white fluffy towels, one smaller towel, a pair of shorts, rubber sandals, a shoehorn, a comb, a brush, a hairdryer, some moisturizing skin cream, and a bottle of eau de toilette.

The looks on the faces of the two monsignors are impenetrable, and do not suggest at all to Veronelli whether or not he has brought the right gear, nor can he tell what should be given to the engineer. Fortunately, Nasalli Rocca comes to the cardinal's aid. "The small towel will be fine; I'll wrap it around my waist. And if you have an extra pair of sandals, I'll be all set."

"We'll find you a pair immediately."

"You don't happen to have an extra bathrobe for His Eminence, do you? Something like the ones you're wearing? I think that would be perfect for him," the engineer politely suggests.

"Yes, but not purple, of course. The cardinals should wear white. Here you are, Your Eminence. When you are inside the sauna you'll be able to take the robe off and hang it on a hook."

"Bring one of your towels with you, too, Your Eminence. You might need one if you remove your robe. It all depends on the heat of the sauna and the steam. If my men have done a good job, it should be too hot for the robe."

"They've done an excellent job," one of the two monsignors says. "The cardinals from the East said that it is the perfect temperature, and they're experts."

"All right then, let's go, it's getting late. Is anyone still inside?"

"Of course, Your Eminence."

The chamberlain and the engineer disappear into their changing rooms. Nasalli Rocca comes out first, with the plum-colored towel around his midriff and the sandals on his feet. It's not at all cold in there, as he had feared it would be. Even the changing rooms are warm. In the distance he can hear music, organ music; it sounds familiar. It might be Handel's *Messiah*, though he can't be sure. Ten minutes pass before Veronelli appears from his changing room, bundled up in his white robe, the sandals on his feet a size too big.

"I'll give the benediction another time, when there's no one inside. Or else, Monsignor Attavanti can come on my behalf. I have so much to think about these days. Aren't you cold, Nasalli Rocca?"

"No, I'm very comfortable, Your Eminence."

"Lead the way, Monsignor."

"Follow me, please."

The group moves toward the revolving door at the end of the room. The music gets louder. The Ugandan monsignor enters first, followed by Nasalli Rocca and then the timorous chamberlain.

The interior is humid and dark. It's better this way, the chamberlain thinks; no one will recognize me. His heart is pounding, and for an instant he is tempted to turn around, as he glances back over his shoulder at the revolving door.

"Is that you, dear Vladimiro?"

In front of him, loosely draped in a robe, is a small, round man. In the weak light Veronelli can't make out his face. A jet of steam blows between them, hiding the man's face altogether, but Veronelli recognizes his voice. It is Celso Rabuiti.

As the steam clears, the disoriented chamberlain sees other white shapes moving about, indistinguishable in the penumbra. The music suddenly grows louder; it is indeed Handel's *Messiah*. Someone has forwarded it from the pastoral symphony to the triumphant finale of the "Hallelujah."

"Dear Vladimiro, we put on this music especially for you. We put it on as soon as we heard you were with us." The baritone voice belongs to Siro Ferrazzi, the archbishop of Bologna. Veronelli is now sweating profusely, and no longer knows where to look, for with his eyes accustomed now to the shadows, he can see several conclavists as nude as God made them.

In that mystical atmosphere, the men in white robes remind him of the extreme dignity of the white vestment that one of them is destined to wear. The garment already hangs waiting in a closet in three different sizes, to accommodate the physique of the new pope.

He can no longer bear the heat, so he loosens his belt, letting the robe slide down on his shoulders. It seems to weigh on him like a leaden cloak — the same gilded cloak of lead that tormented the hypocrites in Dante's *Inferno*.

"You must come this way," Rabuiti invites him, "to see the Finnish sauna."

"Where's Nasalli Rocca?" he asks, feeling incapable of proceeding without his guide, the person who had accompanied him through his metamorphosis from the chamberlain into a man who could strip off his clothes and soak in the steam; the only witness capable of reassuring him that he is not living out one of the worst nightmares of his life.

"Here I am, Your Eminence, right behind you. Can't you see me?"

"Now I can! I thought I had lost you."

If he ever emerges from this adventure, the first person to receive his wrath will be that demented Paide. To whom, though, will he be able to confess his sin? Who will be able to absolve him for agreeing to turn the Apostolic Palace into a spa? And how can his brethren walk around in there like seraphs in Paradise? What about that "Hallelujah," which is just now reaching the acme of its jubilant force? How on earth could they have welcomed him with that piece? Until then, he had heard it exclusively from the glory of his altar, where he stood dressed in his most sumptuous vestments, encrusted with gems and gold, under a miter embellished with gilded needlework, and the hymn was performed only during the most solemn occasions, when he was celebrating Mass with two other bishops in attendance. Now it was being played as he stood there half-naked, his weary flesh encouraging him to remove even that last layer that preserved his decency. That white robe! That white robe on those nude and semi-nude bodies! If it is so hot in this antechamber, what must it be like in the other room? Behind that door, no one could possibly tolerate wearing a robe. In an act of desperation, he blurts out: "Nasalli Rocca, isn't there a Turkish bath too? Take me there, please."

"All right, come this way then, back where we saw those jets of steam."

He follows Nasalli Rocca to a wooden door with a porthole in it that looks in on a darkened room. In crossing the threshold the penumbra gives way to an artificial blue light, though the steam makes it difficult to discern any details. Along three sides of the room there are benches where people are sitting, their robes removed. At least that blasphemous resemblance to their vestments has disappeared. But who are these people? He sees them rise to their feet. "Oh my God," he thinks, "they've recognized me, and they want to pay their respect. And here come the final notes of the 'Hallelujah,' too."

"It's an honor, Vladimiro."

"Welcome, welcome, dear Vladimiro."

"What a pleasure to see you here!"

"Please, please don't get up," he says, recognizing among the dulcet voices the man who had instigated all of this, Matis Paide, while Nasalli Rocca invites him to sit down.

"Relax, Your Eminence. The beauty of the Turkish baths is the relief that it provides to our weary bodies. Sit down here, next to me. Allow me to hang up your bathrobe, just keep your towel on your waist, but let it be loose, let the air circulate. Like this."

He lets himself be guided like a child, surrendering all efforts to resist. He sits down next to Nasalli Rocca and abandons himself to the warmth, to the caresses of the jets of steam, which rhythmically burst from two vents near the floor. The music is still Handel, but the selection is now a slow and formal recitative, far removed from the triumphant intonations of before. It is a pleasure to follow, as a growing languor invades his rigid limbs, slowly erasing the nagging worries that have been tormenting him.

The rats and their biblical infestation. The cats that need to be stolen from the city to become the paladins of the Vatican. The news from the outside world. The recent spate of telephone calls from powerful leaders. The agreements that broke down this morning during the elections. The animosity and polemics that arose from the Palestinian's nomination. Everything disappears; none of it is important enough to cause him continued grief as his body, his exhausted, seventy-eight-year-old body, responds with such readiness to the invitation to take a rest from that tremendous conclave.

Through the steam he catches a glimpse of someone who must be Paide. Even his resentment for the Estonian has dissipated, leaving room for something else, something closer to sympathy and complicity.

The joy of the cloistered life. He recalls the Estonian's words: "The body needs to be conditioned to appreciate it, and the senses, too." He is surprised that he hasn't paid attention to the looks he so feared might have existed in a place like this. He keeps his eyes closed; he doesn't want to see anymore. He doesn't want to subject his mind to the laws of reality; to follow the flow of his thoughts is more than sufficient, for here he is no longer the chamberlain; he is no one.

When he finally reopens his eyes he hears the soft, slow voice of one of the Francophone cardinals talking about the next series of elections. He'll vote for the Spanish nominee, as will many other Spanish and French cardinals.

The chamberlain's thoughts return to the following day.

The manner in which the men are speaking is so different from the way they talk when they are dressed. There is a sense of simplicity, a lack of animosity, an absence of competition. Although he can hear the cardinal clearly enough, he can't discern who is speaking. He listens for a moment to the cardinal of Bogotá, speaking in calm tones, taking nothing too seriously. What a change! It is almost as if here inside, naked, they no longer represent themselves. They don't remember what went on in the Sistine Chapel, or who they are, or what role they play, or how they should be treated by others; or, to be more precise, how they expect others to treat them.

He opens his eyes wide when he notices through the darkness and waning steam a small crucifix on the wall directly across from him.

When Vladimiro Veronelli leaves Saint John's Tower to return to his room, accompanied by the engineer and the three cardinals, it is almost one o'clock in the morning. He hasn't felt so well in a long time. He looks back for an instant on the scene he is leaving, while the two monsignors kneel to kiss his ring.

The gesture brings on a moment of melancholy, reminding him of the gravity of his position, for the ring, along with his garments, defines his persona, and he will soon be faced with resuming the horrendous responsibilities of his role. He suddenly understands that the place that had originally provoked so much repulsion in him could be regarded as a conclave within a conclave. *Cum claude*, closed with a key. But it resides in the heart of man, in his bared flesh, not in the ephemeral role assigned to his costume by power, that director of so many historical spectacles.

As the two monsignors are kissing his ring, Veronelli realizes that they have perhaps accepted the task of working in the spa precisely because they are not insensitive to the stares that he had so feared. For the first time he feels that he can smile at that which had frightened him, and he stops to give them a fatherly benediction.

9

O N T H E D A Y after the inauguration of the sauna and the Turkish bath, while the cardinals are trying anew to elect the future pontiff, Count Paolo Nasalli Rocca leads a reconnaissance mission into the neighborhoods of Rome that are most overrun with cats.

It is a full-fledged hunt, giving many of the older Roman onlookers the impression that the famine they had known during the last months of the war is once again upon them. They are convinced the poor beasts are destined for the frying pan. Furtively, several black limousines make the rounds in the designated neighborhoods: the Pantheon, the Roman Forum, Largo Argentina, the Grillo, Piazza Vittorio, and Piazza Sallustio. Young men leap from the cars, pale and befuddled; they work in groups, faithfully following the orders of their guide, who knows Rome well and shuttles back and forth between them.

By placing cans of food in locations that reek with the scent of cat urine, they lure the beasts out and ensnare them in nets. Clawing and howling furiously, the cats are loaded into the trunks of the automobiles, which head back to the courtyard of San

Damasus, loaded with their precious prey, before returning for another round. Discussions rarely arise between the well-mannered seminarians and the local residents, and those that do are mostly complaints from cat enthusiasts in the poorest parts of the city, who feel that even generous monetary compensation is inadequate for the loss of their beloved creatures. The most rebellious protesters actually manage to overturn the sacks, and hordes of hissing cats escape to the streets.

Some people notice that not all of the license plates are from Rome; indeed, some of the vehicles carry Vatican City plates. Even more extraordinary, the cars have thrones instead of backseats, indicating their entitlement to the absolute right-of-way in the chaos of Roman traffic.

Although the hunt continues deep into the night, the cats have made their solemn entrance into the Vatican by evening, slowly taking possession of it. In waves until dawn, the cars continue to shuttle back and forth between the city and the Leonine Walls, and the young seminarians turn the sacks of cats loose on the various floors of the Apostolic Palace.

The cardinals, who had been warned by the secretary of state about the plan to rid the palace of rats, prudently retire to their chambers earlier than usual. Not all of them share the same sense of comfort around felines, and the idea of letting the cats wander freely about amid their personal belongings provokes a certain irritation.

Hardly anyone so much as closes an eye that night. The miserable animals meow desperately, losing themselves in the vast spaces of the palace, which seems more a tortuous labyrinth than a lodging for living beings, and they forget to eat and drink from the bowls left for them. Instead, they look for an exit to the conclave, not knowing it is impossible even for the cardinals to find one. The most feral, made even more aggressive by fear, hunger, and cold, begin to hiss and spit as soon as they see the scarlet vestments of a cardinal, and if the unfortunate man dares to come too close, the cats scratch and claw at his robe.

The next day many of them are found dead from fear, apparently unable in their old age to give up the filth and liberty of the Roman streets and piazzas.

After the second night, though, things begin to change. The atavistic war between felines and rats explodes in all its glory, much to the satisfaction of the Sacred College. Immediately, the chamberlain is urged to send a platoon of cats over to the Vatican Museum as well. Once they have adjusted to their new surroundings, and once their weakest members have fallen by the wayside, the cats' predatory instincts take over in response to the presence of such an exquisite enemy. The infernal commotion that ensues is beyond belief.

Everywhere — under beds, above the cabinets of the sacred furnishings, on top of the altars, on the thrones and baldachins in the Sistine Chapel, up and down stairwells, in the kitchens, in the Swiss Guards' gunneries, even in the pope's apartments and in the courtyard of San Damasus — there are struggles to the bloody end.

The rats, terrorized by the massive numbers of the enemy, seem to tap unknown resources in their threatened genetic makeup, turning their mild squeaks into shrill screams. And with the smell of death so near, they rise up on their back paws, turn their narrow faces and long whiskers toward the cats, and throw themselves into battle, baring their sharp teeth and striking out at the felines' eyes and noses.

Soon the sacred halls are brimming with dead rats and exhausted cats, giving every indication of a battle grown increasingly more abnormal and sinister.

"Enough! I can't take it any more, Cerini. This has got to end," says the cardinal of Dublin to his Milanese colleague. He has just been assailed by two rats that launched from a chandelier toward a white cat at his feet. "We must make a decision, we must reach an agreement at once, otherwise we'll go crazy in here." He studies the Bohemian glass sparkling in the rodents' wake, creating a strange play of light against the red satin-covered walls, and he is surprised to hear the Milanese cardinal say, "Oh, but John, this is only the very beginning."

"Just the beginning? Isn't this enough?"

"Last night I found scorpions all over my room."

"Are you serious?"

"My two secretaries helped me kill them, but it took hours, just ask them."

"Scorpions? How horrible!"

"We'll have to fight this scourge of evil, too. They're the strangest color; they aren't black, but dark green, an iridescent green, like the color of a serpent's scales."

"No . . ."

"And when you see them in a group, all together, like a legion, the way I discovered them under my bed, as well as on the floor of the bathroom and in my closet, they truly look like awful, luminous snakes."

"Could it be that they are only in your room? Maybe the sewers aren't working in that part of the palace."

"I hope so, for all our sakes."

But it was not an isolated case.

The scorpions appear first on the lower floors of the sacred halls. Apparently tempted by the idea of new conquests and higher dominions, they gradually take over the third, the fourth, and then the fifth floors, finally reaching the pontifical apartments on the highest floor.

And indeed their claws and tail are of a strange, unnatural color: a dark, iridescent green.

The chamberlain is the last to accept the arrival of this new plague, discovering the scorpions in his lodgings on the fifth floor as he prepares to say Mass before the morning round of voting. While fastening the silver buckles on his shoes, he lets out a yell: inside his shoe, a scorpion has stung his big toe.

"Squarzoni! Call the doctor!"

The corpulent physician is slow in reaching the chamberlain because the elevator isn't working and he is forced to scale the stairs, a rather fatiguing endeavor at his seventy years, not to mention a strain on his ailing heart. But professional obligation and the elevated rank of his patient do not allow for delays. When he enters

CONCLAVE ❖ *71*

the chamberlain's room the physician is so pale that Monsignor Squarzoni wonders if he should call in a doctor for him, as well.

But the tired old man is a proud descendant of Clement VII, one of the oldest pontifical nepotists in history, and his spirits are irrepressible. He pulls a syringe and flacon out of his bag and prepares an injection to counteract the effects of the sting, having already been advised of the chamberlain's situation by the chaplain. Immediately after injecting the antidote into the chamberlain's arm, he asks for a chair and collapses into it as he regains his breath, his duty fulfilled.

News of the chamberlain's sudden indisposition spreads quickly, resulting in the cancellation of the morning elections. Shortly afterward, a group of cardinals offers up a new initiative, underscoring for Veronelli just how dangerous the recent events have been for the unity of the Church.

The cardinals of India, Japan, Australia, and the Philippines present a written proposal to their colleagues nominating the Ukrainian Uniate cardinal, Wolfram Stelipyn. Another provocation, Veronelli immediately thinks as he reads his copy of the document, like the maneuver to elect the Palestinian cardinal.

"Tell Rabuiti to call a meeting of the Italians," the chamberlain tells Squarzoni. "I'd like to see them tonight, after dinner, but not here in my chambers. In Saint John's Tower."

Reassured that he will feel better in a matter of hours, thanks to Aldobrandini's timely intervention, Veronelli orders the cardinals to gather in the chapel at four o'clock in the afternoon, hoping to squeeze in two rounds of voting before evening. Later on, he will discuss this problematic nomination with his most trusted confidants, unless something else arises that afternoon regarding the Ukrainian.

As he is organizing the details of the afternoon agenda, Squarzoni announces a phone call from Nasalli Rocca.

"Pass him to me immediately. Hello?"

"How are you feeling, Your Eminence? Any better?"

"I think so. This afternoon we'll try to vote twice. I'm glad you called."

"I have an idea that could help us solve the problem of the scorpions." The engineer is smiling as he recalls the chamberlain's reluctance only a few days earlier to acknowledge the problem.

"You're very good at solving certain difficulties, I realize. The cats worked exceptionally well, but I confess that at times it's a little disturbing. You seem to catch us at the most scabrous of moments. I also confess to have doubted in you, indeed one night I even dreamed that you were the one who infested the palace with the rats, hauling them here instead of the cats in the trunks of our cars. You're not receiving kickbacks from the city on cats, are you?"

The engineer breaks into laughter. "You'll take me for a chicken farmer when you hear my new idea."

"Why, what is it? Tell me."

"Well, the scorpion's natural enemy is the chicken, an animal that is far less stupid than people usually think, and in any case, the most intrepid against scorpions. Their pecks deal mortal blows."

"Now that you mention it, I clearly remember my mother occasionally letting the chickens run wild through our house in the country for that very reason."

"I was thinking we could let them run through the Sacred Palace."

"What an abominable thought!"

"I can easily get my hands on a few thousand of them. I made a few calls to a chicken farm not far from here, in Colleferro. I've calculated how many we'll need for each floor, not including the Sistine Chapel."

"The Sistine Chapel? Are you crazy? Chickens in the Sistine Chapel — never!"

"Your Eminence, maybe no one has told you but they're there, too, and they are beginning to damage the frescoes. There's a strange geometry to their devastating work: they're scratching away at the part above people's heads, where the color is lighter."

"No, I haven't heard a word. As soon as I can walk again, I'll rush over and see for myself. At four o'clock we're having an election. How will we manage? It's already eleven."

"With your permission, the chickens will be in place by then. They are well-fed and strong, as well as accustomed to being woken up in the middle of the night in order to eat a little extra; you'll see, they'll do a fantastic job."

And the chamberlain of the Holy Roman Catholic Church finds himself envisioning the mythical figure of the archangel Michael, the Devil's greatest enemy, as he listens to the ineffable engineer explain his plan in his usual dispassionate manner, for like Nasalli Rocca, the archangel knew how to chase evil back into the shadows from whence it came.

"Are you still there, Your Eminence?"

"Of course, Nasalli Rocca. You know, you're very much like Michael, the archangel, for this conclave threatened by . . ." but the chamberlain doesn't have the courage to finish his sentence, to specify who precisely is threatening them.

"I'm only doing my job, nothing more. I certainly don't have the strength you attribute to me, but thank you anyway. May I proceed?"

"Go right ahead. Just leave me time to warn my closest collaborators. It won't be easy letting . . . how many hens did you say?"

"Thirty-seven hundred, Your Eminence, at least for today."

"Well, let's hope that's enough."

"I'll have them arrive through Vatican Station, to draw less attention. They're not silent animals you know."

"That seems like a good idea."

"Thank you, Your Eminence, I'll see you later today. I'm off to Colleferro now, to get my chickens."

What would his colleagues say about this newest plan, which is entirely out of keeping with the dignity of their distinguished assembly? Many of the cardinals were upset enough by the cats. He can still hear the thundering voice of Oviedo, the cardinal of Madrid, after being scratched by an enormous black tomcat. How he had railed against the chamberlain for creating an unholy atmosphere by allowing all those beasts to fight among themselves inside such a sacred space!

Veronelli cannot bear to think of how disastrous and humili-
ating it would be to see the conclave overrun by chickens. Had it
not been for Nasalli Rocca's disconcerting warnings about the risk
of damage to the *Last Judgment*, he never would have permitted
the chickens inside the conclave, but given the current state of af-
fairs, they could be considered as assistants to the angels against
the forces of Evil.

*T*HE CHAMBERLAIN arrives at the threshold of the Sistine Chapel, accompanied by the cardinal dean and a group of dignitaries, who carry the Pavilion of the Vacant Throne and the red velvet dossiers holding the confidential documents of the conclave. At the sight of Michelangelo's fresco, the chamberlain stops in his tracks, seized with terror.

The entire upper part of the stunning masterpiece — where the Blessed are aligning themselves at the Savior's side, called to eternal life by the blare of the angels' trumpets — is covered by an immense dark swarm, a monstrous carpet of scorpions that renders the colors and figures of the fresco indistinguishable.

All the cardinals are stunned. Some of them shake their heads; others have tears running down their faces. Some, devastated by what they've seen, fall back onto their chairs and cover their faces with their hands. Others search through the crowd for someone, perhaps for the chamberlain himself. And indeed, after Veronelli enters the chapel, it is to him that a trembling Malvezzi turns.

"They're attacking only the good figures, only the saints. What should we do? We can't just stand here wringing our hands!"

Veronelli, who is still feeling the effect of the antiserum, experiences a moment of light-headedness. What, he wonders, did Malvezzi want them to do? Sing the *Veni Creator* as if nothing were happening? Call someone to help clean the fresco, and risk ruining it? Malvezzi had never been much help to him.

"I can see that, Malvezzi. If you return to your seat and without losing your head, if you allow me to reach the altar, I'm sure we can find a way through this together. But we're not leaving this conclave until a new pope has been elected."

He moves with determination toward the back of the hall, through the throng of cardinals who have not yet had the courage to take their seats. Not even the chamberlain's example convinces them to ascend their thrones. The atmosphere is tense, the group too stunned and unsettled to be governed. But Veronelli doesn't give up. He sits down on his throne near the altar and beckons Monsignor Squarzoni to his side.

"Go tell Nasalli Rocca that he should bring those birds in through the back door immediately; people are becoming irrational."

He knows that the scorpions, like metastases of Evil, are spreading across the fresco directly over his head. Out of the corner of his eye he can see that the holy figures of both the Savior and his venerable Mother are intact: the same phenomenon that struck the holy paintings in the Vatican Museums has repeated itself in the chapel, and this realization infuses him with courage enough to continue the battle, certain that the forces of Good will prevail.

As if in a trance, he declaims a Latin phrase so loudly that the words carry all the way to the back of the room. *"Vade retro, vade retro, Satana!"*

In that precise moment, with the mesmerized cardinals scattered throughout the chapel — standing in the main corridor, or beside their thrones, or already seated, or waiting in groups near the exit — the hall is suddenly inundated with white chickens, and their deafening squawks muffle the chamberlain's final words as they fill the room.

The spectacle unfolding before the princes of the Church could easily be a dramatic parody of the imaginative forces that originally prompted Michelangelo to paint the *Last Judgment*. An immense green wave, undulating like the open sea, quivers on the walls. The hens, crazed by the odor of the scorpions overhead, seem to have attained their long-lost dream of flight as the frightened cardinals retreat to the opposite end of the chapel, near the exit. The rats that still remain in the chapel, having taken refuge under the wooden scaffolding of the thrones, scurry toward the exit, trying to outpace the band of cats in close pursuit behind them. The cats, in turn, create such a fury during the onslaught that several of the older cardinals are knocked to the ground.

But the floor has already been taken over by the hens. They throw themselves at the scorpions, which fall from the frescoes in bunches, freeing the faces of the Elect, of the angels, and of the dead as they rise again in the valley of Jehoshaphat. To everyone's amazement, some of the hens even fly a few feet into the air and stab at the scorpions with their beaks. Gradually, the infernal mass loses its vigor, and clumps of the iridescent creatures drop from the wall.

The chamberlain and his prelates, who haven't moved an inch during the entire fray, stand stoically at the main altar, praying intently in Latin — who knows what words. At the doorway of one of the rear entrances, barely visible for the dust that has rendered the air almost unbreathable, stands the imposing director of that liberation from the forces of Evil, Count Nasalli Rocca, the archangel Michael of the conclave.

Although the fresco has been saved, the aftermath of the battle is most notable for the tumult among the conclavists: the coughs of the older cardinals as they struggle to breathe, the pleas for help from those who fell to the ground and were trampled by chickens and cats, the furious yowls of the felines, the mad flapping of hundreds and hundreds of hens, the desperate squeals of rats in the clutches of death; all combine to evoke a world of universal suffering.

Hours go by before silence and peace return to the holiest

place in the Vatican, hours in which all of the chaplains and personal assistants are called in by the indefatigable Nasalli Rocca to aid the wounded princes of the Church.

None of them can hide his horror upon witnessing the scene, and some of the weaker men faint after only a few steps inside the chapel. It takes the iron will of the chief engineer of the Vatican, along with the efforts of the stoic chamberlain, who remains rooted in his place but capable of giving directions with his eyes, to restore some semblance of order to the hall, where the hell that had encroached now seems to be in retreat.

The most seriously injured cardinals are taken to the infirmary, and calls are made to nearby hospitals. As soon as the chamberlain realizes that the tempest is over and that he can come down from the altar, he orders the press office to block all telephone communications and to disconnect any computers with Internet access. But he does not want to leave the Sistine Chapel until all of the dead animals and scorpions have been cleared away. The victorious cats and chickens that survived the encounter are lured with offerings of meat and birdseed into the sacristies and gardens of the Vatican, where pens are set up for them. He takes full responsibility for his unusual decisions, which are surely incomprehensible outside the Vatican, where the world is ignorant, and should remain ignorant, to the truth behind that cancelled voting session, the sixty-sixth round since the doors of the conclave had been closed.

Many hours later, after a state of calm had been restored, with the windows opened to clear the air and the floor swept clean with sawdust, with the candles on the altar once again lit and the thrones tidied, Veronelli finally submits to the pleas of Squarzoni and Nasalli Rocca, who have grown increasingly concerned over his pallid complexion. He gives in to their admonishments, physically and emotionally exhausted, and lets them carry him back to his room on a gestatorial chair. As he passes through the hallways, the rocking of the antiquated chair nearly lulling him to sleep, he catches a glimpse of the doorway to the room where the cardinals'

portraits had been ruined by rats. He wants to know how the
storage room has fared, for there, too, Nasalli Rocca had sent a
number of cats. He takes great comfort in hearing that the cats
have killed all the rodents, and that the remaining works of art have
been moved to a place deemed safe, at least for the time being.

It is almost eight o'clock when he finally reaches his chambers.
Squarzoni has lit a fire for him, which crackles and emanates a
welcoming heat as he enters the room. He also finds a message
from Cardinal Malvezzi waiting for him. He opens it: "You were
brilliant today. Now I really know that we won't leave here until a
new pope has been elected, and it could even be you."

There is a message from the cardinal of Palermo as well: "I don't
know how many of us will be able to convene in the Turkish bath
after dinner as you requested, but I, for one, will try to be there."

He had already forgotten that he called a meeting of the Italians for that evening. But none of this had happened yet. His secretary passes him the list of phone calls that had come through
before he had ordered communications cut off. It is so long he
can't even run through all the names. There are calls from every
corner of the globe. For a moment he thinks about the many time
zones that divide up the world and create countless difficulties
when attempting international communication. He won't answer
any of them. He does, however, give orders for the operator and
the press office to reconnect with the outside world at exactly
midnight. A continued silence might otherwise be misinterpreted
as a sign that a pope had been elected.

He rereads the messages from the two cardinals. Malvezzi is as
unpredictable as ever. Trying to nominate him as a candidate! As
if everyone didn't already know that he is too old. As if everyone
didn't know that he is considered a Curia politician with a rigid,
centralized vision of the Church. Malvezzi would be the right
age, at sixty-three. But what was going on in the Asians' heads by
proposing the Ukrainian? The Uniate church is a powder keg and
could potentially reopen the wounds with Russia. He really ought
to make his way to the Turkish bath to see what those cardinals
are plotting.

"Squarzoni, prepare my bag for Saint John's Tower. Wake me up in half an hour. I'll eat when I come back."

Once alone, eyes half closed, he envisions the terrible spectacle that took place in the Sistine Chapel. Finally, he breaks down, allowing himself the liberty of crying, which he could not permit himself to do earlier in front of all the cardinals. The infernal scene had reminded him of the *Dies Irae*, the Latin prayer that he and his prelates had repeated during those interminable moments of battle as they stood immobile at the altar.

While recalling the words of that prayer, Veronelli falls into a deep sleep. So deep that when Monsignor Squarzoni returns to the room, he can't bring himself to wake the cardinal, even though he has prepared His Eminence's bag and a platter of food for his return from the tower.

The chamberlain sleeps, and in his sleep he dreams. He is still at the altar in the Sistine Chapel, but the events unfolding in that room, which has for centuries housed the conclave, seem perfectly appropriate and no longer require his supplications. Standing in two rows in front of him are a multitude of men and women, either naked or loosely swathed, enveloped in whirls of steam from the Turkish bath. He recognizes the people. On the far left is the Condemned Soul, his hand over one of his eyes in fear. All the figures before him are from the fresco: they are the Elect and the Damned from the *Last Judgment*.

The florid flesh of the Elect and, to a greater extent, the vigorous, tanned skin of the Damned can barely withstand the loincloths and modesty veils that Daniel of Volterra was ordered to paint over them while Michelangelo was still alive. All the figures share the same expression of anticipation, even though they continue to be aware of the distinction between the redeemed and the rejected. A respite has been called during the execution of justice. A pause, a hiatus. Caught between time and eternity, both Judge and judged are allowed to rest.

The women rub their arms, legs, necks, and breasts in the soothing warmth of the steam, smiling gently, their eyes half shut. Some of them turn their gaze toward the altar, toward Veronelli, but not in search of him. Rather, they are looking for someone who must be hiding, or who is perhaps late in arriving. The chamberlain's embarrassment in front of the women is tempered by the knowledge that he is invisible to them. He knows they are waiting for the Judge, he knows their eyes seek out the Savior, and that they are making themselves beautiful for him.

One of the younger women catches his eye. She is in the first row and has long blond hair that goes down to her knees, concealing her nudity. Her head is reclined as she sings; he sees her lips moving. To her alone, he would like to be visible and speak. A man stands next to her, his back turned, revealing his broad shoulders and muscular buttocks. He has one arm draped over the woman, and for a moment the chamberlain wonders if he isn't one of the Damned, taking leave of his lover, saying goodbye in a final affectionate gesture.

Her fair complexion and his dark skin seem to be the codes for Good and Evil in the color scheme of the *Last Judgment*.

The woman's companion is about to turn around. Without letting go of the woman, he switches sides, putting his other arm around her and letting his first arm fall as he faces the chamberlain. It is Matis Paide. He is naked, just as he had been in the sauna, but "with a glorious body, at the height of his youthful splendor," as he had said that evening when speaking about the resurrection of the flesh. And the lovely young woman next to him, singing with her head reclined, is his sister Karin, the sister whom Paide spoke of as the only girl he saw in all his years on the Baltic island of Sarema.

Then something happens to disrupt Michelangelo's fresco, which has become so alive and palpable. Matis Paide stares at the chamberlain as though he sees him. In fact, he recognizes him and beckons him to descend from the altar. He hears his name spoken in Paide's distinctive northern accent. "Vladimiro, come and join us!"

But he can't move from his throne. He can't join them, can't remove himself from a life that has become as immobile as Michelangelo's fresco. An infinite amount of distance exists between the living and the dead.

"Come, Vladimiro!" the young and beautiful Matis Paide says, pulling his sister even closer. "Come and listen to my sister sing!"

Veronelli moves his mouth to tell him that he is unable to move, but no sound comes out. A great cloud of steam wafts over him, concealing the siblings for a moment, and an acrid, pungent smell invades his nostrils. When the cloud fades he sees them again. He had been afraid of losing them, afraid they would vanish, because something tells him they aren't real; they might disappear from one moment to the next. But he does not want that to be so. He wants them to be real. He wants to touch them, to hear Karin sing. As if in answer to his prayer, he finally hears her voice: *"Wir sind durch Not und Freude, genangen Hand in Hand."* "Together we've traversed suffering and joy, together, hand in hand" — it is the *Vier letze Lieder* by Richard Strauss.

But the pungent odor that constricts his nostrils grows stronger, and the vision of the Elect and the Damned grows dim. Karin's voice softens until it disappears all together. Something is erasing the living fresco of the dead, erasing the colors and the voices. He is no longer in the Sistine Chapel.

He wakes up in his room. The odor that dissolved his dream and woke him up is coming from three hens scratching at the floor near his bed, in search of remaining scorpions. He recalls that during his return trip from the Sistine Chapel in his gestatorial chair, Nasalli Rocca had suggested letting both the cats and hens wander freely through the rooms of the palace to kill the remainder of the vermin. In his state of distraction, he had consented.

II

As on so many other mornings, Ettore Malvezzi is awakened by the light shining through the window in the room across from him. The shadows moving behind that yellow glass call his thoughts to the new day ahead. What will happen in the Sistine Chapel next, after the infernal turbulence of yesterday?

The stubborn meow of a small ginger tabby rubbing up against his bedcover reminds him that the cats need to be fed. Contarini has probably already tended to the chickens and prepared the altar for Mass. They had to divide up their tasks because Contarini has a most idiosyncratic dislike for cats. There he is now, knocking on the door; it is 6:30.

The cardinal gets up and drinks the cup of decaffeinated coffee that his chaplain prepared for him. What a sleepy face Contarini has. His hair is a mess, too, rebelling against the gel that usually keeps it in perfect symmetry, parted in the middle. How strange of Contarini. But with everything going on, it is only normal that even the most intimate early morning routines have been disrupted. Still, the request that he hears from Contarini leaves him utterly dumbfounded.

"Your Eminence, before celebrating Mass this morning, I'd like to confess."

He hadn't asked to confess in years. After a few seconds Malvezzi replies that he would be glad to hear his confession. Contarini shuts his eyes in relief and embarrassment, surprising Malvezzi yet again. As he performs his libations, keeping one eye on the hen perched on a stool near him, he thinks about Contarini's behavior over the past month and seven days of conclave. His behavior here has been completely different from his normal demeanor at home, where he spends much of his time alone. Here he has often invited the young Swiss Guards to dinner: the last vestiges of youth, no doubt.

Once shaved and combed, perfumed and dressed in his cassock for Mass, the cardinal of Turin sits down next to the prie-dieu, where Contarini waits, having not just kneeled, but thrown himself down under the gothic crucifix, as soon as he saw that Malvezzi was ready.

"How long has it been since you last confessed?"

"Since we entered the conclave, Your Eminence."

"And what do you have to confess in front of God?"

"Negligence in my work. Smoking. You have no idea how much I've been smoking."

"You're wrong, I know perfectly well. But I also know things haven't been easy in here. However, it's bad for you, as you well know. Forgive me, Contarini, for talking to you as if I were speaking to my nephew, but he has the same vice."

"But that's not the worst of it, Your Eminence. I have no idea how you will forgive me for what I have to tell you."

"God forgives all wrongs if the confession is sincere. Tell me. Tell me without delay; we can't be late this morning." Malvezzi hears the pendulum clock ring a quarter past seven.

"Your Eminence, I have fornicated, if only in thought. The temptation is always there, even now."

So that explains the companionship of the Swiss Guards — but with what women? And why did he say "even now"? And why is he looking at the two hens like that, as they cluck and peck at a few stray crumbs near the confessional?

"Contarini, what's wrong?"

"Nothing, Your Eminence. But can't you see how shameless they are? They love to provoke people, look how they show off their private parts, tipping their bodies forward like that!"

The cardinal turns to look at the two innocent animals that have come toward the center of the room. While they continue to peck at the ground, they give a quick shudder before answering the call of nature, their rears in full view. Even the cardinal knows that those precious birds have simple needs.

"Forgive me, Contarini, but what on earth do you have against those poor creatures? You don't want to force them to wear underwear, do you? You know as well as I do to what we owe the honor of their presence in the sacred palace!"

"But Your Eminence, they're females! They're nude, scantily clad females that can't stop teasing us. . . . I just don't know how long I'll be able to resist!" Contarini breaks down in tears, holding his head in his hands.

There had always been something odd about that young man with the mysterious past, so torn apart by his tragic marriage. His fragility is now evident; his repressed and problematic afflictions are coming to the surface. Oh, this conclave, what damage to the psyche it has inflicted on the weak among them!

And the poor confessor. Malvezzi happened to enjoy widespread fame for his marvelous capabilities in that compassionate ministry, so much so that he had even been called to Rome to confess the pope, an appointment that unfortunately never occurred because of the pope's untimely death. But now he is speechless. If he brings his anxious chaplain back to reality by denying any relationship between the hens and feminine wiles, he might provoke a violent reaction, and then what? Contarini could stand up and embrace a hen to demonstrate the affection he has for them, causing no end of fear and commotion. People were sure to come running, and he might even be charged for the mistreatment of animals. But if he gives in to his secretary's folly, he fears he will only encourage him over the coming days, jeopardizing his chances for recovery, as well as disrupting their longstanding relationship, for which there is no imaginable substitute.

Ultimately, laziness prevails, along with a fear of change and a reluctance to lose a precious companion. "Contarini, don't you think I see it, too? Don't you think I see how the wenches behave? Do you think I don't know they were sent here with the pretense of catching the scorpions, but in reality they're here to tempt us — poor priests that we are? Try to do as I do: exercise the virtue of patience, reinforce your chastity with prayer, and try not to be alone with them. You'll see, we'll be stronger because of it. This conclave puts our virtues to the test. Think of taking part in it as a privilege, as does your unworthy archbishop. Remember that Saint Pachomius, Saint Anthony Abbot, and the saints of the Thebaid were presented with the Devil in the form of a woman, as we are here." He watches the expression on the chaplain's face slowly soften. His furrowed brow relaxes, his customary demeanor returns, and Malvezzi delivers the absolution, without delay, with one eye on the clock.

"Let us now celebrate Mass, asking our Holy Father to give us the strength necessary to face this new day. As penance, you must hand over all the cigarettes that you've hidden away, and say ten Ave Marias to the Madonna."

"Of course, Your Eminence. May I also shut the chickens out of here?"

"Do as you wish, Contarini, but I think we should make all efforts to show our spiritual strength and not let them affect us, as if they didn't exist. As if they were just hens."

Malvezzi sees his secretary bow his head in prayer, but not before glancing furtively at the two animals scratching at the floor near the cardinal's worktable, stopping occasionally to peck and preen themselves.

During the Mass Contarini behaves normally, leading Malvezzi to believe the confession has eased his agitated mind. But as the young monsignor helps Malvezzi remove his vestments, his words reveal that he is still not himself. "I thought Zaira and Zenobia behaved quite well during the Mass. They never disturbed us, never even moved from their little corner."

Better not make a fuss this time either, thinks Malvezzi. "They behaved excellently Contarini, you're right. It means that they will also behave well later on. But now we really do have to leave, for the love of God, or else we'll be late."

Where on earth did he get the names Zaira and Zenobia? Malvezzi can't think of any personality associated with the first name; the second one, yes, that would have been the queen of Palmyra, who rebelled against Rome. And as he sips his caffe latte, he envisions the strange game he will have to play, if indeed time won't remedy the situation. Maybe he should talk to the doctor about it, he thinks, foreseeing his secretary's worsening condition.

But he will have to wait for a more opportune moment, for when he reaches the Sistine Chapel he finds a large sign at the entrance:

> The conclave is suspended today due to the urgent need to clean the frescoes in the Sistine Chapel. The eminent and most reverend cardinals will receive word as to where and when the next elections will take place, in case the chapel must remain closed.
> VLADIMIRO VERONELLI
> Chamberlain of the Holy Roman Church

It is not so much the news of the suspension of the elections that upsets him — though that is disturbing enough — rather, it is what he hears from the rest of the cardinals who are gathered in front of the closed doors. Their whisperings and intimations reveal that many of the young prelates are suffering from the very affliction that has affected Contarini. His first indication is a vague comment from the archbishop of Rennes.

"I never would have believed that such hallucinations could occur in here."

Then a more explicit reprise comes from the cardinal of Dublin, primate of the Church of Ireland. "They say the hens are like odalisques. It's incredible, but that's what they see, even my youngest choir member, who is more innocent than Abel. You should hear him describe those lascivious creatures."

And the archbishop of Westminster seems equally disconcerted as he listens to his colleague from Montreal. "It's a hallucination that only we are immune to; it seems to have infected only the young among us."

Malvezzi resolves to consult the doctors for advice as to how he should behave with Contarini. It seems to be a problem for everyone, though some of them, like Rabuiti and Cerini, feign surprise and argue that not all of the young clergymen have been contaminated by these hallucinations.

How on earth will he be able to convince Contarini to talk to a doctor? How can he frame the argument? He discusses his concerns with Cardinal Lo Cascio as they return upstairs together. "Isn't there some way we could arrange for all of the assistants to undergo a medical exam? Maybe by creating some kind of warning from the Prefect of the Pontifical House, or from the director of sanitary services, saying there are hygienic problems stemming from cohabitation with chickens?"

"But that's exactly what we should avoid. We mustn't mention the chickens or speak about the hygienic problems they bring on. Those young men would become even more worried and suspect us of some underhanded trick to enjoy the hens' favors ourselves. Just ask Dunvegan!"

"I heard. But isn't there anything we can do to make them see a doctor?" Malvezzi insists, still worrying about Contarini.

"Listen, if I may be sincere, I don't think they need to be seen just now, in this atmosphere of — how should I put it? — amazing complexity. I have the feeling that we'll all need to see a good doctor when this is finally over. Don't you agree?" Lo Cascio replies as he dodges a band of fleeing rats, and then a pack of cats as they bolt through his robes. "Better to move ahead and learn to live with our little maladies; sometimes the cure can actually be worse. It won't last forever. You'll see. When the pope is elected the illness will disappear."

"Yes, but how to elect one?" Alfonso Cerini interjects after hearing the last few words between Malvezzi and Lo Cascio. "That's the real problem! *Facilus descensus averni*, but to end this . . . thing . . . if it can still be called a conclave, seems to be getting more and more difficult." With his usual acuity, the archbishop of Milan — still the most revered Italian candidate — expresses the fear that has taken hold of all 126 cardinals after those thirty-seven days: the fear of never being able to leave those rooms, which truly have become a byzantine prison of visions and nightmares.

Many of them reconsider various indiscretions that have come from the pressroom, where the Internet picks up the echo of the world. A crowd of people from the Liberation and Communion party, together with the followers of Opus Dei and a group of Polish nuns and priests, had been marching in front of the Bernini Columns protesting against the cardinals' inertia, against the incredible amount of time being spent on their decision and the irresponsibility of their attitudes, which threatened to create irreparable lacerations in the heart of the Church. Apparently some of the national churches, primarily in Africa and Latin America, were even disseminating the idea of electing their own pope somewhere else.

Yet the fear of a schism wasn't the most troublesome news from the outside. Even more worrisome was the growing indifference to the conclave, as demonstrated by many foreign newspapers and television channels, but especially by the Italian media. The front pages of the papers no longer mentioned what went on behind the bronze doors of the Vatican. Signs of boredom had started to appear in the most important fonts of information, which had been inclined to delay an article on the conclave by a day, and then by two days, in hopes of hearing something slightly more concrete, more definitive.

It could be argued that nothing had been leaked regarding the extraordinary events that had so upset those poor successors to the apostles, preventing, on the one hand, the negative public reaction that would have followed, but creating doubts, on the other, as to how long the people could be kept from discovering the truth behind the destruction that had been wrought by such a malicious and mysterious power. For it was not entirely normal that nothing had been leaked about the occurrences inside the Sistine Chapel. The chamberlain's decision to interrupt all communication for twelve hours, though commendable, was not a satisfactory explanation for the silence. And once that period of time had passed, was it possible that everyone resisted the temptation to let such a juicy morsel slip to the press? Or that not even a word of gossip had escaped, in an ambience so torn by conflict and rivalries, so prone to jealousy and revenge as the Vatican?

Thus, the waning interest of the press, which had taken to publishing articles only on alternate days, always relegated to the back pages, no longer promoted the tranquility of spirit that had been so welcome at the outset of the conclave. Instead, it compromised any sense of serenity remaining after all that had happened, increasing the anxiety and pain of living in solitude, deprived of any access to the outside world.

12

*I*MMEDIATELY AFTER THE shutdown of communications, as the conclave approaches its fortieth day, symptoms of that claustrophobia start to manifest themselves.

Suffering most acutely are those adverse to the "delights" of the cloistered life so dear to Cardinal Paide: the cardinals accustomed to living in the center of the most important dioceses, in constant reach of their telephones, fax machines, cellphones, and e-mail, with airplanes and automobiles always at the ready to transport them to all the corners of the earth.

The first urgent cases are taken to the Vatican infirmary. With its windows looking out onto the pope's private gardens, through the brilliant crimson November foliage of the plane trees, the building offers a semblance of liberty and an aperture to the outside world not available to the cardinals from their chambers.

But an attempt to escape through one of the windows, there on the second floor, by Cardinals Horace Winnipeg of New York and Anthony O'Hara of Philadelphia clearly shows to what degree the illness is a psychosomatic manifestation of a single ailment: the fear of remaining trapped in the conclave; driven mad by the desire to escape.

The two cardinals, seventy-three and seventy-nine years old, respectively, had decided to escape at night, when there were fewer staff members on duty. They selected a window that opened onto a roof about ten feet from the ground, from which they could lower themselves along a rain gutter rich with handholds, and they fashioned a rope by tying sheets together. They threw the rope from the window, but in the dark they were unable to direct its fall, and a clamor of chickens gave them away, attracting the attention, to their misfortune, of the dozing aides. The noise came from one of Nasalli Rocca's enormous henhouses, just outside the palace, where the chickens had been brought as reinforcements from Collefero, from Zagarolo and Frosolone, to fill the ranks where animals had been lost to scorpion bites, but also as part of the count's plan to maintain a strong presence of chickens throughout the Holy See.

A short while later the two men were discovered, wearing jogging suits and running shoes, their heads covered by black balaclavas to render them less recognizable; they were in a part of the garden where they might have pretended to be exercising, had anyone ever been encountered there at that hour. An accomplice was waiting for them in a large silver convertible just beyond the Vatican train station. Indeed, a car with American license plates had already aroused the curiosity of the guards, due to the length of time it had been parked there and the nervous manner of the driver waiting inside it, who could not stop checking his watch.

The cardinals maintained a scornful silence as two nurses, obviously embarrassed, helped them reel in their escape rope. They were not sure how they would ever explain themselves to the chamberlain.

"If I had been any healthier, I would have attempted it, too," confessed Cardinal Di Sacramento from Luanda, as he watched the failed escapees untie the sheets. "And you really were unfortunate," he added with a smile. "Better luck next time."

The two Americans didn't answer. They were distracted by a

noise coming from the entryway at the foot of the staircase. It was the commander of the Swiss Guards, accompanied by two soldiers of a most imposing stature. He delivered orders to the cardinals of New York and Philadelphia to follow him to the chamberlain's apartments.

The news explodes throughout the conclave like a bomb. The distraught chamberlain cannot even begin to fathom it. An unthinkable scandal, two cardinals trying to escape from the conclave! There was no hint of a precedent in the history of the Church, at least not since the Council of Trent. What concerns Veronelli most, when he is struck by the news at dawn, are the potential psychological consequences to the other members of the conclave.

"How on earth did they do it?" he repeatedly asks Monsignor Squarzoni, as he rushes to put on his bathrobe. Squarzoni listens while cuddling a large cat in his arms; black with yellow eyes, it purrs contentedly. Unlike his colleagues, Squarzoni favors the cats in his hallucinations, seeing in them more of an ephebic presence than a feminine one, an androgynous object of desire.

"I almost would have preferred that they used the sheets to hang themselves," the chamberlain exclaimed, no longer trying to contain himself in front of his secretary. "We could have written off suicide as a natural death. It's happened before. But this scandal will contaminate everyone. It'll spread like oil on water. Now they'll try to escape in hordes. I can already see them abandoning ship, leaving me here alone."

After giving orders to have the fugitives brought to his rooms as soon as possible, the chamberlain sends word to the Prefect of the Pontifical House, inquiring after the restoration crew in the chapel, wondering if they have worked all night without a rest to return order to the room. He searches through his papers for the list of damages he was presented, but he can't seem to find it. After chasing away the hens roosting on the overstuffed chair next to the fireplace, he finally recovers the missing paper. He takes a can of air freshener and perfumes the stench-filled room with the scent of roses, and then proceeds to get dressed.

Squarzoni returns, bearing the first good news of the day. The
work in the Sistine Chapel is complete; the problems were much
less serious than expected. According to the Prefect of the Pontifical House, there is but one inconvenience, which they had unfortunately been unable to remedy: the persistent and certainly
not pleasant odor caused by the animals left inside the Chapel as
a precautionary measure. As much as they tried to perfume the air
of the Sistine Chapel with incense, the cats and chickens continued to answer nature's call, soiling the floor and fouling the air.
Consequently, a crew of attendants would need to be constantly
on hand, equipped with brooms and dustpans, sawdust and
gravel, to contain the unpleasant phenomenon.

"That's fine. For the good of the conclave, we need the cats
and hens. It's the lesser of two evils," the chamberlain comments.
"Tell the dignitaries and other prelates to be here by 8:30, ready
for the official entry into the conclave. What? The American cardinals are here already? Show them in."

Monsignor Squarzoni announces the archbishops of New
York and Philadelphia, who appear just then at the threshold to
the room, escorted by two Swiss Guards.

The first thing to strike Veronelli is the clothing they are
wearing. They still have on their escape clothes, as there had not
been time to change into their cassocks. The cardinal from New
York is wearing a blue athletic suit with black stripes and the
name of a famous tire company across the front, while his colleague from Philadelphia sports a pink athletic suit with a penta-
gram on it bearing the opening lines of the song "Cheek to
Cheek."

The lengthy conversation that ensues between the three cardinals is naturally not without its difficult moments: their raised
voices reach the ears of the dignitaries who are gathering to escort
the chamberlain to the chapel. Hoping both to drown out the
noise and to profit from the delay, Antonio Leporati, who is
guiding the procession, invites the choristers to sing the *Veni Creator Spiritus*. While this succeeds in muffling the cardinals' voices,
the feverish meows of some of the frightened cats grow increas-

ingly louder, and the chickens, for who knows what reason, feel compelled to start squawking as if they had each just laid an egg.

"What is all this pandemonium!" Veronelli exclaims, throwing open the door and releasing the two cardinals in athletic suits.

The scene before him is far worse to the eye than the cacophony of human and animal voices had been to the ear. For the younger choir members have succumbed to the seductions of the hens, which in their eyes seem enraptured by their singing. In their efforts to overcome the temptation to watch the birds, they are missing their cues, losing the beat and the tempo, and managing only to infuriate the dean.

"Let it go, Leporati, let it go," the chamberlain says. And at the thought of a repeat performance, he whispers in the dean's ear, "It's better if they don't sing in the chapel, either. We'll have to indulge our able custodians in there, too."

The entourage makes its way to the chapel, while the two cardinals who have just received their reprimand hurry to their chambers to change into their red-trimmed robes, which are so much more in keeping with their dignified station than their athletic suits. Only after the last choir member has left Veronelli's room does the babel from the cats and hens quiet down.

The scene that awaits the chamberlain when he and the cardinals enter the Sistine Chapel is far more reassuring. The rows of thrones to both left and right appear in perfect order, as does the central corridor, where every few feet an attendant priest helps the cardinals take their seats or assists the older members to ascend the narrow stairs. The room fills with the laborious drone of an assembly that, while no longer tranquil as it sets to work, is determined to let nothing interfere with the task to which it has been called.

The marvelous fresco of the *Last Judgment* has been freed from every hideous tumor that defaced it; indeed, that grand allegory of the encounter of Good and Evil appears disinfested and cleaned, with no sign of even a single scorpion. And so joyous are the cardinals at seeing it restored to the splendor that has illuminated the conclave for over four centuries that they can even bear the stench of cat urine and chicken feces that seemed so offensive upon entering. Here and there between the thrones, on the stairways, in the corridor, and in front of the altar, careful observation reveals the discrete presence of some of the older chaplains, ready with brooms, dustpans, and small trashcans to meticulously attend to the floor — the younger clergymen having been prohibited from this duty in light of their vulnerability. The objects of all the attention — the cats and the chickens — stroll about the chapel with familiar ease, having apparently forgotten all about their Roman streets and piazzas, or their safe havens in Colleferro.

A cat curled up on the seat of a throne stares diffidently at an approaching cardinal; he will have to choose another spot for his afternoon nap, once he has devoured yet another rat. A chicken scratches at a crack between two steps, her movements the signature jerky struts of her species, head down, eyes fixed on the prey that still threatens her dominion. In fact, some of the surviving scorpions, taking advantage of the dark cracks in the baseboards of the damp and peeling walls, continue to stage their revenge. They spring from their hiding places, their outspread pincers as inciting as a battle flag or a red cape in front of a bull. At this, the hens lose what little intelligence nature gave them and throw themselves with open wings over their enemies' lairs, hammering their beaks against the ground in vain.

Veronelli can't long enjoy his pleasure at finding order restored to both the chapel and to the *Last Judgment*. He is immediately unnerved by the director of the Sistine choir, Maestro Antonio Liberale, who invites the young choristers to enter the chapel for the singing of the *Veni Creator*. And yet his orders to the dean could not have been more clear. "Squarzoni, tell them we're not singing this morning! Tell them immediately, for heaven's sake, before those young men come in!"

The stunned and mortified expression on Maestro Liberale's face assures him that the directive has been received. But one of the choir members, perhaps the most zealous, the most eager to have the cardinals hear his beautiful voice, has already entered. In his efforts to read the music in front of him, he doesn't notice the

desperate gestures being made to him by his maestro and Squarzoni. Another song, however, does succeed in making him lift his
head, upon which he, too, becomes overwhelmed by shock, and
in spite of his confusion and disappointment, he heeds the bids to
withdraw himself from the room.

A rooster who had somehow managed to stay with the hens,
perhaps an escapee from the hands of Nasalli Rocca's men, begins to call. He crows with glorious ostentation, with strength and
joy, with a conviction sure of calling forth the sun and helping it
rise, or, rather, of helping it rise again even in that room full of old
men, in the midst of the clouds of incense, the cats, rats, scorpions, and the immobile faces on the frescoes that look as though
they are only awaiting permission to come down. For an instant,
no one moves. As if urged on by such immobility, from the living
in the chapel and the dead on the walls, or perhaps thinking he
hadn't put enough strength into his song, the rooster begins to
crow again. This time he is accompanied by two more roosters
hiding among the hens, and in unison they carry out their duty to
greet the rising sun.

It is definitely not the morning reveille the rooster normally
sings to his harem in Colleferro, where light comes pouring
through instantly in the heart of the night to his multitude of hens.
This is a sad henhouse, where one must struggle to summon the
light, which is why he and his brethren have been called. His song
can make the sun rise even here, and he knows it; no other rooster
can call as well as he, not even those two roosters accompanying
him. Naturally, they don't dare sing over him; they chime in at opportune moments during his hymn to the dawn.

The cardinals remain silent, listening attentively to that extraordinary variation in the chapel's musical program. Some of them
recognize a motif in the rooster's song: the triple warning to Peter,
the first pope of the Roman Church, who denied Christ three
times. Those who look up at the sibyls and the prophets think of the
incongruous imposition of the rooster's song on that sky of saints,
heroes, and royal spirits. Others close their eyes instead and ask
themselves in fear what trials still remain to be surmounted before

they can see the new Peter. Just then, the two fugitive American cardinals enter the chapel, thoroughly confused by what greets them, and a loud voice disrupts the captive audience.

"Someone silence that creature!"

The Florentine accent marks the voice as belonging to an Italian. Indeed, it is Zelindo Mascheroni, the Prefect of the Congregation for the Doctrine of the Faith, the son of a caretaker for the noble Cenami family in Lucca, and one of the most unwavering paladins of Catholic orthodoxy. It was he who had inspired the rigid treatise on family ethics that had been upheld by the deceased pope. And he was responsible for the most vigorous attacks against civil legislation favoring abortion, birth control, divorce, and the cohabitation of unmarried couples.

13

CARDINAL MASCHERONI does not limit himself merely to silencing the impertinent rooster, which has been dutifully captured from amid the hens by a few domestic prelates. He takes the floor before the chamberlain even concedes it to him and launches into a severe rebuke, above the squawking protests of the hens, who are enraged by this inquisitor of their fellow feathered Giordano Bruno.

And he unleashes his rage on everyone. On the chamberlain, the dean, the cardinals — in particular the two who tried to escape — and on those reporting in sick. He is furious with the choristers, with the young chaplains, with Nasalli Rocca, and with the head of the pressroom, Monsignor Michel de Basempierres. Even with the cardinals who have received the most votes.

He spares no one. Everyone has behaved reprehensibly, invoking the justifiable wrath of God upon that congress of cowardly, lustful, weak men, who are unworthy of receiving the Holy Spirit into their hearts or minds. The chamberlain of the Holy Roman Church has reduced the conclave to a veritable henhouse, and not only because those creatures, through a questionable decision by Count Nasalli Rocca, offend the sense of smell and the sanctity of the chapel. Rather, the chamberlain's lack of resolution and his inability to navigate Saint Peter's boat have reduced the voting sessions of this august congress to little more than the squabbling of chickens. Indeed, the conclave has become nothing but the empty blathering of hens.

As if to underscore the cardinal's words, the rooster's crows become more acute, more shrill, more irreverent and imperative than ever, until finally it is snatched up by Monsignor José Felipe Gomez, as the incensed Tuscan cardinal continues his henhouse metaphors.

A good many other chamberlains have successfully guided the Church in times no less delicate, always showing the necessary mettle! Cardinal Mascheroni continues to rage as poor Veronelli and his embarrassed dignitaries finally reach their thrones. Seeing the chamberlain in his place, resigned to listen, appears to satisfy him, for Cardinal Zelindo Mascheroni, Prefect of the Congregation for the Doctrine of the Faith, then turns toward a wing of the chapel behind him, where the two archbishops from New York and Philadelphia are also just sitting down.

Immediately, he embarks on a topic many would prefer not to discuss. Certainly not the chamberlain, out of fear for the effects it will have on those who haven't yet learned about it; not the two guilty men, who have already promised Veronelli to make amends, guaranteeing him never again to attempt an escape; and not any of the cardinals who sympathize with the two Americans, who would prefer to mask the sufferings of a divided conscience with silence.

The cardinal of Shanghai, Zacarias Fung Pen-Mei, who is deaf, only makes the situation worse. For when Mascheroni pauses, momentarily unsettled by a resurging fracas among the hens, the Chinese cardinal all but shouts to his neighbor, "What did he say? Who escaped?" And Aldo Miceli, his Venetian colleague, is compelled to whisper to him repeatedly that no one, absolutely no one, has escaped.

But Mascheroni, annoyed by the interruption, and by the

whisperings of the deaf man and the Venetian, shouts out, "That's right, Your Eminence! Our brothers from Philadelphia and New York tried to escape!"

The amazed expression on the Chinese cardinal's face appeases Mascheroni. But Zacarias Fung Pen-Mei, not having clearly heard the reply, turns to his Venetian colleague to ask the reason for the two cardinals' attempted escape. He hadn't known them ever to be imprisoned, as he had, languishing for years in a Chinese jail. He knows them, they are two outstanding people. . . . And there has never been a word about religious persecution in the United States; he's been living there in exile for years now.

Meanwhile, Mascheroni launches himself full steam against the two guilty cardinals. The horrendous consequences they would have faced, had they succeeded in escaping from the conclave: The ridicule of the Sacred College, which declares itself inspired by the Holy Spirit. The television orgy at their expense; it would torment and brand them for life. The use made of their case by enemies of the Church, who would like nothing more than to see the House of God undermined to its core.

At the first few words of the fiery discourse, the two imputed cardinals stop chomping on their chewing gum and bow their heads, lacking the courage to confront their accuser. But the scene now unfolding restores their will to raise their heads, although astonishment still keeps them from chewing their gum.

Directly over Cardinal Mascheroni's head, on top of the trim that adorns his baldachin, perches a white hen. Either viscerally agitated by the continued shaking that the cardinal's declamations and violent gesticulations are delivering to the throne, or annoyed that her elevated position is impeding what is generally a ground-level procedure, she juts out her bottom and defecates squarely in the middle of Mascheroni's bald head, interrupting his speech.

The incident takes all the urgency and drama away from the protagonist, and as he wipes his forehead with his handkerchief, he can't overlook the chuckling and the hands being raised to cover faces as this audience attempts to hide indecorous expressions. In the silence that follows, the sound of scuffling and the beating of wings can be heard from the back of the chapel. It is the rooster struggling in the hands of his captor, Monsignor Gomez. The chaplain has been pecked numerous times by the rooster and is tying the bird's feet together before transporting it outside.

The chamberlain, who has missed nothing, can't help but connect the two events. How on earth did that hen manage to get up there, above the head of the man who had demanded silence? At any rate, the rooster who had called upon the sun, following his own innocent instincts, has been vindicated by a most sensible hen.

Then Cardinal Mascheroni resumes his discourse. But he no longer has the power to rattle the consciences of the cardinals, as he had done before the malicious hen selected him as a repository for her most intimate offering. Thus, he can touch on the behavior of the choristers, who have succumbed to the most shameful form of lust, abandoning themselves to a fantasy more befitting geishas practicing the art of *fan-chung* on their customers in Shanghai than young Vatican seminarians. For the same reason he can feel scandalized that men of such intense religious experience as the cardinals' secretaries have given in to the temptation of envisioning women waiting everywhere to ensnare them. He can scold Count Nasalli Rocca for a kind of pragmatism more in keeping with an assembly of railway workers than a conclave of cardinals from the Holy Roman Church. He can fume at the ineptitude of the Vatican press officer, Monsignor De Basempierres, who is losing contact with a world grown increasingly less interested and less involved in the most important religious event in the Occident. He can even berate the archbishop of Milan, who has managed to paralyze the elections because of his personal ambitions, and Cardinal Nabil Youssef, who is guilty of having brought politics aboard Peter's ship. He can then attempt to destroy each and every one of the parties that has formed in almost two months of conclave, berating their most outspoken leaders and the cardinals who have received the most votes. But he can no longer manage to command the same attention.

Throughout the entire ranting speech of Cardinal Zelindo

Mascheroni, the tension ought to have provoked resentment, self-defense, and counterattacks. But the audience's gaze is unanimously directed toward one object only, up above, over the orator's head. The irreverent hen continues to remain perched on the canopy above Mascheroni's throne, not impressed in the slightest by the gravity of the arguments levied by the cardinal. The possibility of a repeat performance on her part destroys all sense of guilt, reducing to the ridiculous every suggestive passage of Mascheroni's vibrant discourse, and snuffing out any desire for rebuttal.

Consequently, no one except the Prefect of the Congregation for the Doctrine of the Faith is surprised when the chamberlain rises after the tempest has subsided. He thanks Mascheroni for his generous intervention, and then opens the floor to anyone who would care to offer a word.

Several minutes of complete silence pass, followed by rustling from the cardinals near the entrance, where word eventually issues forth that a cat has given birth to five beautiful kittens in an old box of candles.

Immediately, a debate breaks out among the cardinals regarding the advisability of sterilizing the cats, given that many of them are pregnant and about to give birth. The question places in a new and paradoxical light those fundamental ethical principles that Cardinal Mascheroni has long defended, often generating intense criticism and confusion throughout northern Europe and South America. If it was not acceptable for the daughters of Eve, how could it ever be permissible for cats? How should the problem of birth control be applied to the animal world?

At the other end of the chapel, Cardinal Veronelli can't understand why it is taking so long for someone to speak up. But the persistence of the commotion, which is growing louder and more animated, tells him that something else has captured the audience's attention, further depleting Mascheroni's already diminished authority.

"Your Eminence, five kittens have been born," the Maltese Prelate of Honor, Thomas Tabone, whispers in the chamberlain's ear.

"Five? Where?"

"Here inside, Your Eminence, at the entrance to the chapel, in a box of candles; the cats are all looking for safe places to have their kittens."

A few of the cardinals near the chamberlain's throne overhear him, and with understanding smiles they assure him that this curious and unexpected event is what has caught the attention of the conclavists.

"You should see how darling they are. One is tiger-striped, like the mother, the others are —"

But the chamberlain is no longer listening; instead, he is studying the vexed and offended expression of Cardinal Zelindo Mascheroni, who certainly is not interested in talking about cats or kittens in the conclave. Veronelli looks above the cardinal's head; someone is waving a candle snuffer at the audacious hen that has attacked the cardinal's dignity and dissolved the tension into laughter.

What should he do next?

The Maltese cardinal then leans toward Veronelli to let him know that the birth of the kittens has raised the question of whether to sterilize the other cats, and that the principle of animal dignity is dividing the conclave.

And now what should he do? Never before has a chamberlain of the Holy Roman Church been faced with such a dilemma.

He should proceed with the election, but he realizes he will get nowhere until the frivolous question of the cats ceases to bother the cardinals. And he better do something quickly, because there, centered around Cardinal Paide, the discussion is growing increasingly more fervent, drawing in Cardinal Rabuiti and a few other Italians who are perhaps less inclined to favor animal rights. He can sense the ever more sullen stare of Mascheroni, who is well aware of the trifling that has robbed him of the spotlight.

Suddenly someone stands up to take the floor. He asks the chamberlain for permission to speak in Latin, as he is unable to express himself fully in Italian.

Silence returns to the assembly. Who could have the courage
to speak after Mascheroni? Could it possibly be the Uniate archbishop of Lviv in Ukraine? Slender and shy as he is, he often goes
unnoticed. His name is better known as a card to be played than
as an actual person. His health is not good; at times the doctors
have forced him to stay in his room during the elections.

The archbishop of Lviv opens his speech with a tribute to the
prudent chamberlain of the Holy Roman Church, who has received the difficult task of guiding the assembly in one of the most
delicate moments in the history of the Church. He then pays
homage to Cardinal Zelindo Mascheroni, the Prefect of the Congregation for the Doctrine of the Faith, whose noble anxieties for
the outcome of the conclave can be nothing but shared by all
who have been elected by God to this difficult task. There are no
precedents in this dark hour. It is as if threatening forces hover
over the Sistine Chapel and the Apostolic Palace, evoking spirits
from the distant past, when the forces of Evil seemed to prevail,
when schisms and divisions had even taken the seat of Saint Peter
from Rome to Avignon.

But where is Saint Catherine of Siena today? She knew how to
advise and guide the movements of the Church, should its leader
make decisions inspired by the Devil instead of by the Holy Father.

The word "devil" is dropped among the cardinals in the assembly like a stone into a pond, and artfully left to create concen-
tric circles in the previously smooth water. For the cardinal
enunciates the word clearly, repeating it three times, then stands
in silence, eyes fixed with intention on Michelangelo's fresco, on
the lower part, where the Damned and the devils are gathered.

He begins again, after having stopped to drink a glass of water,
directing his discourse toward his eminent brothers, who listen intently to his simple words, uttered in a Latin more worthy of Saint
Jerome than Saint Thomas. "*Summa hac Ecclesiae Magistrae
tempestate novam animam in proximo pontifice necesse esse . . .* we
must revive our weakened forces against the ancient adversary.
The youngest soul of the world belongs to Africa, a land where
evangelization flourishes most strongly, it is true, but where the

battle between Good and Evil has reached its acme. In Africa, racial and tribal wars, and endless struggles for power, have assumed the character of primitive encounters between a humanity still warm from creation, only recently exiled from earthly paradise. There, Cain and Abel renew the fratricide based on the opposing, yet complementary, powers of love and hate on a daily basis. There, the main protagonists of the Fall are still alive: Adam, Eve, and the serpent. The world must return to Africa; it must depart again from the point marking its terrible innocence, its loyalty in the struggle between light and dark, which has grown unclear and overshadowed by the progress of the West, that great ailment of the Earth. The new pope really must be "new," must bathe himself in the regenerative waters of Africa and experience a true baptism. The new pope must borrow from that land the kind of spirituality that knows no doubts or ambiguities, exceptions or mediations; the same spirituality that gave dark-skinned Tertullian and Augustine the strength to fight their enemies, in the spirit of the heroes of the Iliad. The Prince of Darkness has launched his final attack against the Church, which now stands orphaned of its father. He has planted the arsenal of darkness here, in its heart, in the conclave."

And while the Slavic cardinal takes another brief pause to drink, his eyes turn back to the fresco, and everyone follows his gaze in profound silence. "Perhaps you are amazed to be confronted in this way by one of your brothers from Eastern Europe, a man whom a great many of you have favored with your votes, thinking that he could solve the problems that torment you. Perhaps you think of it as weakness, as fear, or as flight from responsibility. But it is not so. My land is as sick as the land of Western Europe. Its Christian heart no longer beats strongly enough to constitute the rhythm of a nation, as it did in the times of Dostoyevsky or Tolstoy. The materialism of poverty over seventy years of Communist regime has wounded it in the same way that the materialism of wealth has corrupted Europe. Look for the new pope in Africa, I say! Look for a man who knows how to interpret the most basic formulas of faith, a man who is in touch with the most earthly and primordial of forces, capable of fighting Evil and vanquishing the Devil who is about to seize our souls, who is set to overtake us in our exhaustion, in our timidity as we grope in the dark, as we doubt our faith and fear solitude. There is a man here from Africa, and in his country he is a most beloved priest. He is worthy of all these hopes. I plead with you to cast your votes for him, dear brothers."

Wolfram Stelipyn concludes his speech and sits down, wiping away the sweat that has formed under his scarlet zucchetto.

He didn't mention the name of the cardinal he invoked, leaving the assembly more nervous than ever, disturbed by the intensity of his words, by the force of a reckoning so rigid and convincing in form as to redefine the dualistic conflict between the Devil and God. And yet, the enticements to return to their origins, as evoked by the portrait of Africa, sound to many Europeans like a condemnation of their own constitutions, and of their own choices for the government of the Church. A sense of agitation and intolerance arises that underscores, in the minds of those inclined to self-reflection, the precise conflict painted by the words of the Slav.

14

WHY ON EARTH did that man — whose speech was inspiring to even the least convinced among them — neglect to mention the name of the African candidate? Many ask themselves that very question later that evening at Saint John's Tower, gathered in the Turkish bath for rejuvenation after the fatiguing events of the day. Both the morning and the afternoon elections had resulted in scattering the votes among the eleven African cardinals and the Ukrainian.

"There was just no getting the words of that blessed name out of his mouth," Cardinal De Jouy of Paris says, more to himself than to Matis Paide, his eyes closed as he abandons himself to the benefits of the heat.

"All he said was that we have to know how to look for him. It's almost as if he is afraid to name him, as if caution prevented him from taking that responsibility," Paide replies.

"And yet he had the nerve to tell us that we've been surpassed by history," says Rabuiti, who has removed his robe, unable to tolerate the steam.

"I could be mistaken, but there must be something beneath all this," adds Siro Ferrazzi of Bologna. "There's too much mystery. That Uniate is hiding something; maybe he's sending us a message in code."

"A message? To whom?" Rabuiti asks.

"To the person in question, to the new Tertullian, or to Augustine, if you prefer," Ferrazzi says jokingly.

"It's true, it's as if he were inviting that man to reveal himself," adds Paide, "as if he were waiting for him to nominate himself."

"Meanwhile, he has succeeded in setting the Africans against each other, that's the real result of his silence," adds the cardinal of Palermo, who has had enough of the heat and is turning toward the showers.

"But that's not the only result he obtained," says Paide, as the aria by Albinoni playing in the background picks up its tempo. "He's managed to give a sense of direction to this conclave, which is something. There is no going back now. Many others also believe there is a need to return to the origins that he sees coming from his African choice. All that remains is to learn whether it will be the cardinal of Luanda or Kinshasa or Lusaka or Nairobi or Dar es Salaam or Antananarivo —"

"Or Maputo or Dakar," Ettore Malvezzi says, throwing himself into the conversation in order to repress the impulse to leave.

"I think there are cardinals from Addis Ababa and Kampala, too," the cardinal of Genoa adds.

"Careful, one of them is here," Rabuiti says, returning from the showers.

At that point, the glass door opens and the African cardinal enters, his white robe in stark contrast with his dark skin, his face unidentifiable in the thick steam. At the sight of him, the cardinals' thoughts go back to the morning's events, and to the afternoon elections following the Slavic cardinal's invocation; an invocation that had not fallen into the void, but that had not fostered any kind of accord, either.

Immediately after Wolfram Stelipyn's speech, the chamberlain had thanked him, and had begun the distribution of the ballots in order not to lose the reflective ethos he had engendered. The chamberlain had not wanted to clarify which of the eleven black priests the orator had been referring to: Stelipyn's cautionary approach would gradually prove its worth. He must have had reasons of his own for his silence, all of them directed toward a solution and not intended to further obstruct the illumination of the Holy Spirit. At any rate, four or five of the African cardinals were beyond the optimum age. The name would surely come up after the next few rounds of voting; it would eventually be revealed, even if the initial attempts to evoke it generated nothing new. They had already waited almost two months; they could be patient a bit longer.

When the 126 ballots were brought back to him, he had a strong feeling as he read the names out loud that the identity would forge its own path to the hearts of the voters. There were twenty-three votes for the cardinal of Uganda, twenty-two for the cardinal from Angola, nineteen for Madagascar, seventeen for Mozambique, and nine for Cameroon. The other twenty-five votes were distributed between the cardinal of Milan, who still received seven, and Stelipyn, who had three, in addition to a few others who received one or two votes, like the Palestinian and the cardinals from Bombay, Sarajevo, and Buenos Aires. Malvezzi continued to get his single vote. There was even one blank ballot. Each one of them was perfectly eligible, the oldest among them being the cardinal of Cameroon, who was sixty-nine. And he was a young lad, considering the average age of the cardinals. The twenty-three votes for Cardinal Joseph Masaka, the Ugandan, broke the record for the conclave; no one had obtained that many votes in any of the previous elections.

When they resumed voting in the afternoon, after intense meetings that seemed to fuel the general tendency toward an African, the tension was palpable. No one cared about cats or kittens; no one noticed the stench, even though it had grown worse. The box containing the kittens had been entrusted to the African nuns in the kitchens. The roosters had been isolated and taken out to the chicken coop near the infirmary, where they immediately returned to their crowing. The chapel cleaning crews, with their brushes and silver dustpans, continued to work, but with a discretion that seemed to make them invisible, nimbly moving about on tiptoe for fear of attracting attention. There had even been a request for them to sing the *Veni Creator Spiritus* in the absence of the young choir members, who had been banished to their cells on account of their lascivious visions. So their weary, aged voices were raised to greet the Lord in a dissonant but hopeful chorus.

Only then did the animals give any indication of renewing their inquietude, alarmed by the confusion. But patience prevailed, and none of the cardinals protested the cat that hissed or the chicken that squawked and laid an egg under a throne. And the hymn was heard all the way in the back of the chapel, down to the final phrase bleated out by the deaf archbishop of Shanghai, well after his colleagues had already fallen silent.

The results of the afternoon election created a good deal of astonishment. The dispersion of votes actually expanded to include all the Africans, even those who hadn't received a single vote in the morning, at the expense of the Ugandan and the Angolan, who surrendered votes to the Ethiopian, Senegalese, Zairian, and Tanzanian cardinals. Only Rabuiti's position had remained unchanged, with seven votes to his name. Everyone else had lost ground, some of them even surrendering their only vote, like Malvezzi, the Palestinian, and the cardinal of Sarajevo.

It was clear that the invitation to vote for an African continued to motivate the cardinals, but it had also caused an internal struggle among the African candidates. No one wanted to be excluded from that initial pronouncement; perhaps they were all asking for the honor of that call to arms, or at least a place on the front lines, which would save their dignity and allow them to capitulate in favor of the cardinal whom Stelipyn had in mind.

The Ukrainian's absence at the second round of voting did not go unnoticed, although his physical condition had never been stable. Or perhaps, given the pressure he must have received in those recent hours, his absence had been a diplomatic choice, giving free reign to the process of reflection. On the eve of the eightieth day of the conclave, the chamberlain felt that things

were moving along and that the machine had truly begun to
churn again, albeit with a few reverberations and physiological
obstacles after so much inertia.

The cardinals in Saint John's Tower are entertaining similar
thoughts as they bask in the sauna and the Turkish bath, when it
is announced with great excitement that the Ukrainian cardinal
has entered the spa and is already putting on his white robe. His
poor health had not allowed him to leave his bed for the afternoon elections, but it has warranted that he seek relief in a steam
bath that evening. Maybe in his country it is just one of the daily
rituals. Or perhaps the pontifical physician, who had visited him
in his chambers, had prescribed it.

The simultaneous presence in the sauna, where so many age-
weary bodies have come to seek comfort, of both an African cardinal and the man who invoked an African choice, creates a
strange tension. The cardinals had already been marveling at the
sight of the cardinal of Turin, who hadn't previously set foot in the
spot, and word is on the lips of many that none other than
Zelindo Mascheroni is about to join them, too. They can already
hear the Swiss Guards who are accompanying him, singing their
anthem: *"Notre vie est un voyage / dans l'hiver et dans la nuit, /
nous cherchons notre passage / dans le ciel ou' rien ne luit."*

What could such a procession possibly mean? Will there be
enough space for the guards in that room reserved exclusively for
the cardinals? And what if this was merely a provocation on the
part of the most intransigent among them, to chastise them for the
unseemly casual nature of their bathing attire? They don't know
what to expect from this man. Unfortunately there aren't any hens
in the sauna or the bath to buffer the fury of his moralizing.

They learn that he requested permission for the four guards to
enter, and that the African and Philippine monsignors did not
know how to refuse him. And now, from where the Italians are
gathered in the Turkish bath with Paide and the African cardinals,
there is nothing to be done but await the arrival of the archbishop
of Lviv, the Prefect of the Congregation for the Doctrine of the
Faith, and the four young soldiers.

The moments spent waiting give the Italians and Paide time to identify the African cardinal, recognizing the smile on his broad face as belonging to Carlo Felipe Maria Dos Angeles of Maputo in Mozambique. In the second round of voting he had received twenty votes, one more than in the morning. That nude man before them, who had taken off his robe the moment he was seated, could well be the first black pope in history. It is a thought that crosses everyone's mind, and it leaves each of them dumbstruck. Their uneasy silence, compared to the fragments of vivacious conversation he had overheard on his arrival, embarrasses the African cardinal all the more for being the cause of it.

Dos Angeles accepted Stelipyn's suggestion to visit Saint John's Tower, where the inner nature of things could better be understood, without suspecting that the other African cardinals had been urged to go there, too. In a matter of minutes, they all begin making their appearance, squeezing in beside one another on the unoccupied benches, until finally all nine of the black cardinals who received votes are present.

From the surprised expressions, which none of them are able to hide, it is clear that not one of them expected to find his fellow companions there. Some of them, like the cardinal of Luanda, regret having come, and reconsider the wisdom of Pascal, who said that all man's miseries derive from not being able to sit quietly in a room alone.

The glass door opens, and the archbishop of Lviv appears, wrapped in a bathrobe that trips him as he walks, so long is it for such a minute body. As soon as he crosses the threshold, the nine African cardinals rise to give him their seat, but he waves away the attention and sits down in the corner, near Malvezzi. "What lovely music. What is it?" he asks the cardinal of Turin in his heavily accented Italian.

"Baroque, I think."

"We always have background music playing in my cathedral, just like in here. My choristers are excellent. We had them recorded; that way they never stop singing."

Matis Paide leans over toward them. "If you'd like a really fine body massage, dear Stelipyn, with birch branches, we had some brought in. You should try it; it's good for the circulation," he says, indicating the pile of branches on the floor next to him.

"How very kind of you. You're Finnish, aren't you? You know how these things work."

"Actually I'm Estonian, from an island off the coast of Finland where birch trees grow like linden trees and acacias here in Rome."

"So how does this massage work?"

"I'll show you. You take a branch and rap it gently, but continuously, across my back," says the former Trappist monk, who had so strongly advocated the delights of the cloister. He finishes undressing, then rises to his feet and offers his bare back to the improvised whip in the Slav's hand.

The sight of the massive nude body of the Estonian cardinal makes a curious contrast with the hunched, weak figure of his timid flagellant, who, although presented with the smallest twig available to use as a whip, begins striking his subject's ample back with a vigor unexpected in a man of seventy-six years.

"Harder, Wolfram, harder," Paide pleads.

And the little Ukrainian, whose hood makes him look more like an elf than a prince of the Church, begins applying greater force. The fatigue and heat make his face turn red, while his movements loosen the belt on his bathrobe.

The Africans seated across from them, either moved by the spirit of emulation, or hoping to overcome their unease through any sort of action, stand up one by one, pick up birch branches, and begin lashing each other, following Paide's lead. Kinshasa lashes Dar es Salaam, Maputo flogs Antananarivo, Douala and Kampala pair up, while Dakar takes on both Addis Ababa and Luanda.

Enraptured by the silent rhythms of their gestures, the Italians soon pick up branches and, selecting their consenting victims, begin flogging each other without ever taking their eyes from the lead flagellants, Stelipyn and Paide, the two great advance guards of the Northern Church. The only words heard are Paide's repeated invocation to Stelipyn, "Harder, harder," which, like a

mantra, urges them all on and calls the ancient practice of mortification to the minds of many.

Paide knows he should ask Stelipyn to interrupt his massage in
order to switch roles and be flogged in his turn. But the weakened
condition of the Ukrainian priest makes Paide hesitate, fearing his
partner won't be able to withstand the blows. To his surprise, it is
Stelipyn who remedies the situation.

"I think it's my turn now," he says, removing his white robe.

In the eyes of everyone present, the sight of that small, stiff body
— with its flaccid muscles and wizened, jaundiced flesh, its protruding bones and hunched back, offering itself up to flagellation —
could not better epitomize the penitential experience. Paide's
hand is as light as a feather, but still Stelipyn begins to stagger, and
the Estonian thinks it wise to stop.

"No, keep going. Harder, harder," Stelipyn says. He does not
want to lose the battle in the mortification of the flesh as he
watches the Africans, whose energy greatly exceeds that of every
other prince of the Church in the force of their lashes and the an-
imation of their gestures.

Just then, as Stelipyn is marveling at the vibrant energy powering
those naked black bodies, the door opens. Immobile in the doorway,
paralyzed with amazement, is Cardinal Zelindo Mascheroni, Prefect of the Congregation for the Doctrine of the Faith. Behind him
stands his entourage of four blond Swiss Guards.

15

CARDINAL MASCHERONI does not have the courage to enter. He can only stare at the naked flagellants, enveloped in steam, standing at the base of the crucifix on the front wall. The scene attains its height of pious intensity in the weak figure of Stelipyn, who has submitted himself to Paide's violent lashes. Completing the picture, and reminding him of the infernal scenes that he contemplates daily in the Sistine Chapel fresco, are the nine black cardinals intent on beating the sense out of one another. The Prefect of the Congregation for the Doctrine of the Faith shuts his eyes and prays to God, asking for words that will serve him better than they had in the conclave.

It had taken him no small effort to don the white terry cloth robe that seemed so mocking of the papal vestment. But he thought an inspection was warranted, having heard that the Africans and their supporters would be there. He had chosen to come, however, with the Swiss Guards and one of their officials, fearful that some sort of impropriety might harm his dignity and force him to call for help. He had never been in a Turkish bath before, but he had been adamantly opposed to its installation.

But with what he now sees unfolding before his eyes, his greatest fears instantly vanish. Never would he have believed that one could indulge in the practice of mortification so ascetically and so severely in such a place. Genuinely confused and ashamed of his suspicions, he doesn't know how to respond when the cardinal of Naples gently asks him to close the door so as not to let the warm air escape. He obediently lets himself be guided by Rabuiti's damp hand to the inner sanctum of the spacious bath. Behind him, trailing like shadows, the four Swiss Guards slip inside as well. They have been ordered to remain constantly by the cardinal's side, yet they feel slightly ill at ease, nonetheless.

Mascheroni's entrance brings the cardinals' group massage to an end, not because the men are intimidated by his presence, but because they are still reeling from the thought of the hen that defecated on his head. For a moment they stand motionless with their branches in their hands. When they turn to seat themselves, they peer through the wisps of vapor, smiling, searching for any chickens that might have managed to sneak inside.

Paide gathers the birch branches from each of the cardinals, noticing the malicious glimmer in their eyes as they regard Mascheroni. The prefect, meanwhile, has seated himself in front of the largest vent in the room, which is spraying him with great blasts of steam. He is approached by the Swiss Guard who has been assigned the task of escorting him, and he starts to cough, his chest rattling. Wrapped only in a towel, Lieutenant Kapplmüller asks His Eminence how he feels.

"How do I feel? A bit strange, but it will pass," he says, peering through the white steam that continues to cascade over him. He can make out only a tall, indistinct form in front of him, though he is fairly certain he recognizes the voice. When the emission of steam stops, his cough finally ceases and his eyes adapt to the dim light in the room. And then he clearly sees the lieutenant, the young Hans Kapplmüller, who turns his back to him as he walks toward his three companions. The sight of that back with its perfect musculature, of that strong neck crowned with a head of honey-colored curls, of those legs as solid as columns; it is more than he can bear. Also in front of him are the decrepit remnants of Stelipyn's wrinkled body, as well as that of the archbishop of Palermo, who has been transformed by obesity into an obscene caricature of himself. On his right stands the cardinal of Naples, whose arthritis has buckled his body into the curved shape of a parenthesis, his chin practically attached to his sternum. His thinning white hair is tousled from the steam and sticks up from his head like a scarecrow. The laborious, hobbled footsteps of the cardinal of Genoa intimate that he will soon be unable to walk at all, while the purplish tinge to his complexion reflects the difficulty with which he breathes. In contrast, the breathing of the young Swiss Guards seated next to their official remains as effortless and natural as a gentle sea breeze.

What kind of place is this?

What kind of torture are his eminent brothers subjecting themselves to? It takes great courage to look the realities of approaching death squarely in the face, and that collective removal of their clothing is truly an exercise in patience and mortification worthy of Saint Ignatius of Loyola. To think he had feared some kind of impropriety would result from the bathrobes they were wearing!

He is struck by the incongruity between the absolute dignity maintained by their sacerdotal robes of royal purple and the reality of those bodies that no hand had ever caressed at night in the privacy of the nuptial bed. Their flesh had never known the sweetness that could mitigate their decline. If their bodies had ever been vigorous and beautiful, like the physiques of those magnificent young men, they had never been so to the delight of the eyes of a woman. Young and virile for no one, their bodies had been offered to God and to time, which was consuming them in its passing. But the community of the faithful had received the benefits of their silent martyrdom; a sacrifice that no longer occurred in the grips of wild beasts in the Coliseum, but in the face of the blossoming love experienced by their brothers and sisters, and in the births of their descendants. The Church was rich in that renunciation, a wound that one could learn to live with while still occasionally wondering how things might have been different. Those young men enrolled in the oldest military corps in Europe, like all soldiers, would return home one day and meet a woman. For them, this period of service, this conclave, this long separation from the other half of the world, would only be a memory of youth.

Meanwhile, he sees Lieutenant Kapplmüller turn toward him, his face rosy and glistening with sweat, chest broad and firm, and thighs pressing tightly against the towel wrapped carefully around his waist. The smile on his face, the remainder of something said to his companions, quickly disappears, erased by his sense of duty: the duty to keep vigil over those old men without asking too many questions, without making comments, and without contesting the orders of his commander. What shame Mascheroni feels, presenting himself to that man in the same nudity as the other cardinals! He feels his authority vanishing over that official, that soldier who is trained to receive his commands without so much as looking him in the eye, or letting him see if his face bears signs of fatigue. Sitting on his bench next to Stelipyn, who is eager to speak with him, he understands that in comparison to the guard standing before him, he is indeed small, but not merely in stature.

Cardinal Zelindo Mascheroni closes his eyes, his aging eyes that have unlearned their love for beauty, and he forgets about the kingdom he has governed on earth. For a few moments, while receiving a long, powerful jet of steam, he surrenders to the pleasure of disappearing into its clouds, far from the insults of time and the isolation of old age.

"Your Eminence, I'm so glad you joined us," Stelipyn's honey-eyed voice brings him back to the present. Because now Mascheroni understands that all the talk about a meeting in the Turkish bath had only been a ruse created by the Slavic cardinal to bring him there, too.

He opens his eyes to the stooped presence of Stelipyn, whose wrinkled face has seen many Russian winters, some even spent as a prisoner of the Soviets. He forbids himself to look at the Swiss

Guards, and responds to the courtesies extended by the old cardinal, who has shown such strength in spite of his age. "I'm glad
to see you here, too, dear brother. Please, let's speak informally
with one another."

"We're not here simply to enjoy the Turkish bath, as I'm sure
you are aware. We must try to leave here with clear ideas; we must
be much more clear than we were this afternoon."

"Allow me to dismiss the guards. It's better if they leave."

"Why did you bring them?"

"Because I was afraid that . . . I'll tell you another time. It's late
now, we don't have much time." Pulling his robe around him, Cardinal Mascheroni takes a few steps toward Lieutenant Kapplmüller
and his soldiers. All four of them have remained standing, leaning
up against the wall, and not daring to take a seat next to the cardinals. Dripping with sweat, their towels cling to their skin, accentu-
ating the muscular thighs of men who obviously adhere to strict
exercise regimes to keep their bodies in such perfect shape.

One of the cardinals also rises, indistinguishable in the steam,
but revealing his sex as his bathrobe falls open. Mascheroni turns
away so as not to offend his poor brother, who has inadvertently
committed such a distressing indiscretion. The prefect is reminded of the biblical story of Ham, son of Noah, who comes
upon his drunken father in his nakedness. He remembers, too,
the offense taken by the humiliated patriarch. Mascheroni turns
again, in order to speak to the lieutenant, and feels a claw seize
him in the chest, urging him to look at that body, where his sex
can only be imagined. His thoughts go cloudy, while he whispers weakly to Hans Kapplmüller that he and his soldiers may
take their leave. He has only enough energy left to add that he
will be expecting the officer later, in his cell, to draw up the
day's report.

He leans against the wall, a large mirror above the sink in front
of him reflecting his image. Over his shoulder in the mirror's reflection, he sees the group of soldiers leaving. What is happening
to him? At seventy years old, how can he give in to such anxieties?
He, who is the standard measure of ethics? He, who has received

from God the power to scrutinize the hearts of believers, granting them the mystery and gift of sexuality? He, who has chased from the Church those who abandoned themselves to desire. But the same desire now rises up within him with a most frightening force, a force that can be opposed only by renouncing himself.

This, then, must be the suffering that afflicts the rejected and the wicked, whom he bans from participating in the sacraments. The very horror that, in the name of Christ, he has caused people to endure.

As a youth in the seminary of Prato he had been the most implacable accuser of his professor of theology, who was inclined to certain acts of attention toward the young seminarians whom he received in his studio. He can still remember the reddish beard and pallid complexion of Monsignor Esmeraldo, the Colombian theologian who had been parked there for forty years, as if hidden away by his superiors. And even now he can feel the priest's clammy hand caressing him on the neck — there, against the skin under his white collar; it is still the same shiver. And on the day the rector of the seminary interrogated him after he had denounced the Colombian, he didn't even hesitate to sign the declaration that would send Monsignor Esmeraldo away. The conversation with his roommate still echoes in his mind:

"What did that poor guy ever do to you? So what if he touched us? He was still a good teacher."

"No, he was a revolting human being."

"What's the matter, Mascheroni? Do you feel dizzy?" Paide asks, taking his arm in concern. "Maybe you'd better leave. It's dangerous to stay in here for more than fifteen minutes."

Mascheroni pulls his arm away, as if bitten by a snake. Paide looks him straight in the eye. What kind of man is this Mascheroni? Coming in there with his squadron of Swiss Guards, as if he wanted to chase them all away, and now he trembles, so pale and fearful, so incapable of being himself without his cassock. He can't even bear to be touched.

"Yes, maybe it's better if I go out for a moment. I feel strange. I'm very thirsty."

"That's normal; you've been perspiring a great deal."

Zelindo Mascheroni leaves the Turkish bath unsteadily. The Philippine monsignor escorts him to a small room furnished with a refrigerator and beverages, and gives him something cool to drink.

He asks to change back into his clothes, and is accompanied to his changing room. When he comes out again dressed in his vestments, with his zucchetto and diamond pectoral cross, he doesn't feel any better, as he had hoped. His cassock has not restored any semblance of order to his innermost thoughts, where the images of that semi-nude body, with its hidden sexuality, still reign. He asks for a mirror. Immediately, he is brought before a full-length one, and he slowly recognizes in his reflection the mask of the man whom he doubts he can return to being. He again feels compelled to renounce himself, in order not to succumb to the desires that are taking possession of him. Whatever had prompted him to visit the baths? He cursed the very idea. Rivulets of sweat run down his face, and he wipes his handkerchief repeatedly across his cheeks and forehead, where he had been marked by the chicken earlier that day. It truly seems as though the mask will never again succeed in covering his face. He should leave; perhaps once he is far removed from that place he will regain his composure.

"Please tell the cardinal of Lviv that I am not feeling well and that I've gone back to my room. I'll talk to him tomorrow."

The conclave doesn't matter to him anymore, even though he had gone to the sauna with the intention of helping the cardinals resolve their differences. Far more pressing is his impulse to leave.

He wants to prepare himself for his appointment with Kapplmüller, whom he has asked to report to him. He has no idea why he gave him that absurd order, as he won't be able to withstand a meeting with the young lieutenant. He can't do it, simply can't do it. He has no idea what he will tell him, alone, inside his room. Nevertheless, he must hurry back to receive him, must prepare himself for their encounter. There must be a way of living without the horror he felt amid the clouds of steam, when he had secretly witnessed such beauty. There must be a way for that young man to continue working for him without having to suffer such shame. There must be a way to save everything: his honor, the desire that is rattling him like an old bush struck by a bolt of lightning, the entire life that he has devoted to judging people like him. And he must be able to appear without fictions, but disappear immediately after revealing his true self. A gesture, a mask, an hour of this life that is already outside of life.

The news that Zelindo Mascheroni left the sauna because he wasn't feeling well seems to concern only the archbishop of Lviv. Everyone else had viewed him as an unnecessary entity there, someone who had come to unearth who knew what secrets or behaviors, with his usual air of superiority. And to bring those four soldiers with him! How indiscreet, how tactless! Stelipyn's gentle overtures had simply made him feel all the more ill at ease, and had convinced him to take his leave.

"That man is not well, and he's going to get worse. He needs help," Stelipyn says, as if thinking out loud.

"We have other things to take care of now, Wolfram. We're here to help our African brothers," Malvezzi says, sure of speaking for many of the cardinals, some of whom had left the Turkish bath to lie down and relax on the foam mattresses, wrapped in their cotton towels, or to move to the sauna.

"I'm afraid of what will happen to him, and how he'll take it out on us," the Slavic cardinal adds in a thin voice. "We must pray for him."

"Let's go into the antechamber, it's too hot in here," Matis Paide says, helping Stelipyn to his feet. The rest of the cardinals, who had remained in the steam bath, follow his lead, and after most of them are seated on the benches and chairs in the antechamber, which opens to the dressing rooms and the partitions containing the beds, the cardinals in the sauna are called to join them.

"We've almost got the entire Sacred College here now," Rabuiti jokes, his face bright red from the heat. In his heart he swore against that physical practice, longing for the beautiful sun

of his beloved Sicily, where a body could be warmed by the light
and the open air.

The conversation that unfolds between the cardinals in their
white robes, intent on drying their hair, their legs and arms, their
faces, is immediately taken over by Joseph Masaka, the cardinal of
Kampala, who that morning had received a respectable twenty-
three votes.

In the name of the other Africans, he expresses his gratitude
for the faith placed in them. None of them had the intention of
excusing himself from his responsibility, but he did want to express a few doubts they shared about the suitability of such a rad-
ical choice. In ancient times, the civil wars that had shattered
imperial unity, and ultimately Rome itself, were initiated each
time the throne was seized by one of the colonies of the Empire.
Thus, there had been Spanish, Illyrian, African, and Arab em-
perors, until finally everything dissolved in the hands of the barbarian Odoacer, who sent the imperial insignia of the Roman
Empire back to Byzantium. Handing the papacy to an African
would incite the rest of the Catholic nations to claim their right to
it in the future. The consequence would be the demise of the
centrality of Rome, the debatable results of which had already
been seen with the last pontiff. A partial vision would prevail over
a universal one, to the detriment of the mission of the bishop of
Rome. If one of them were elected pope, he would inevitably
bring the weight of his culture, of his traditions and limitations
along with him.

Africa, he went on to say, was not just the myth that his eminent brother from Lviv had depicted. It was animism, black
magic, belief in the occult, witchcraft. It was rejection of Western
thought, tribal cults, primacy of physical strength over reason,
sexual promiscuity, polygamy, ingenuousness, and cruelty. They
were fervently proud to belong to that melting pot, to that coali-
tion of forces, but they feared it could inflict harm upon the
Church if it were to become the general vision of Saint Peter's
Cathedral. They weren't trying to shirk from their duties, he repeated; they were ready to sacrifice, to accept the papal tiara. But

they felt obliged to make their brothers reflect carefully on such a risky choice, convinced as they were that the Church would be most strengthened by the election of an Italian pope.

The pronouncements of the Ugandan create no small stir throughout the room. That support for the waning prospects of Italy should come from Africa is the ultimate bombshell. Cerini, Rabuiti, Malvezzi, Bellettati, Rossi Del Drago, Ferrazzi, Capuani, Leporati, Marussi, and Lo Cascio suddenly feel in the running again; and to think they had been expecting to see the doors forever closed to Italy.

The weak voice of the Ukrainian prelate raises the first response, begging his brothers to listen to him. It is a serious error to fear that local cultures will weaken the papacy. On the contrary, they will invigorate it. The centrality of Rome is nothing but an empty formula, a lifeless ritual, which is no longer meaningful to the younger generations, to the humanity of the future. Rome's desire to stand for everyone without being part of anyone has always been presumptuous. It might have made sense at the beginning of the history of the Church, when the city was still the heir to the Holy Roman Empire. But it has been superseded for centuries. Do we pretend to forget why Luther had such a great following? And what about the Schism with the Orient? He, who came from those lands, felt that only by accepting variety in the mosaic could the design of the whole be preserved.

He is interrupted by the loud voice of the cardinal of Turin. "Only a saint can save the Church. We need a saint at the apex, someone who can demonstrate the divine origins of the Church through the power of a miracle. The world wants realities, hard facts, clear arguments, sharp reasoning —"

"And who among us is a saint?" Matis Paide asks, ironically.

"No one," Stelipyn replies. "None of us is a saint, yet. Saints are only discovered afterward, when death has illuminated their saintliness. Although present among us is perhaps someone who will become one."

"But God doesn't want to reveal it to us," says Alfonso Cerini with his customary theatrics in voice and gesture. "Or are we so blind that we can't see His footprint among us? We, who believe ourselves to be illuminated by the Holy Spirit here in this conclave. Dear Ettore, saints don't come from a given country. They don't belong to history, but to eternity. I don't think a saint could govern the Church — an institution, after all, compromised by its very task of governing men, who aren't saints."

"But an exorcist, yes!" exclaims Malvezzi. "An exorcist could help the Church with the conundrum in which we now find ourselves. Look at the state we're in: we're oppressed by the forces of Evil, not inspired by the Holy Spirit!"

16

*I*N THE MIDDLE of the night, Vladimiro Veronelli is awakened by his faithful assistant, Squarzoni. "I'm sorry, Your Eminence, but something serious has happened. You must come with me."

"What's wrong?"

"It's Cardinal Mascheroni. They asked me to let only you know, and they recommended that you go immediately to the room of the Prefect of the Congregation for the Doctrine of the Faith. They didn't give me any details."

Veronelli dresses with great effort, cold and tired as he is. He doesn't bother asking any more questions, for Mascheroni is a dangerous enemy; he must proceed carefully, and not underestimate the threat. And he had best not alert Dean Leporati, either. It would just complicate matters, especially if the situation warrants confidentiality.

While walking down the dark corridor behind Monsignor Squarzoni, who is carrying a flashlight, something suddenly seizes him by the hair. Frightened, he stops and puts a hand to his head to free himself from whatever it is. He immediately lets go, horrified by his hand's contact with the warm and velvety body that shrieks and pulses between his fingers. Only then does he comprehend that he is holding a bat, and he sees that his secretary is struggling to free himself from one as well. The oscillating flashlight in Squarzoni's hand sends a beam of light up to the ceiling, revealing a swarm of the animals. There are legions of them: on the beams, on the doorframes, on the paintings, and now that they have been startled by the beams of light, they are also in flight, all shrieking at once in an unbearable concert.

The chamberlain is certain that he is dealing with yet another infestation of the Apostolic Palace once he reaches the doorway of Mascheroni's room, where the cardinal's private secretary, Tommasini, and the lieutenant of the Swiss Guards are waiting for him. They tell him that not a single room or hallway is free of the creatures, and only with great difficulty have they been able to keep the bats out of their hair. In fact, they have been forced to keep their hands above their heads to chase them away.

"Why did you call me here at this hour of the night?"

"Follow me, Your Eminence. You must see for yourself," Tommasini says, his eyes red from crying.

They cross the foyer and pass through the cardinal's study into his small bedroom. The chamberlain then understands what grave reason has forced them to wake him up. Lying on the cold bed, in the immobile posture of death, is Cardinal Zelindo Mascheroni, the Prefect of the Congregation for the Doctrine of the Faith.

He is wearing his bathrobe, and is lying on his left side. His arms are extended in an evident attempt to ring the bell on his bedside table for help. But the cardinal's face is not his own. It is the face of a woman who has not yet finished putting on her makeup. The cardinal's half-closed eyelids have been brushed with color, the lashes on one of his eyes have been painted with mascara, one eyebrow is darkened, his cheeks are contoured and brightened with blush, and he is wearing a dark blond wig over his thinning hair.

Veronelli cannot hold back the tears. A few seconds of absolute silence pass before he can find his voice. He clears his throat. "But who . . . who reduced him to this?"

"No one, Your Eminence. I found him like this when I came to report, as he asked me, at one o'clock in the morning," Lieutenant Kapplmüller says. "He must have died suddenly of a heart attack. Given the circumstances, we waited for you before calling the doctor. Also because there was nothing left for us to do."

"You did well. But . . . the wig? And the cosmetics?"

"He found them in the closet near the staircase, where the cleaning women keep their things. He knew all of the women; he was the one who gave them their orders. They must have left their personal belongings there before the conclave started," Monsignor Tommasini says, crying freely. "The wig . . . he took the wig from the statue of Saint Zita, the one in the chapel. He was so devoted to her. She was from Lucca, too. He had the statue brought here from Lucca."

"Let us pray for his soul," the chamberlain says, and he slowly imparts the benediction to the corpse, walking around the bed while Squarzoni and Kapplmüller recite the *Requiem aeternam*.

He can't take his eyes off that face, off those closely studied features that must have been his only concern during his last hours of life. Could it be possible that death had taken him while he was intent on transforming himself, consigning him forever to that monstrous new face? Now who will have the courage to remove his mask? For in its current obscene condition, the cardinal's body could never be buried in the Duomo of Frascati, his titular church. And he would have to give the orders.

"Monsignor Tommasini, before we call the doctor, I must ask you to perform an act of pity for the man whom you served for so many years."

"What can I do?" asks Mascheroni's private secretary.

"We simply can't put the corpse on view in this condition."

"Yes, I understand. I'll take care of it. I'll do it myself."

"We'll tell everyone that His Eminence died of a heart attack in his sleep. Isn't that right, Lieutenant?"

"Yes, Your Eminence, I understand perfectly."

"Do I have your word?"

"Yes, Your Eminence. Of course," all three men reply.

"You were the last one to see him, Lieutenant, is that right? You had an appointment to fill out your report; did I understand you correctly?"

"Yes, but he had never asked me to do so before. We were in the Turkish bath earlier this evening, and he hadn't felt well."

"What was wrong with him? Did you notice anything unusual?"

"He was having difficulty breathing."

So this was how he was preparing for the encounter with the lieutenant. He must have wanted to show his death mask to the young Swiss Guard. He watches as Tommasini gently slips off the wig, and then brings some sterile cotton from the bathroom to erase the traces of that grotesque makeup. The secretary slowly cleans Mascheroni's face, which is growing increasingly pallid, and the chamberlain waits beside him, his eyes closed.

When he reopens his eyes, the sturdy figure of the Swiss Guard fills his field of vision. He had come without his helmet, with his shirt unbuttoned, and wearing the casual attire permitted by the late hour — that hour of night that almost all of humanity pass together, joined in the conjugal bed. Veronelli suddenly comprehends the emotion that Zelindo Mascheroni's heart could not sustain. And he is moved to recite the *Requiem aeternam* for a second time.

Someone knocks at the front door of the apartment.

"Don't let anyone enter, Monsignor, Cardinal Mascheroni is sleeping and he absolutely does not want to be disturbed," Veronelli says.

"It was only Cardinal Malvezzi," Tommasini says when he returns. "He couldn't sleep. He said he was walking by and saw the light on and became worried. After everything that happened to Cardinal Mascheroni in Saint John's Tower today, he feared that His Eminence might not be well. But I told him that he was sleeping; that he was fine. He also said that bats have invaded the Apostolic Palace, and that the cardinals were attacked as they were leaving the Turkish bath."

"At dawn the physician will come to write the death certificate that I shall dictate to him. We'll celebrate the funeral immediately, as soon as the relatives and the authorities in Rome are advised. You will receive instructions in due course. For now, you must remain in total silence. Until tomorrow. Good night, Monsignor. Good night, Lieutenant. Let's go, Squarzoni, and may God help us."

The chamberlain, still quite chilled, wants to reach Malvezzi at once, to find out what had been said in Saint John's Tower, and if need be, to disclose the tragic news, excluding certain details. He needs to know what kind of reaction to expect, and to hear what, if anything, had been decided.

He finds Malvezzi on the threshold of his room, hair mussed, skullcap dirtied, fingers scratched: the unmistakable signs of an encounter with the bats. Unable to sleep, as eager as ever to vent his anxieties through conversation, he seems glad to see Veronelli, and he briefly relates what was said in the Turkish bath.

The Africans had raised some objections, fearing the loss of centrality of the papacy should one of them be elected, and they sustained the choice of an Italian pope. But the resistance of their "patron," Stelipyn, had been strenuous, and it gave rise to a rather incendiary discussion. One of the Africans, the archbishop of Kampala, above all the others, resented the demands placed on him, opening up a veritable onslaught of excuses and pretexts between the other eight of them for withdrawing their candidacy. The cardinal from Addis Ababa backed out next, invoking his imminent retirement. The cardinal of Kinshasa complained about his poor health. The cardinal of Mozambique said he couldn't abandon his country on the verge of civil war, since he was working as a mediator between fierce rival factions. And then there was Angola, who had just begun the most delicate phase of a second evangelization in a country still ravaged by war. And the cardinal of Cameroon could not let his immediate subordinates carry out his mission, as they were still too young and inexperienced. The cardinal of Tanzania needed to perfect his translation of the Bible into Swahili — an indispensable tool for the dissemination of the faith in a country such as his, where Islam was rapidly gaining proselytes.

In conclusion, they all seemed united against the idea of an African pope. Until Malvezzi himself, at the height of a discussion on sanctity, had ingenuously suggested electing an exorcist, given the climate that surrounded the conclave, although he really had no one in particular in mind.

"During the entire conversation that followed, they were exchanging glances while making their own excuses, and then they fixed their eyes on one man," explains Malvezzi. "It was as if I knew about his powers and had singled him out, and they didn't want to fall into my trap."

"But you really didn't know that there was an exorcist among the Africans?" Veronelli asks, not trusting the oblique and tentative manner of the Turinese cardinal. Malvezzi responds only with a perplexed look, and the chamberlain grows impatient waiting for an answer. "Who was it?"

"The Tanzanian, the archbishop of Dar es Salaam, Leopold Albert Ugamwa," Ettore Malvezzi replies. By the end of their talk, Ugamwa was forced to admit that he had exorcised the demons from many souls in his diocese, but he never wanted anyone to know about it."

Veronelli tries unsuccessfully to recall the features of the African cardinal, confusing his physiognomy with the other Africans who sit close to him, in the first row to the right of his throne in the Sistine Chapel. But Malvezzi's mention of the remarkable sense of unease conveyed by Ugamwa's eyes triggers his memory. Enormous, round, jet black eyes, always looking about, and yet downcast, as if attempting to keep their rebelliousness in check. Yes, now he knows, he remembers the fire in that gaze, which had occasionally even crossed paths with his own.

Suddenly Veronelli envisions Mascheroni's colored eyelids, closed forever by death. He gives the news of the prefect's unexpected death by heart attack to a stunned Malvezzi.

"So, that's why! That's why!" is all the cardinal of Turin can say.

"That's why what, Ettore?"

"That's why he wanted to leave. That's why he repeatedly touched his forehead, as if he wanted to chase away a thought that

was tormenting him. Paide noticed it too, and urged him to go back
to his room. But what is really amazing is what Stelipyn said after
Mascheroni left. It was as if he foresaw a tragedy, but it was also a
reference to some other obscure consequences to the conclave."

"What consequences?"

"He didn't say in particular, but I remember his words: 'I'm
afraid of what will happen to him . . . and how he'll take it out
on us.'"

That Ukrainian monk, the chamberlain thinks, he is gifted
with prophetic powers, as well. Fortunately, he didn't specify the
painful details of his prophecy, allowing us to conceal a part of
the truth that needn't be revealed.

"What should we do tomorrow? Will we vote?" Malvezzi asks.

"No, Ettore, we must observe a day of mourning for
Mascheroni."

"It's probably better that way. As you can imagine, we all left the
tower even more uncertain than before. It's almost as if that African
who chases demons has made our fear all the more tangible."

But Veronelli does not want to continue the conversation. He
has too many worries already. He must prepare the funeral rites
for Cardinal Zelindo Mascheroni, the Prefect of the Congregation for the Doctrine of the Faith, one of the foundations of the
Holy See, in spite of his scandalous exit from the stage. Then
there is the new plague of bats to contend with. But a solution will
be found, just as in the other instances. And finally, he must find
Stelipyn, whose foresight might be providential in that troubled
conclave, and who perhaps has already offered up his most precious gift, by exhorting the choice of an African.

Veronelli takes leave of Malvezzi, wishing him good night,
even though he can see the first rays of dawn coming through the
window, and someone behind the illuminated yellow window
across the courtyard is already on his feet and moving about. The
only relief he finds in the late hour of that terrible night is that the
first beams of sunlight are chasing the bats to their hidden corners, leaving the palace to the hens and the cats.

Back in his room, he finds Squarzoni waiting for him. "We

have to arrange the program for the funeral, Your Eminence. And we must impart the burial rites at once."

"Yes, I know. Were you aware of Mascheroni's problems?"

"No, Your Eminence. Cardinal Mascheroni was the epitome of the dignity embodied by his robe. I have never heard anyone say anything but the most irreproachable of comments about him."

"He had a brother and sister in Lucca. Please communicate the news to them on my behalf, with the proper protocol. I'd like to speak to the lieutenant again. What was his name?"

"Hans Kapplmüller."

"Who knows if we will find time for him; we won't have a moment's respite all day. I have already explained to the cardinal of Turin that Mascheroni died suddenly in his sleep. Did anyone ask you any questions?"

"A few colleagues, but I told them the same thing. And yet, it's strange. It's almost as if no one was interested in finding out the details."

"Why do you think that's so?"

"I can't say for sure. Maybe because he was unloved, poor cardinal. He should have lived his own life, the way he wanted to; he would have been more human, after all."

The chamberlain, who had already removed his pectoral cross, his skullcap, and his scarlet cape, turns around quickly. "Monsignor Squarzoni! I'll pretend I didn't hear that. Remember that the wife of Caesar must never be suspected! We are that wife — the Church is the wife of Christ. We can pardon, and we must have compassion, but we must never consent. I urge you to remember the cassock we are wearing."

17

*T*HE FUNERAL RITES of Zelindo Mascheroni are held in Clementine Hall, where owls have been sleeping during the daylight hours, as in every room in the palace. Upon waking at night, these raptors, brought in by Nasalli Rocca, will resume their battle against the bats. Fire, that natural enemy of bats, will also be enlisted, as torches will be lit throughout the palace to frighten them off.

The funeral services are performed by three of the Roman Curia cardinals — Rondoni, Rafanelli, and Lo Cascio — all of whom had worked for years alongside the deceased. Despite the formality of the hall, where the body of the deceased pope had also been placed for viewing, the funeral has an austere tone in keeping with the conclave. No hymns, no guests from the outside, no representatives from the Italian government. The family members of the departed will be able to receive their beloved only at the cathedral in his bishopric of Frascati, where the formal entombment will be held.

Cardinal Dean Antonio Leporati is placed in charge of the commemoration. During his speech in front of the seated cardinals, he frequently glances at the ceiling to keep an eye on the owls, distracting the cardinals likewise, and redirecting their focus from the coffin, the candles, and the four Swiss soldiers who are serving as Honor Guards at the corners of the open casket. From his seat in the first row, the chamberlain observes for the final time the waxen mask of the cardinal, whose face has been graciously restored by his secretary.

Out of pure coincidence, one of the Honor Guards presiding over the princes of the Church is none other than Lieutenant Kapplmüller, his face partially concealed by his helmet, his expression impenetrable. It seems as though the actors in that tragedy, after the final catharsis, do not yet know to take their leave. Among the crowd of prelates at the back of the hall, Monsignor Squarzoni and Monsignor Tommasini note the inopportune presence of the young guard. Upon seeing him appear, calling cadence to the other soldiers, they had immediately exchanged glances. They have not discussed the event that occurred during the night, but both would have preferred that he not be present.

Antonio Leporati concludes his commemoration. His speech interspersed with lengthy pauses, he expounds on the rigor and the extraordinary doctrinal riches that had characterized the life and ministry of the Prefect of the Congregation for the Doctrine of the Faith. He does not neglect to mention that among the probable causes of such a sudden death was surely the anxiety derived from participating in the difficult task that had called all of them to Rome.

At this point, the chamberlain, seated a few meters from Kapplmüller, notices a barely perceptible trembling in the lieutenant, his tall figure almost seeming to shiver.

In the first row, a few seats from Veronelli, is the Uniate archbishop, Stelipyn. On more than one occasion, Veronelli receives his long, sorrowful glance; he is perhaps the only one present to shed tears during Leporati's speech. That man knows, thinks Veronelli, even without having witnessed what the chamberlain had discovered upon being awakened in the night. He must try to speak to Stelipyn alone; surely the Uniate will not deny his powers of clairvoyance to the man who has the supreme responsibility of the conclave.

When Cardinal Mascheroni's corpse is escorted through the Leonine Walls after the service, the cardinals return to their lodgings. Another day has been lost, saddened once again by death after the passing of Emanuele Contardi, the archbishop of Rio de Janeiro. The shadow of their forced reclusion only grows longer and longer, there in that palace infested by bats like a medieval ruins, presided over by cats and hens like an abandoned citadel.

It seems as though the only means of escape from that infinite conclave is the route that Contardi and Mascheroni have taken: the first after exhausting himself through suffering, as though his prolonged struggle had earned him a way out; the second with the speed of light, like someone who did not want to miss a unique opportunity. Some of them still hear the echo of Stelipyn's words, alluding to "what will happen to him . . . and how he'll take it out on us," as Mascheroni was leaving Saint John's Tower to go to his death. It is not difficult to acknowledge the truth in those words, in that climate of heightened depression caused by the sudden loss of the man who only twenty-four hours before his death had thundered against the inertia of the conclave. To whom should they turn now?

To Stelipyn, with his contagious burden of apprehension for the future of the Church and humanity, as he calls for a return to their origins, away from progress? To Leporati, the refined, Eurocentrist Italian, who brings Roman primacy back to the Church, and who has the ability to weave, in a web made up more of political connections than pastoral concerns, a future for the Church?

Or should they turn to the archbishop of Dar es Salaam, whose fame as an exorcist has spread like fire, evoking magical powers and ancient prophecies against the presence of Evil at the heart of the Church? Or to the Maronite patriarch, Abdullah Joseph Selim, who raised his voice to contribute a wisdom suffused with a fatalism born of the times, and consigned to God's design?

Or maybe to the former Trappist monk, Paide, who, despite his asceticism, nurtures a vision open to ecumenical dialogue? Or to Nabil Youssef, the Palestinian, whose possibility of ascending the throne of Saint Peter rests in his ministry to a people at war, people who have come to symbolize extreme oppression and re- ❖ venge in the name of justice?

As if an ancient directive has made its way into the minds of so many disparate people, numerous meetings are held throughout the palace that evening, over the pretext of dinner.

In the rooms of the commander of the Swiss Guards, who returns home to his family every evening, Lieutenant Kapplmüller entertains the least powerful, but perhaps the most influential, members of the conclave. At least thirty private secretaries and ten domestic prelates gather there, each contributing a dish to be shared and something to drink. The meeting room, with its one long table, has meticulously had every animal removed, at least for the time being.

Monsignor Giorgio Contarini and Kapplmüller act as hosts of the evening, standing at the door, receiving bottles of wine and platters of food, which immediately disappear into the kitchen. And as the diners at the table await the arrival of their spaghetti *all'amatriciana*, the conversation takes flight.

The evening is marked by a conscious schizophrenia as each secretary, in the self-serving manner of a spy, reveals private details of the cardinal he serves. Resentment, jealousy, and intolerance are confused with pride, admiration, and affection. There is cross-questioning, the passing on of intimate details, and ostentatious laughter. There are marvelous and scandalous theatrics, requests for witnesses to verify what is being revealed, bets placed, and oaths taken. A lid raised from a pot of boiling water could not liberate as much steam.

Kapplmüller is often tempted to raise his voice and call out for silence. But something both indulgent and affectionate stops him from doing so. Those lively faces and feverish eyes, those pallid hands waving through the air to accentuate their speaker's words, those rebellious bodies in their black garments, reveal a residual

youth and a resistance to the mortification of the senses that is letting them enjoy the last rays of their sensuality before surrendering. He has a sense of respect and anguish for them. He knows
many of them, for during those three months of conclave they
have often confided in him, and in the other soldiers. The hallucinations they have suffered because of the hens and cats don't
surprise him. It isn't difficult to follow along in order to appease
them; it gives him a subtle sense of satisfaction.

He had spent hours in Contarini's room, talking nostalgically
about the adventures of his boyhood in Basel. It was the only way
he could fend off Contarini's stories, his delusions about Zaira
and Zenobia, and what they had said to him that day, displaying
their femininity to him in such a provocative way, showing up in
the most unheard of places, as if the secretary were the object of
their desire. When he returned to his quarters after those
evenings, he would learn that his comrades had been forced into
similar foolish conversations, their stories echoing what he had
just heard from Contarini.

There he is now, his good friend Giorgio Contarini, sitting at
the opposite end of the table, intent on preparing supper, on
posing questions and responding to the questions of others, on
opening the door to the late arrivals.

A giant platter of steaming spaghetti is brought to the table,
and a unanimous choir of praise goes up. The diners are served
rapidly, amid much chatter, until finally silence falls over the
room as they each concentrate on the pleasure of eating. In the
kitchen the cooks are feverishly preparing the surprise second
course: *porchetta alla romana*. The scent that comes wafting
through the kitchen door as they are finishing their spaghetti has
them placing bets as to what delicacy will be served next. The
pleasure of eating in a group after the segregation of so many
months restores many of them with the vitality and cheer they
had lost, dispelling all the ghosts of their solitude.

When they finish their first course, the tone of their conversation changes. The unconscious pleasure of revealing facts about
the private lives of their veritable doubles, the 125 cardinals to

whom they are so inextricably linked in that prison, diminishes in the face of their desire to speak about themselves. The barometer of the conversation changes, and the mirage of the future appears, reflecting the lives that are being carried on outside those walls, and their own lives, which will soon return to normal, too.

Information of all kinds flies from one end of the table to the other: soccer, politics, sports, the price of fuel, the reduction in interest rates, the war in the Middle East, the stock market, the euro against the dollar, Lucio Dalla's most recent concert, the next San Remo music festival. The most prevalent language remains Italian, but just barely, with English a close second among the many foreign chaplains and secretaries.

The many months of reclusion have resulted in a hunger for the most ephemeral of news, a need that is normally sated through television, that master of trivial information. Some of them, like Contarini, can't help but think that all those pieces in that orgy of news, the brief highlights along the difficult walk toward the unknown end that is the journey of life, must nullify one another algebraically, with an end result of zero.

For a moment Contarini exchanges looks with Kapplmüller. His friend's smile seems to communicate the same mixed feelings that he has for that lively assembly of people, all of whom are eager to return to normalcy after such exceptional times. But could Kapplmüller also share his sense of boredom at the idea of returning to the outside, to the agony and longings of normal life?

He is afraid not. No, Contarini does not think the lieutenant's life will face the same torments that aggravate his own. But maybe many of his colleagues who have dreamed of running off, as opposed to the two cardinals who actually tried to escape, will feel the first inklings of that boredom as soon as they return to the prison of their everyday lives.

Finally the *porchetta alla romana* appears on the table, welcomed with an ovation for Monsignor Bini, who stands on the threshold of the kitchen in an apron and a chef's hat. The roasted suckling pig has a large lemon in its mouth; all it seems to need is a touch from a magic wand in order to come back to life, so

stunned and enchanted does it look, as if death caught it by surprise. Again, as the bottles of wine come and go, the conversation
dwindles, the voices fade, until the only noise is that of the silver-
ware clinking on the china. Some of them are already glancing at
their watches, thinking of the early morning ahead. But nothing
in the world could make them want to leave the room. They are
willing to stay up for hours in the hopes of gleaning valuable information, any hint at all that will shed light on what they are all
asking themselves by the end of the second course: where is the
conclave going? Who will be chosen?

They return to these questions while salad and fruit are being
served after the roast pork, conversing with the tranquil concentration that accompanies a full stomach. Many of them study the
secretaries to the cardinals of Dar es Salaam and Luanda, whose
mouths remain sealed, without even smiling in response to the in-
cessant questioning. Or else they reply only in monosyllables, so
as not to reveal too much. The secretary to the cardinal of Hong
Kong, originally from Zanzibar, can speak Swahili, and is no
longer able to contain himself in the face of such obstinate indifference. Hoping to incite his fellow Africans, he begins a strange
chant that is accompanied by a series of gestures, a kind of
singsong that ends on a brief sharp note and a stamping of feet.
The song has a contagious effect on the other two Africans, who
chime in, stamping their feet in unison with Augustine Marangu,
the Zanzibarian. And the rhythm's steady crescendo, which is
heedless of all interruptions, and by no means seems to be an embarrassment to the three Africans, renders everyone else in the
room speechless.

Then something happens that will keep people talking for a
long time.

One by one the secretaries are overtaken with the uncontrollable desire to join in. Beginning with the people already
standing, and proceeding to those still seated, who rise as one
from the table, they start to stamp their feet. They keep time with
the three Africans, who have intensified their motions and their
strange litany under the direction of Marangu from Zanzibar.

Soon, the song turns into a dance performed throughout the room. No one can stay still — arms, hands, feet, and fingers move as if following an invisible choreographer. Most incredible of all, they all appear to understand the Swahili words. They respond with purely invented sounds, yet their utterings seem to make sense to the three Africans, who have begun using the table as a drum, banging out a rhythm on the wood with their hands.

Even Monsignor Squarzoni and his assistants, the most reluctant among them, are pulled into the vortex of the dance as they come out from the kitchen with the salads and desserts, holding up the trays in their hands with surprising skill, never spilling a drop.

Marangu passes on to a more complex rhythm. Taking his partners by the hand, he begins a new dance, shaking his body from the waist down, letting his voice rise louder and louder. After a gesture from the three of them, the rest join hands and dance in a chain around the table, slowly at first, and then increasingly faster, until finally they assume such a frenetic pace that some of the men are forced to drop out. A few collapse to the ground, unable to keep up, emerging from that diabolical *sardana* stunned and out of breath, but determined to follow the three Africans with their eyes.

Marangu lets out one final shrill note and everything ceases, as if by magic. The first to come to the aid of the ailing men on the floor are the Swiss Guards and Kapplmüller, who had also succumbed to the draw of the contagious dance.

18

THE PAUSE LASTS just a few minutes, for the dance has only begun its infectious seduction.

At the stroke of midnight, the three African prelates each take up a torch from the hallway, as if in tacit agreement, and the diabolical frenzy resumes. The African monsignors, following Marangu's lead, return to their rhythmic chants and motions, this time with an intricate counterpoint of tones and footfalls. They nod toward the door, and it is opened. And the band of corybants links hands and dances its way out of the Swiss commander's room.

They follow the long corridor that leads to the courtyard of San Damasus, and they then descend the staircase to the first floor, where they wend their way through the rooms of the various offices of the secretary of state. The sight of the dancers makes the chickens take cover, their squawking only adding to the unbearable clamor. The cats are no less frightened, retreating behind wardrobes, armchairs, curtains, and anywhere else that offers protection against the creatures that have invaded their domain.

With a sign from Marangu, after they have occupied the first

floor of the palace, the Dionysian fury of revelers heads back upstairs to the floors where the eminent cardinals are sleeping.
Upon throwing open the doors, they find the cardinals awaiting
them with rosaries in hand, awakened by the noise at the foot of
the stairs, which they assumed to be the onslaught of another
plague. Most of them, foreseeing another trial to surpass, are
praying to the Holy Mother for stamina in their weariness. Still, a
sort of tertian fever takes over their limbs, enticing them to join
the chain of dancers, dressed as they are in pajamas and night-
shirts, and they proceed along with the chaplain, whom they
barely recognize with his uncombed hair, bare feet, and disheveled clothes. Before losing all command over their actions,
however, the cardinals intuit that the spell's origins must trace
back to the African prelates, to the culture embodied by the
powers of their obscure magic.

The procession of dancers makes its way to the third floor, and
then to the fourth, reeling in new prey from every wing of the
palace, as the cardinals fall victim to that infectious vocal and
motor disease. Not a cardinal is spared, afflicted by an absolute ir-
reverence, by a feverish madness. They surrender to the necessity
of expressing themselves no longer in words, but in the gestures of
a hypnotic and contagious dance, which undresses its participants
in its vortex and lasts all night long, illuminated by torchlight
under the crossed eyes of the owls, awakening the eminent cardinals one by one with meticulous precision, excluding no one, not
even the chamberlain.

The mad antics do seem to have missed one person sleeping
soundly in his chambers on the fifth floor, where the dancing
chain was not led. That person is the archbishop of Dar es
Salaam, Leopold Albert Ugamwa, the exorcist whom Stelipyn
hoped would ascend Saint Peter's throne. But His Eminence does
notice the increasing noise coming from the lower floors when he
awakes as usual around six o'clock, shortly before his alarm clock
is set to go off. In his drowsiness, something coming from the
rooms below begins to disturb him; he recognizes the echo of
something familiar in that music, those voices. He doubts it to be

only the fragment of a dream, set in the missionary school of his youth in Domana, where he sang with his brothers as a child, but he tries to go back to sleep. Then he is jolted to wakefulness by a voice he knows far too well, a voice that is repeating a word he only dares utter in his exorcisms.

He immediately gets up, throws on the first clothes he finds on the chair next to his bed, and puts on his pectoral cross. He runs out the door and through the halls, following the sounds of the ruckus down two flights of stairs. And finally he sees what has turned the Apostolic Palace upside down: an invasion by a force he knows only too well. Filled with compassion for his poor brothers, he gives the same shrill call that initiated the frenzied dance earlier that night, gesturing furiously with his arms, and everything suddenly ceases.

To guarantee absolute efficacy, Cardinal Ugamwa repeats the cry a few moments later, and then he feels certain the spell has been lifted.

The revelers collapse in exhaustion, dropping to the bare floor, onto the rugs, into chairs, or leaning their backs against the walls, and a jeremiad of wailing, exclamations, invectives, and insults rises up against the three Africans who led the dance. The three men stand bewildered in front of Ugamwa, as if they too were waking up from a nightmare, and they listen with profound contrition to his severe rebuke.

But the Swiss Guard halberdiers are already intervening, arriving with their colonel, Tobias Kellerman, to arrest the three prelates for disturbing the peace during the conclave. The irate colonel embarks on a tirade against the cardinal of Dar es Salaam. He is not interested in reasons or excuses, those three witches will be taken away where they can do no further damage to the conclave — which, incidentally, must let itself be heard soon, as all humanity is awaiting the name of Christ's successor.

People begin appearing from the stairwells and elevators: more Swiss Guards, domestic prelates, medics from the Vatican Sanitary Corps, the pontifical physician Aldobrandini, the choristers, Count Nasalli Rocca, and others who had not been caught up in the contagion in the Sacred Palace. They are rendered speechless by the sight of that miserable crowd. The discussion between Cardinal Ugamwa and Kellerman grows more and more animated, for Ugamwa understands what must have happened to the three Africans. He believes they acted against their will, but needs to verify his suspicions in a more private interrogation. To complicate matters, the reactions of many of the chaplains are becoming increasingly threatening, making it necessary to move the African monsignors to safety, away from those most intent on harming them, like the Italians, who have already begun to strike out at Augustine Marangu, the Zanzibarian secretary to the cardinal of Hong Kong. Forced to choose between his urgent desire to speak with the disgraced men and his wish to protect them, the African cardinal opts for the latter.

The three "witches" are rapidly escorted through the angry crowd toward the Swiss Guard cells, where no priest has ever been detained. The exhausted cardinals and their secretaries begin to vacate the floor, and as they are returning to their rooms Ugamwa approaches Stelipyn, the archbishop of Lviv, who is lying exhausted on a divan.

"Forgive them, dear Wolfram. They will be punished appropriately."

"I've already forgiven them. I just hope it doesn't happen again. They have hurt the cause of Africa, and I fear it was sabotage," the Slav replies in a tired voice.

"I don't know, it was definitely the formula of an ancient ritual, a dance used for chasing away evil spirits of the night. It scares them away, but it is also a means of annulling the night, by filling it with sound."

"Why didn't they stop when they saw the havoc they were wreaking on us?"

"They said they didn't know how to stop. They tried, but they felt a force rise up against them, stronger than their own powers, and I think I know who it was."

"But why give us a glimpse of these powers?"

"That's what I still have to determine, Wolfram, although there are signs making me suspect it was only a joke after they had a little too much to drink; they wanted to fend off the excessive attentions of their colleagues."

"The problem with this conclave is the lack of discretion: the palace is full of holes, everyone is spying," says the chamberlain. "If only our secretaries and chaplains, as well as our fellow cardinals, knew how to keep their tongues from wagging, there would be far fewer problems!" He is beside himself, his face red, his clothes little more than sweat-soaked rags, his breath uneven, and a doctor is checking his pulse.

"I'm so pleased to hear you use the euphemism 'problem,' dear Veronelli, " Cerini says, making no effort to curb his temper. "You are too much for words, but I'd use a different term to describe the diabolical witchcraft the Africans have induced inside these walls!" Cerini has described the event in the manner Stelipyn most feared. Still, Veronelli manages, even in his nightshirt — in spite of his shortness of breath and his disheveled appearance, pulled as he was from sleep — to maintain his sense of dignity.

A group of domestic prelates approaches to extinguish the torches and lanterns that have been lit to frighten off the bats. The owls return to sleep in the corners of the hallway and the antechamber, disappearing from sight in the maze of the fifth floor. The cats and hens called in by their caretakers for their morning meal seem such a welcome sight, a light diversion in a fairy tale, compared to what has just happened. Perhaps only the vision of the scorpions crawling over the *Last Judgment* can begin to compare with the horror.

That morning, Masses are celebrated with unparalleled fervor in all the private chapels. The need for recollection and prayer is felt as never before. The chamberlain must sense their urgency, as he grants his brethren a pause for silent reflection. He exempts them for the entire day from appearing at the Sistine Chapel for the elections, which are now nearing the end of their third month. The most eminent and reverend cardinals are asked to appear the following morning at nine, and again at four in the afternoon, in case of black smoke during the first round of voting.

Unlike his colleagues, Veronelli does not have much time for introspection that day. From the outside, from the world beyond the bronze doors, have come renewed signs of alarm and intolerance at the long delay in proclaiming a pope. Immediately after hearing Monsignor Squarzoni proclaim Mass — he lacked the strength to remain on his feet and say it himself — Veronelli read the mail that the secretary of state had received from several embassies. Three heads of state — two kings and the president of a republic — had written to express to the eminent chamberlain the grave anxiety felt by their citizens over the lack of action by the most important spiritual guide in their respective countries.

Two of them, in singular harmony, point out the same worrisome phenomenon: the tendency among fundamentalists in the Catholic community to search within their own ranks, amid the bishops in their own dioceses, for an authority to replace the bishop of Rome. The reemerging threat of Gallicanism, the French resistance to papal authority, cannot be underestimated at this time. The growing numbers of converts to religions and philosophies other than Catholicism must not be ignored, the letters go on to say. Significant too are the ever more frequent invitations made by certain religious circles to the fourteenth Dalai Lama, Tenzin Gyatso. He has been coming to their countries in search of proselytes as he campaigns against the Chinese and for the defense of the people of Tibet, who are threatened by ethnic cleansing. The king of Spain, the most Catholic nation among the three states, raises the point that the politics of ecumenism practiced by the deceased pope have only encouraged an outflow from the Church to other religions, as it has fueled the metaphysical anxiety that always underlies religious projection.

The chamberlain, lying in bed looking over the papers consigned to him by the secretary of state, lifts his eyes to contemplate the crucifix on the wall. He puts the letters down on his white bedsheets and removes his glasses. He aches throughout his body from dancing for seven hours; still, sleep is late in coming, in part because of the odd hour. While the daylight is not conducive to sleep, it is the missives that are robbing it from him definitively. The responsibility of a schism or of many schisms weighs heavily on his heart. But he must not, he cannot, let himself despair. Maybe the African card can still be played, but he first needs to understand the nature of the powers enjoyed by priests from that part of the world. Or, if that possibility no longer exists, given the horrendous occurrences of the night, perhaps it is providential that Africa showed its true soul.

Suspended between these diverse hypotheses, the chamberlain doesn't even notice that a few hens have wandered in through his half-closed door and have begun pecking about at the base of his damask bedspread.

Meanwhile, on the second floor of the Apostolic Palace, someone does notice the chickens, and he promptly chases them from his room. It is the cardinal of Dar es Salaam, who is waiting to receive the three black prelates. He finally obtained permission to interrogate them privately in his rooms, following another discussion with the commander of the Swiss Guards. He threatened the colonel that he would appeal to the chamberlain, whose power in light of the vacant throne was almost absolute, that the detention of the prelates was an abuse of authority, and he had won.

Now that he sees the three monsignors waiting at the door to his study, where he has just finished celebrating Mass, he becomes overwhelmed by the delicacy of the discussion he faces, and by the irreparable damage their behavior has inflicted on the sanctity of the palace and the conclave.

"How could you ever let such a thing happen?"

"Your Eminence, it was my fault. I wanted to tease them."

"I had to join in, after the first step."

"It was the only way to make them be quiet," says the secretary of Luanda to the cardinal. "We couldn't take any more of their questions. We thought we remembered the incantation, but then —"

"One at a time! Please! There's already enough confusion in here," the cardinal says, noticing the obstinate return of the hens, drawn by the sight of a few scorpions in the cracks of the wall. "You go first, Marangu. You seem to be the ringleader here."

The lengthy, rambling explanation that follows confirms his suspicions. Versed in the secret rituals of a form of magic that had been passed down through the ancient tribal lore of his descendants, he had invoked a force, almost as a joke, but perhaps with a touch of exhibitionism, that had escaped his control. It was not a place where one could toy with such powers with impunity.

What should have been an innocuous display of the capacity to dominate the rhythms that pulse through the body, governing the voice, the breath, pace and tonality, the will to awaken, and the will to fall asleep, had become something completely different. Whoever had raised his terrible hand to destroy the fresco of the *Last Judgment* by releasing that malicious horde of scorpions over the figures of the Saved was still waiting in ambush for the opportunity that has been recurring ever since the Fall of Adam: the choice between Good and Evil. This struggle would only know rest during the moments in which Being was liberated from the chains of Becoming. And this was the power of the rituals passed down through centuries of history, passed from distant places, far from Rome, where the Savior had shown a slightly different face, thereby liberating the purity of Being from the prison of Becoming, rising out of the furrows of time, and accessing the eternal, if only for an instant. It was the power that Monsignor Marangu, with the collaboration of his two inexpert assistants, had managed to call forth through that frenzied dance, void of tempo, memory, and conscience. It was also the power, unfortunately, that had been usurped by those not wanting liberation from the battle between Good and Evil, who had taken advantage of the poor monsignor's faulty memory.

The secretary, who had been born in the same part of Africa as Ugamwa, listens along with his companions to the cardinal's harsh response, without so much as a remark, perhaps without even fully understanding the weight of the words. But at the end, a question falls from his lips, directed more at himself than at the archbishop. "Why did God make us so weak?"

But Ugamwa immediately has the answer. "Because he made us free, Marangu."

19

"*DEUS AMENTAT QUOS vult perdere*," Cardinal Alfonso Cerini of Milan reads later that night in an essay from Bossuet's *Sermons*. The Latin citation, regarding the Book of Zacharias from the Bible, could not be more pertinent. Indeed, how true, he thinks. God takes away the judgment of those who want to wound Him. That is certainly what is happening here, within these walls. Cerini is seated at a table piled high with books — his preferred company over the past three months of seclusion, and but a fraction of the volumes he brought with him from his personal library in Milan.

What more can they bear, after that infernal dance through the halls of the Sacred Palace? Who can deny that Evil has scored another point in the struggle that is taking hold at the heart of Christianity?

In spite of the mandates of tradition, is a conclave held in isolation from the rest of the world no longer ideal, or even wise? To Cerini it now seems to be a trap, which through fear is ensnaring those called to participate. He knows their contact with the external world is weakening. He knows that across the globe the tendency to envision a possible autonomy from Rome has appeared. He can sense apathy and boredom growing like weeds around the walls of the Vatican. And the strategies of Evil have been exceptionally subtle, suspended between playfulness and terror, malice and violence, entertainment and folly, suggestion and force. *"Deus amentat quos vult perdere."* It is so true.

It was as if a sorcerer had aroused their senses, relaxing their strict morals through physical practices unbefitting ministers of the Church as they gathered in Saint John's Tower. And he had been seduced, too. Their collective imagination had been pressured, evoking specters of biblical plagues with the infestations of rats, scorpions, and bats. This sorcerer had taken advantage of their fading sense of reality, nurturing a desire to escape the claustrophobic surroundings that had slowly begun to terrify them, as had been the case with his two brothers who attempted to flee. He had tried to upset their equilibrium, displaying the enormity of his powers with the horde of scorpions that teemed across the fresco of the *Last Judgment*. Their minds had been toyed with, their wits dulled by the enervating travails of ephemeral alliances that changed from one day to the next. With that night-long rendition of Saint Vitus's dance, he had taken possession of their aged bodies in a violent and desecrating manner that struck the dignity of the Sacred College at its heart. But the most atrocious act of all had been to lift their hopes so high with the proposition of an African cardinal, only to dash them with a blow that grew out of that very choice. The mystery behind the death, so silent, so unexpected, of Zelindo Mascheroni, that cornerstone of Catholic orthodoxy, only a day after his brilliant intervention, had also been a staggering blow to the conclave. Two of their brothers had passed away during those three months. That specter, too, prods the imaginations of those whose advanced age already has them feeling close to death.

And the thought of madness, which Cerini reads about in Bossuet, only adds to the confusion. What misadventure will rain down on them next, after that tarantella? Chasing after a world still in its infancy by taking refuge in Africa, with its archaic simplicity and magic, by retreating to a primordial state through an African pope, will not save the Church. If anything, they should aim higher, to the Romanic tradition, to that divine equilibrium between the Roman and barbarian worlds that ultimately gave birth to modernity, carrying on the works of the apostle Paul, Roman citizen of Tarso, who brought the supremacy of Rome to new heights. The world still needs a center, a beacon, a pastor. All of the evil that the Church has shared with humanity throughout history is the price it paid for guiding it, for never abandoning it. Turning their backs on the Church now that it has suffered so many wounds for the sake of human nature, with all its imperfections, would be most ungrateful. To cling to the illusion of a second youth, immersed in the waters of Africa, would be vile. Tradition has not evaporated with time; the past is not an arabesque of smoke to be blown away in order to liberate the mind and attain a new understanding. The past is a rock; tradition is a treasure. As such, Cardinal Alfonso Cerini, heir of Saint Ambrose and of Saint Charles Borromeo, continues to believe in his candidacy for pope.

The cardinal of Milan reads deep into the night, absorbed in the eloquent French of Bossuet, and ruminating over the Latin commentary. Just a short distance away, Contarini reenters his room in the same wing of the palace. He is returning from the apartments of the Swiss Guard, where he has been the dinner guest of Hans Kapplmüller. All is not still in his lower legs after the abundant libations of the evening. Not trusting his balance, and fearful of waking Cardinal Malvezzi, he pays careful attention to where he steps. The last thing he wants is to have the cardinal discover him in that state.

He puts his ear to the door of His Eminence's study. Total silence. He opens the door with caution, trembling when the hinges creak. A ray of moonlight shines down on the desk and hardwood floor. Everything is in perfect order — newspapers, missives, documents, books, pens, pencils, erasers, medicines, the photo album with pictures of the cardinal and his young seminarians in Turin — just as he himself had left it a few hours earlier, without saying what time he would be back. The light under the door tells him that the cardinal's habit of reading into the night remains unchanged, even on the evening following that unholy dance.

Through the yellow-paned window across from the cardinal's room comes a stream of light.

When the alarm goes off at six o'clock, Contarini does not recognize his room, so deep has he been sleeping, and he would happily continue to sleep, as he can still feel the effects of last night's wine. But he can hear the sounds of the cardinal on the other side of the apartment as he paces up and down the length of his room, waiting for him. He reaches for the packet of cigarettes that Kapplmüller left for him and smiles. The sight of the first hens of the day leaves him entirely indifferent, and he gets up to give them something to eat. Their hold on him seems to have passed.

During the morning Mass that he performs for Malvezzi, who has come down with a miserable cold after perspiring profusely during the night of dancing, he makes every effort to have the cardinal notice his indifference to the hens as they roam about the room. Kapplmüller had confided rumors to him of a plan to replace the younger secretaries and chaplains with older clergymen, called from throughout the dioceses, and the comments were worrying him.

Ettore Malvezzi is indeed relieved to note a recovery in his precious yet unpredictable secretary, who had been out all night without a word as to his whereabouts. Malvezzi had turned out his light only upon hearing him come back.

Both of them are extremely punctual, appearing at five minutes to nine at the doors to the Sistine Chapel, where the elections that were suspended the previous day will be held. As soon as the chamberlain finishes roll call, one of the cardinals near the marble balustrade in the last row rises and asks to speak.

"It's the cardinal of Brasília," one of the scrutineers, Cardinal Luigi Lo Cascio, whispers to the chamberlain.

"The floor is yours, Your Eminence," the chamberlain says.

He has never heard the Brazilian cardinal speak before, neither in public nor in private, and is somewhat wary of his eagerness to do so. He leans toward the other scrutineer, Attilio Rondoni, vicar general of Vatican City, and asks if he has any idea what the cardinal will speak about.

"No, Vladimiro, but he's not an easy one to fathom. I only know that last night all the cardinals of South America met in his room for a conference."

The cardinal of Brasília, José Maria Resende Costa, is indeed a master schemer. During his speech, which is calm and analytic despite his impatience to take the floor, he presents several diverse but convincing arguments that destroy any remaining hopes in the African camp. He then counters with his own aspirations, presenting them openly for the first time. In the name of justice they should turn to someone new, someone never before taken into consideration: a Latin American.

One by one, he introduces his brethren, the twenty-two cardinals who have defended the part of the world most oppressed by the economic imperialism of the Unites States of America, where millions of people face hunger and prostitution, where children are enslaved in sweatshops, where drugs are manufactured and sold, where the inhumane exploitation of laborers ensures that the people of the United States can enjoy their supremacy. They need only look to the folds in their dioceses to see the truth behind that monstrous falsehood that upholds the United States' image as custodian of piece and arbiter of justice throughout the land.

And one by one he calls them by name, asking them to stand, as if he were presenting witnesses for the prosecution to a tribunal of justice, who have come in front of the supreme judge for a trial that can no longer be postponed.

And they stand, affirming the truth of the terrible accusations that afflict their sons and daughters: The cardinals of Buenos Aires, Bahia, Bogotá, Tegucigalpa, Santa Cruz de la Sierra, Belo Horizonte, Caracas, Medellín, Lima, São Paolo, Brasília, Mexico City, Quito, Aparecida, Managua, Havana, Cordoba, Guadalajara, Monterrey, San Juan, Santiago, and Port Luis. The death during the early days of the conclave accounts for the absence of the final Latin American, the archbishop of Rio de Janeiro, Emanuele Contardi.

For centuries that marvelous corner of the earth, which the Lord blessed with industrious people and copious natural resources in its plains, seas, and mountains, had been denied its destiny of prosperity and expansion because of the tether its citizens bore around their necks; a mournful servitude that pits the rights of the strong against those of the weak. South America had never been free, the messages of Simón Bolívar and Saint Martin had yet to be understood, because only on paper had the nations that revolted against Spain won their right to self-determination. The country that had been the first to raise a rightful protest against its oppressor, ignited by the spirit of liberty, equality, and the pursuit of happiness, now betrays these same ideals. These rights have been denied to the rest of the Americas, substituting the tyranny of the king of England with that of the president of the United States. If the conclave could acknowledge, and this they truly believe, the place where the Holy Spirit would enact a broader scope of His redemptive powers, the choice of one of them would be most providential. Because a South American cardinal could offer the Church a change that no progressive force in two centuries has succeeded in effecting. The Holy Ghost could not be manifested in the powers of black magic that had befallen the Sacred College that night. The horror of the tribal dance that had wrung their flesh had been a message all too clear. Africa was not yet mature; it would have to wait its turn to offer up one of its pastors to the apex of the Church. But beware falling victim to the spell of those sinister powers! An exorcist pope? It would be like returning to the dark hours of the Middle Ages when Gregory VII had been accused by Henry IV of being a —

The cardinal of Brasília's words are interrupted by shouts rising up from the back and center of the room. Fingers point to the ceiling, confused faces turn upward; no one is still listening.

Michelangelo's fresco of the *Last Judgment* is slowly vanishing into thin air. The faces of the saints and the Damned are graying:

they are without features, without eyes, without wrinkles or flesh. Good and Evil are becoming indiscernible. Clothes are disappearing, along with the angels' trumpets, the boat and oars of Charon, the wheels and arrows of martyrdom, the column of Christ's flagellation and his crucifix, the clouds and tombs, the flayed skin of Saint Bartholomew where Buonarroti painted in his own face. Fading away, too, are beards, hair, hands, thighs, and the loincloths covering the figures' naked sexuality. Only the faces of Mary and the Savior remain in the center of that gray shadow, which in the minds of millions of people for centuries has embodied the justice that will await mankind at the end of time. Even the prophets and sibyls submit to the same fate. Bare walls are regaining possession of the Sistine Chapel, painted by an artist who has depicted the void as the barren earth, now emptied of humanity, with the monuments and works of art that have brightened so many lives destroyed and torn to the ground.

"Ugamwa, do something! Stop this from happening!" someone shouts in English.

"But he's the one causing the destruction! It's one of his spells!" cries the cardinal of Cologne in German, shouting from the other side of the room.

The chamberlain rises and calls to the most eminent archbishop of Dar es Salaam, acknowledging for the first time the prevailing sentiment in the chapel. "Your Eminence Leopold Albert Ugamwa! I command you to make this stop!"

In the confusion following the chamberlain's command, the tall black prelate rises from his throne and walks to the center of the chapel, accompanied by the Swiss Guards. A blunt object, hurled from one of the thrones, barely misses his head: someone threw a missal at him. He turns around slowly, toward where the projectile came from. The stream of tears that runs down his face speaks for itself, silencing those nearest him. Then, as if fighting a strong wind, his vestments blow up around him and he raises his arms to protect himself from the gale. The effort required as he approaches the altar, walking toward what was once the *Last Judgment*, seems to command superhuman strength. Immediately the tumult that caused the hideous destruction of the fresco begins to subside, although everyone in the chapel continues to feel the violent gusts that are raging against the exorcist. The wind has not entered through the windows, which are all well-sealed. Nor is it a sudden draft. It is the cold breath of death, penetrating the bones and chilling the blood.

Then something happens that makes even the most skeptical cardinal believe in Ugamwa's powers. He utters a few words, then repeats them over and over, his voice growing increasingly louder, his solemn figure almost doubled over from the effort. Suddenly, the *Last Judgment* reappears on the ceiling, its marvelous colors and myriad forms returned to their former splendor, and the wind in the chapel abruptly ceases.

But there is no trace of the African cardinal who performed the spell against the spirit of Evil. The exorcist has disappeared, just as the colors of the fresco had disappeared, only to return, brimming once again with life. The four Swiss Guards look for him in vain, making their way through the open spaces where only a few seconds earlier they had done battle against the wind. They search for him throughout the chapel: in the entrance, in the antechambers, in the sacristy. The great exorcist has left the conclave.

20

*T*HAT EVENING, the Maronite patriarch Abdullah Joseph Selim visits Malvezzi in his chambers to return some books and accepts an invitation to stay for dinner. The isolation of the conclave is taking its toll on his health, rendering him increasingly weak, though unwilling to resign his position, to the eternal amazement of his Turinese colleague, whose throne is adjacent to his in the chapel. Sitting together in front of the fireplace while Monsignor Contarini clears away the dinner plates, the two friends reexamine the events of the day, starting with the afternoon election, which had been held in spite of sparse attendance.

In fact, most of the members of the Sacred College stayed in their rooms that afternoon, terrified by the disappearance into thin air of one of the most influential candidates in the papal election. The results of the voting had been seriously influenced by the Brazilian cardinal's speech, as twenty-two votes were cast in his favor. But his position was still precarious, still far in number from the simple majority that had been sufficient after the first two days of voting.

Malvezzi was surprised to have received another vote in his

favor, in addition to the one from the Lebanese patriarch, from whom he had heard the question, "What do you know about the capabilities of God?" The words that had so struck him have now taken on a more tragic, more unnerving sense, for in allowing such devastation to occur, God seems to have retreated far away from his sons. One of them, guilty perhaps of having exerted magical powers, had even been swallowed up by the forces of Evil.

At what point would God allow them to leave this battlefield? Historically, there had been conclaves that lasted only a few days, their elections guided by divine inspiration. This one dragged on endlessly, proof of God's withdrawal. What if his presence were to be found elsewhere? What if he had chosen others to receive his graces and represent him?

Malvezzi had lain awake the previous night, pondering the biblical passages that recount the folly of Saul, who realized he had been abandoned by God but remained unaware that the young David had secretly been anointed King of Israel by Samuel. King Saul's distraught soul had been claimed by the Devil, and he would soon face death. What if the Church, like Saul, has distanced itself from God? And if so, where will the young David be hiding?

These are the questions that Malvezzi confides in the Maronite, who has been listening in silence for several minutes, staring into the fire as a cat rubs up against his leg. The silence continues after Malvezzi has finished speaking. Then, slowly choosing his words, Selim invites his colleague to create a vision more ample than a battle between only Christians and the enemies of Christ. The Lord is retreating not just from the Church, but from half of humanity, leaving his spiritual legacy only to the most forgotten souls, the impoverished among them. Egoism — disguised as economic progress, as the race for success — combined with narcissism, the final stage of discontentment that is rife throughout Western societies, is Evil's victory. Good lives in silence, where it has neither voice nor power.

It exists in the people about whom the cardinal of Brasília spoke, as well as in the impoverished in the underdeveloped nations of

Africa; in the millions living in Russia, marginalized by want, forced to their knees under the power of the mafia; in the Kurds, the Burmese, the Iraqis, and all others rejected from every negotiation table; and in those shackled in chains, like the Iranians living under the yoke of the ayatollah. The Church is not alone in its struggle; the rest of humanity is involved along with it. But he, who comes from a part of the world ravaged by war between opposing faiths and diverse races, feels qualified to say that at times, the Divine is not where the official Catholic Church erects its tents, but in the opposing camp. In his martyred country of Lebanon, God has changed the signs, often appearing not among ranks of the wealthy Catholics, but among the poor Muslims.

At this, Malvezzi lifts his hands in astonishment and moves his chair closer. A proposition like this could bring on the Apocalypse. What will happen to the Church's authority to teach religious doctrine and to bear witness to the truth, over which it is the custodian and headmaster?

The patriarch pauses a moment before replying. Finally, he says that he is most glad to have voted for Malvezzi, because no one can manifest the Romanism or the Italocentrism of the papacy with more cogency. The problem, however, is in asking oneself if voting for the pope still means calling on Christ to guide humanity through his age-old vicar. Aware of having said something of utmost gravity, something that visibly disconcerts his interlocutor, Joseph Selim falls silent once again.

Now the question that had so illuminated Malvezzi, "What do you know about the capabilities of God?" takes on yet another meaning, confounding his feelings of certainty. It invites him to see the paralysis of the conclave not as a perverse intrusion of Evil, but as a new choice for the side of Good, which is abandoning Rome and its exclusive right of representation, a realization that coincides perfectly with his doubts during the long night while he reread the biblical passages on the folly of Saul.

The pendulum clock in his study sounds nine o'clock. The patriarch reaches for his walking stick and slowly stands to take leave of his friend. Afflicted with pulmonary emphysema, the cardinal is accustomed to being away from his bed for only a few hours at a time, even during the day. He approaches Malvezzi, embraces him three times in the Oriental fashion, and then leans on Contarini's arm to be escorted out.

Ettore Malvezzi remains on his feet, staring at the door long after the problematic man has departed. He walks over to the window that opens onto the interior courtyard and is surprised to see large flakes of snow beginning to fall. After an excessively warm autumn, the winter has begun unexpectedly early, the chill in the air rendering their isolation in the Apostolic Palace all the more distressing. The sunlight has been disappearing earlier and earlier with each passing day; at four o'clock in the afternoon he is now obliged to turn on the desk light in his studio, as are the unknown inhabitants behind the yellow-paned window across from him, whose lights are now shining in the dark. The heat from the fireplace and the antiquated radiators struggles to chase away the humidity in those vast rooms. So, the votes Selim has cast for him don't constitute a strong conviction, but are merely a concession to a ritual that he no longer holds dear to his heart. And he, an archbishop full of doubts, who says Mass every morning with the torment of not always seeing the Savior in the host that he himself has consecrated, has become a pillar of those ancient and outmoded beliefs.

He reconsiders the appeal made by the cardinal of Brasília, which had momentarily swayed him, allowing him to envision a promising outcome from a definitive choice. But the cardinal's plea had been motivated by political passion. The North American cardinals, ever in contact with their countries, would see that it never happened. The chamberlain and the Brazilian cardinal have both received tremendous additional pressure for not observing the proper channels of diplomacy during the segregation.

A shiver runs through him as he watches the snowflakes strike the glass and melt down the panes in rivulets. The window across from him teems with shadows, lives that continue to keep him company without ever revealing themselves. It is 9:15. He could still go to Saint John's Tower to warm himself. Surely many of his brothers would be there, seeking refuge from the cold, like him, or perhaps in search of someone with whom to exchange a few words, or to comment yet again on the most recent inexplicable events.

Selim left him prey to the doubt that few in the conclave still nurtured the ancient beliefs, while the rest of the world, which had lost its navigational beacon with the demise of bipolar politics, seemed to accept a vague and syncretistic deism: the very danger that men like the archbishop of Milan had most feared would erupt.

He is just about to leave his room when the telephone sounds an imperious ring. He is tempted not to answer, but then it occurs to him that he hasn't heard from his family in more than ten days. He picks up the phone, and the operator passes him to his sister, calling from Bologna.

"Clara, how are you? I haven't heard from you in so long."

"We're fine, Ettore. We're fine now, but something happened and I didn't want to worry you."

"What happened?"

"Francesco had a bad accident, but he's all right. Just a few fractures, that's all."

The silence that follows on the other end of the line gives Clara an idea of just how wise she had been for waiting until after the danger had passed. At the same time it transmits to her, more forcefully than any of their other phone conversations, a sense of his acute suffering. The isolation has become far too burdensome on her brother, the only brother left to her after the death a few years earlier of their sibling Carlo. She hasn't seen Ettore since the beginning of September, when she went to visit him in Rome, just before the conclave.

Malvezzi focuses all his energy on the illuminated yellow glass panes of the window across from him. The horrible news, though somewhat mitigated by the knowledge that Francesco is alive and well, penetrates him to the core, generating in him for the first time an uncontainable impulse to escape. "But he's all right now, Clara?"

"Yes, Ettore, he's fine. He has a broken hip and a few broken ribs. But he'll recover after several days of bed rest. When you get out, he'll be back on his feet, you'll see."

"When I get out? Who knows if I ever will!"

It is the first time she has ever heard her brother make a comment like this, a clear sign of exceptional fatigue and worry from a man known for his patience and ability to accept the trials of his calling. "How are things going? The last time we spoke it seemed to me that something was looming on the horizon."

"Well, you can't see anything now. People are disappearing like ghosts."

"I heard about someone who asked to be sent home on account of his health. I read about it in the papers, but that was a long time ago."

"No, that was . . . oh, let's not talk about it. You wouldn't believe me if I told you. At times it seems even to me like a dream from which I can't wake up. Let's talk about Francesco instead; where is he now?"

"He's at the hospital. We decided to move him to a small private clinic near Bologna where Eugenio has some friends who are doctors. They had to perform a small operation. But he's all right now. His only diversion is the friends who come to visit. He's bored, and he often asks about you."

"Give me his phone number."

"I will. You should see him. His hair is so long. As vain as he is, he makes his girlfriend wash and comb his hair, but he'd never let her cut it."

"Does he still have the same girlfriend?"

"Yes, Caterina. She's very bright. You'll meet her. Francesco will be home by Christmas, and if you have nothing against the idea, Eugenio and I thought we'd invite her over on Christmas evening."

"That's right, it's almost Christmas." He is filled with nostalgia by thoughts of the holiday. He has always spent Christmas Eve with his loved ones, and then celebrated Christmas Day with his parishioners, first as an auxiliary bishop and now as a cardinal in

Turin. He is not sure whether they will have completed their task by then. It would be his first Christmas alone in many years.

The shadows in motion behind the opaque windows have disappeared. He must maintain his composure, reign in that which was about to sweep him away, and which his sister has already noticed. He must also return to the circumspect air expected from a cardinal participating in the conclave. Now the lights have been turned off in the room facing him. The dog that he hears most mornings begins to howl. The cats in his room look up in alarm.

"Ettore, are you there? Do you hear me?"

"Yes, I'm here, Clara."

"So is it all right with you if we invite Caterina over on Christmas Day?"

"Of course, Clara."

"I won't make her wear black; she won't be seeing the pope, after all," his sister laughs. Her voice is without its usual biting irony. But the image she evokes makes Malvezzi break into laughter for the first time since he entered the conclave.

"All I want is to get out!"

"I'll get you out of that jail, even if it means coming in and pulling you from the clutches of those guards," she says, and her voice changes again, becoming slow and guttural, as if a shadow of fear were descending on her as well.

They are no longer speaking, just listening to each other breathing, brother and sister, in the silence.

But then a campanile in Bologna, which he recognizes as the bell tower of San Domenico near Clara's house, begins to strike the hour. It is 9:45. The vastness of the world brings him back to her house, where there was always a room ready for him, which partly in jest and partly out of vanity they referred to as "the cardinal's room."

The sound of the clock tower returns Malvezzi's thoughts to Francesco. "Could you give me Francesco's number?"

"Yes, it's 051-6576332; you can call whenever you want because he has the room to himself."

"Fine. I'll call him tomorrow morning after Mass, at eight. Let him know."

"I'll call him now to tell him. But do try to keep in touch more often."

How can he call more often? How can he explain that he is speaking to them amid a menagerie of chickens, cats, and owls, that he is living in constant fear of seeing some new manifestation of Evil? Or that the cardinals are attempting to escape, and that, like the patriarch from Beirut, the pious are being robbed of their faith, doubting their ability to elect the next Vicar of Christ? She has no idea what it's like. She can't possibly know how enticing is this slope toward insanity. They are on the brink of it already, all of them, from the youngest chaplains to the oldest prelates.

He can't tell her these things. He is gaining a slow and subtle resistance to that climate, with its eternal repetitions and delays. Maybe this is how insanity comes on: like an odd habit that you can't find time to address, always waiting for a more opportune moment, until finally it becomes tolerable, almost insignificant. All of the misfortunes in life have this ambiguous quality, this deceptive cadence. Old age comes on in the same way, its changes muted, its intentions masterfully concealed as the flesh grows flaccid, the perfect arc of the eyebrow loses its definition, the firm breasts and the curves of the hips give way to gravity. Illness, too, practices the same war tactic, that invasion without resistance, knowing how to coexist with a healthy body and covering the apertures from which it will one day erupt. The conclave has entered into this same school of spiritual exercise, more perfect than even the Black Pope, the Jesuit general, could imagine.

No, he would never succeed in conveying what he feels, not to her, much less to his nephew. He will call Francesco tomorrow, not right away, as his sister was surprised to hear. And who knows, perhaps the impulse to call, which now feels so strong, will have disappeared by the time he wakes tomorrow, as has happened with so many other calls for help in the recent weeks. "I have to go now, Clara, but we'll talk again soon," he says.

"When?"

"In a few days. The day after tomorrow."

"Fine, talk to you Sunday. We love you."

After he hangs up he feels weak and has to lean on a chair. An owl perched on a curtain rod swoops down toward him to seize a bat. A ruffling of feathers, a flapping of wings that grows more and more violent, and then a thud on the floor. The bat lies on the ground, dead. But the owl doesn't seem to be faring too well either. He watches the raptor bleed, unable to lift one of its wings, hopping about on the floor near its victim. A cat takes sight of him and crouches, ready to pounce. Malvezzi chases the cat away and moves the owl to his desk, out of the feline's reach.

The phone rings again.

"Uncle Ettore! Are you ever coming out of that lair? Aren't you tired of playing pope yet?"

"Francesco, how are you? I heard you had an accident. How are you feeling?"

"I've got a broken hip and three broken ribs, nothing serious. Just forty days of boredom, almost as long as your conclave. When are you getting out? You know we haven't seen each other since last summer?"

"I know, I know. Did you take your exam?"

"I was supposed to take it the day after the accident. I studied so hard for it, too!"

"Your knowledge won't disappear, don't worry. From obstacles advantages are born; remember that. You'll probably get a higher grade."

"I'm not a perfectionist, you know. Eighteen would be good enough. But how are you doing? I'd give my eye to know what it is you do in there. Every so often we get news and I always look for your name, but they never say anything about you!"

"It's not like soccer, Francesco. Anyway, it's probably better that you don't hear my name mentioned. It's a life full of squandered time, like your days in the clinic, I imagine. Nothing much goes on here at all."

"Well, you are mistaken then. There are plenty of beautiful nurses here, and I think that the doctors and the nurses —"

"Francesco, this is not a conversation you should be having with your uncle, the cardinal. Especially when I'm in the conclave. Anyway, I wasn't telling the whole truth: we enjoy ourselves in here, too, though in our own way."

"And what way is that, Uncle Ettore?"

21

$\mathcal{W}$E PLAY HIDE and seek, dear Francesco, and some people are so good at it that they're impossible to find, even after the game is over. Then we dance all night, with no pauses whatsoever, until we see the dawn, only stopping because we are overcome by fatigue. And then we play magic games; one of the cardinals is so good he managed to make the entire fresco of the *Last Judgment* in the Sistine Chapel disappear and then reappear. We also have fun betting on animals: scorpions against chickens, rats versus cats, and bats against owls. And when we grow tired of all these games, we go and vote for the pope in the Sistine Chapel, or we relax amid the steam in the Turkish bath in Saint John's Tower. You tell me, Francesco, doesn't that sound like fun!"

"You are too much, Uncle Ettore! What a great sense of humor you have."

His young nephew's laughter is contagious, and he soon starts laughing, too, while the owl with the wounded wing flies back to the curtain rod. He had given in to the idea of parodying the truth, and it was just as well. Francesco has infused him with that lively spirit, as he never would have succumbed to such a whim with Clara. His sister would simply have interrupted him to ask if he felt ill.

"So, most eminent uncle, I can relax now. I'm glad you're doing well, and I'll see you at Christmas."

"I'm doing fine! I'll be sure to bring you a couple of chickens from the conclave for Christmas, and for New Year's, too. Wait till you see how fat they are."

And while Francesco laughs and bids him good-bye, the cardinal of Turin feels the noose of folly close in around him, in that futile barrage of jokes and tales, in the foolish confessions of a buffoon who can only pay homage to the truth through acts of desecration. That is exactly what they were becoming, he and the other cardinals in the conclave: court jesters, buffoons, God's idiots, provoked to their breaking points so that God will appear. And the conclave has turned into a carnival in order that He will turn up somewhere, anywhere, so long as He appears. A sun that no longer rises in the East, but in the West, yet at least it still rises.

It is with this sense of despair that he decides, as the bell tower strikes 10:30, to go to Saint John's Tower. He opens the door to the spa's antechamber and is not at all surprised to find a crowd of cardinals already gathered there; it is actually difficult to find an empty changing room. Everyone is there: the French, the Germans, the Spanish, the Italians from the Roman Curia and the dioceses, the Africans, the North and South Americans. He meets up with Cardinal Paide, who is undressing in the room next to his.

"Well, that makes three," Malvezzi says with a sigh, his red and swollen eyes fixed on the austere face of the ex-Trappist monk.

"Three what?"

"Three that have left us, dear Paide: Contardi, Mascheroni, and Ugamwa."

"You can't put our grand exorcist on the same plane as the other two. Ugamwa isn't dead."

"Are you sure? What do you know about magic?"

"You don't need to know about magic to understand that he

hasn't passed on. We do have to pray for him, though; remember to do so during your Mass."

Ettore Malvezzi doesn't reply, and he senses his temperament beginning to change. The echo of Francesco's laughter still rings in his ear, rekindling itself with an infectious intensity, until he, too, breaks into laughter, not caring who is there to listen.

Paide pretends not to have heard that unprovoked euphoria and passes ahead of him into the baths. He is not the first of his colleagues to show signs of psychological weakness in recent days. He has already noticed that Malvezzi is prone to hyperactive speech when he is nervous, perhaps the affliction has been exacerbated by claustrophobia. Paide considers himself lucky to have received a Trappist training, for he can remain in silent isolation for days on end and never feel alone. Actually, he tends to feel solitude in the company of others. That is why he likes the sauna, as it counters his temptation to avoid others. There, as on his island, he is forced into conversation, into confidences, into direct contact with others.

"When do you think our grand exorcist will return?"

Paide recognizes Malvezzi's voice, but cannot see him through the steam. He must have followed him in, unwilling to let the conversation end. Paide chooses not to reply, taking advantage of the clouds of steam that hide him.

"Who knows?" responds a voice, though the speaker is unidentifiable, so thick is the steam. With the snowfall that evening, the workmen had raised the temperature in the baths. "Only the African cardinals can say for sure. Why don't you ask them?"

"You're right. I don't fear them," Malvezzi says. And he calls out, "Are any of our African brothers in here?"

From his anonymity within the clouds of vapor, the indelicacy with which he phrases the question, directing it to a man perhaps wrongly charged of practicing magic, is both provocative and irksome.

"I'm here."

"Who are you?"

"Carlo Felipe Maria Dos Angeles, from Maputo."

"Well then, Cardinal Maputo, let me ask you. Are you going to call Cardinal Leopold Albert Ugamwa back, or do I have to do it? Ugamwa, what are you waiting for? Blow! Blow hard and the wall will come tumbling down!"

A long silence follows Malvezzi's bizarre words.

Matis Paide is about to speak, hoping to ease the tension, when he notices something happening. The steam is rapidly settling, while the temperature begins to fall. The entire group of elderly cardinals is now visible, either standing, or sitting, or leaning against the walls, naked as Adam before the Fall. But in the middle of the room, dressed in his black cassock with crimson trim, stands the archbishop of Dar es Salaam, Leopold Albert Ugamwa. The sound of laughter is heard, at first softly, and then louder, without stopping. It is Ettore Malvezzi, who can control himself no longer. He is asked to contain himself, but can only respond repeatedly, his words coming more and more quickly, that he must make a phone call to Francesco. "A phone call? But, Ettore, can't you see that Ugamwa has returned? Isn't that what you asked for?" Rabuiti tries to calm him down, beginning to comprehend that something terrible is happening to his friend from Turin.

"Please excuse me, I have to call Francesco!"

Several cardinals exit the bath, leaving Rabuiti and Paide alone with Malvezzi. The crowd surrounding the Tanzanian cardinal does not want to let him depart. Many of them touch him and shake his hand, lacking the courage to talk to him, to pose the questions that only a disturbed mind like Malvezzi would have the audacity to ask.

"Poor Ettore, we'll have to take him back to his room," says the cardinal of Venice, Aldo Miceli, who is standing near Ugamwa.

"But he's the only one who had the strength to make me return!" The words of the exorcist surprise everyone.

"What are you saying?"

"His is a good strength, like my powers. Malvezzi understands everything that is going on, but in a different way. That is why he called out to me. Because he saw me. He knew that I was still inside these walls."

For a second time, silence descends on the room. The African has forced the discourse to take a turn, exposing a mode of thinking that can't be reconciled with their own. By defending Malvezzi's fragility, Ugamwa has managed only to cast suspicion on himself in the eyes of the other eminent electors.

"Don't you want to understand? If he didn't have the simplicity of a child, he wouldn't have been able to open the door for me to return."

"What are you saying? How did Malvezzi open . . . a door?" the patriarch of Venice insists.

"Even the highest walls erected by Evil can crumble. Someone, knowing to ask the imprisoned victim to make even the slightest attempt to escape, can turn the imprisonment into a game. That is what Malvezzi knew when he challenged me to blow down the wall. That's how he freed me."

At that moment Paide appears in the doorway with Malvezzi, who is leaning on his arm. An ecstatic smile brightens the Turinese cardinal's face. There is no need for words. That smile without reason, without object, without end, says everything. And it shows everyone present that Ugamwa is right. The man has lost the thread of lies and truths, and Good and Evil have quit lying, have quit appearing to be diverse.

Rabuiti looks at the telephone in the antechamber, thinking to himself that Ettore won't need to call Francesco any more. In fact, the cardinal from Turin walks straight by the phone without even seeing it, allowing himself to be guided by the Estonian cardinal toward the changing rooms.

Someone must have called Monsignor Contarini, because the thin, pale chaplain arrives at the door and disappears with Malvezzi into the changing rooms. The Tanzanian sits down in the antechamber, still surrounded by many of the cardinals. He no longer wants to respond to their questions. He would only answer to the chamberlain, to whom he feels obligated to explain his prodigious powers.

Ettore Malvezzi reappears, accompanied by his chaplain. He looks less confused, although that enraptured smile is still on his lips, suggesting the tenuous grip he must now have on reality. Ugamwa approaches him and asks how he feels, but instead of replying, Malvezzi blesses him, tracing the sign of the cross in the air. His gesture has great dignity; it seems both mindful and as if it were projected from somewhere else. He does not limit himself to blessing just the African cardinal, but turns and begins making the sign of the cross over all of them, with a solemnity that makes them respond by crossing themselves in turn.

Slowly he makes his way to the exit, his hands raised in the air to offer the benediction. Some of them bow their heads, while the Philippine and Ugandan monsignors who work in the sauna genuflect before him.

It is Monsignor Contarini who reports to the chamberlain two hours later, informing him of the mental state of his archbishop, who is already in bed in his room. But the news that Malvezzi is no longer himself has already been communicated to Cardinal Veronelli by Ugamwa, though in terms so suggestive and nonclinical as not to intimate whether the Turinese cardinal would still be able to participate in the elections.

This, in fact, is the only question still to be resolved, as far as the chamberlain of the Holy Roman Church is concerned; he is unfamiliar with any precedents on which to base his decision. The Tanzanian cardinal, for his part, does not doubt that Malvezzi will continue to number himself among the present at the meetings in the Sistine Chapel. He has been consecrated and cannot absent himself from the Sacred College. Quite possibly, the man has now become even closer to the Holy Spirit.

Veronelli, however, already wary of Ugamwa and his manner of speaking, is confused by the recent turn of events, even less able to make a decision. What if the new pope were elected without Malvezzi's vote, even while he is still present in the Apostolic Palace? Would the election be invalid?

He poses these question to Contarini after Ugamwa leaves his chambers, but the secretary does not know how to respond. He can only say that the cardinal has been the picture of serenity, at least in the past few hours since conjuring forth the missing Tan-

zanian cardinal. At the use of that phrase, the chamberlain explodes with anger, interrupting Contarini to say that Malvezzi is
not an exorcist; he does not conjure the dead, nor does he chase
away demons.

Contarini replies that he is no longer certain there is only one
exorcist in the conclave, because the cardinal of Turin has been
speaking with the shadows, even to the two whose recent deaths
have so saddened the conclave.

"With whom?" Veronelli asks, stunned.

"With Their Eminences Emanuele Contardi and Zelindo
Mascheroni. He sees them in his room, seated at the foot of his
bed, as clearly as I see you now. And he talks to them. He told me
that they are terribly lonely and in need of company, and tonight
he's not sure he'll get much sleep, because he doesn't want to
leave them alone. He said some dead people never sleep, that
they envy the sleep of the living. He said that Mascheroni suffers
the most from insomnia due to the strange circumstances surrounding his death and that he's waiting for —"

At that particular piece of information, Veronelli interrupts the
chaplain to tell him that His Eminence should plan to rest in his
room the following day. His absence from the conclave will be
justified. He, himself, will come to visit the cardinal of Turin after
the elections, if for nothing else than to learn whether he needs
anything.

Once Vladimiro Veronelli is finally alone, he lies down on his
bed, turns off the bedside lamp, and reflects at length on what he
should do next to hold back the floodwaters. He had just managed to solve the problem of the young secretaries and chaplains,
substituting them with older colleagues not prone to hallucinations. He cannot admit a lunatic into the conclave; there are already too many eccentrics in the holy assembly, which instead of
being boycotted by manifestations of the Holy Spirit seems to be
overrun by them. And still they have not had a single respite from
Evil. Mystics in the Church spring up like weeds, appearing
when least expected, among the most diverse array of members:
among the monsignors of the Roman Curia, secretly affiliated

with the ranks of the Rose Cross; among the abbots of ancient monasteries, nostalgic for the religious military orders of the Crusades; among Vatican financiers, rigid penitents of Saint Peter's Basilica, and Thomist theologians who become absorbed in the writings of Val Corva. There are numerous devotees of Saint John of the Cross and Saint Teresa of Avila, and a fair number who follow Saint Albertus Magnus, Saint Thomas Aquinas, and Saint Robert Bellarmine.

What a calamity, should anyone outside the conclave discover that there is a similar practitioner in their midst. The armies of mystics would pressure them until his voice was heard. Instead, they needed to keep their wits about them. The election of a pope is a practical process as well as an act of faith, a machine that must choose the best candidate, and ensure that he will last for the most number of years. It is not an emotional act. The emotions have already interfered too much; it is time to return to reason. Kant, his favorite philosopher, explained reason and faith as being two spheres divided by insurmountable barriers, preventing the confusion of one with the other. Phenomenon and noumenon never meet, and precisely because of this autonomy, the two concepts help man seek truth in his condition.

Ettore Malvezzi, poor man, had always been a thorn in Veronelli's side, possessed with that rare gift of knowing how to complicate things; but this unexpected display of madness has truly worsened the situation. Perhaps an exorcist and a lunatic are just opposite sides of the same coin. In fact, they had liked one another immediately, those two men, as Veronelli could tell from the sympathetic and affectionate way the exorcist had spoken just a short while earlier. A state of sanctity is no longer purely an African prerequisite; the movement will spread. Mystics — or, more appropriately, the weak, who can't wait for an opportunity to declare a miracle in order to confirm their faith — are a party of unification, with members in all nations. There are even some among the South American contingent, the most politically driven faction in the Sacred College. It is known, for instance, that the archbishop of San Juan celebrates strange funeral rites that have become an object of suspicion in the Vatican Curia. And the cardinal of Medellín admits to allowing propitiatory dancing when it is requested by the faithful during his Masses.

Then there was the incident with Cardinal Mascheroni. If it becomes known, thanks to Malvezzi's omniscience, what really happened to the prefect, serious problems will ensue. How did he know what happened that night? He might indeed have received a divine gift of clairvoyance during his confusion, but that is not enough to declare him as holy, or above all, to allow him to vote.

Saints are always dangerous; Cerini was right. Only after their death are they recognized, and it is then that they come to be venerated. But while they are alive it is beneficial, even for them, to oppose them, to test their virtue. That way they are better assured their place in paradise. Rushing to elevate them to the altar can bring results similar to what befell the beautiful Lucia of Narni, whose handkerchiefs, soaked with the blood of her stigmata, were sent to devoted sovereigns throughout Europe by the Duke of Ferrara. He had offered her brothers a handsome sum for guaranteeing her presence in the city, but then one unfortunate day the stigmata healed, and poor Lucia had to live out her days in hunger, locked in her convent and forgotten by all.

22

THE CHAMBERLAIN OF the Holy Roman Church begins to tally the first round of ballots with the scrutineers who had been chosen that morning, the archbishops of Cologne and Ernakulam-Angamaly of the Siro-Malabaresi. Immediately it becomes clear that the stalled mechanism of the conclave is being liberated. The names are always the same: Leopold Albert Ugamwa, Leopold Albert Ugamwa, Leopold Albert Ugamwa, José Maria Resende Costa, José Maria Resende Costa, José Maria Resende Costa, Ettore Malvezzi, Ettore Malvezzi, Ettore Malvezzi . . . with occasional votes for Alfonso Cerini, and even fewer for Wolfram Stelipyn, turning up near the end. The dispersion among the 124 voters, absent Cardinal Malvezzi, has finally ended.

The African, the politician, and the mystic seem to Veronelli to be the cardinals' preferred choices, while the Milanese and the Slav are losing ground. Not even Malvezzi's forced absence has been sufficient to erase the impression he left in the minds of thirty-seven cardinals. And he can't be kept in isolation much longer; his pronouncements are being too quickly realized, as

Veronelli has come to accept, given his phone conversation with Contarini an hour before the elections.

"The archbishop of Turin is doing extremely well, Your Eminence," Contarini said.

"Did he sleep? Or did he continue to have . . . his conversations?"

"What conversations?"

'You know, the ones with the dead. The people he saw at the foot of his bed."

"Oh yes, those. They kept him company all night, he said, but toward dawn they left him, taking pity on his fatigue. He only needed a few hours of sleep, though. He already said Mass."

"Does he need anything?"

"No, he's sitting in the armchair near the window, reading his breviary. He did have one request, though."

"What is it, Monsignor?"

"That the thirty-seven votes he'll receive this morning from the Sacred College should go to someone worthier than he during the second round."

Veronelli said nothing in response to that premonition. His sense of caution advised him not to divulge anything to Contarini, who in turn seemed to enjoy keeping the chamberlain on tenterhooks, now that he knew the truth about the death of Zelindo Mascheroni.

Once the tabulating is over, revealing that Malvezzi did indeed receive thirty-seven votes, Veronelli is grateful not to have let his true thoughts be known, not to have revealed his incredulity. He announced the official results, reading from the document presented to him by the Cardinal of Cologne. "His Eminence, the cardinal archbishop of Dar es Salaam, Leopold Albert Ugamwa, has received forty votes; His Eminence, the cardinal archbishop of Brasília, José Maria Resende Costa, has received thirty-eight votes; His Eminence, the cardinal archbishop of Turin, Ettore Malvezzi, received thirty-seven votes; His Eminence, the cardinal archbishop of Milan, Alfonso Cerini, received five votes; His Eminence, the cardinal archbishop of Lviv in the

Ukraine, Wolfram Stelipyn, received four votes. The required simple majority not having been reached in this election, which today would have been sixty-three votes, we are required to proceed to another round of voting later this afternoon, at four o'-clock. I thank you, and I urge you to pray to our omnipotent Heavenly Father, in order that the decision on which we seem to be verging shall truly be inspired by His wisdom." Everyone notices that the chamberlain seems disturbed. He has never made a closing comment like this before. He all but declared that a choice was imminent. Even more telling, he did not raise any objections, he who was such a stickler for protocol, about the votes received by the absent cardinal. Indeed, the cardinal of Turin is still part of the conclave, albeit temporarily indisposed.

At the midday meal immediately following the elections, the cardinals gather at the tables of several eminences — Rabuiti, Stelipyn, Cerini, Shaouguan of Shanghai, Bradstreet of Toronto, Dos Angeles of Maputo, and Winnipeg of New York — and the conversations about this temporary indisposition grow ever more fervent.

Is Ettore Malvezzi incapable of participating in the elections? According to the ecclesiastical laws that have governed the conclave since the constitution of Pope Sextus V, is he in any condition to accept the papacy, should he be elected? This possibility, even though only hypothetical, infuriates no one more than Alfonso Cerini, who doesn't hesitate to voice the possibility of a ruse: Malvezzi is a master of ambiguity and subterfuge, incapable of taking direct action, who simulates madness to draw attention to his candidacy from conclavists who have lost their own sense of reason.

The patriarch of Venice, Aldo Miceli, offers a harsh rebuke at such a suggestion. "You should be ashamed of yourself, Cerini. You know that Malvezzi has always denied any aspirations whatsoever. We also know that he never voted for himself, but instead it was the Maronite who wrote his name on the ballot."

In Rabuiti's chambers, too, the discussion has reached an elevated pitch. In addition to their alarm over the archbishop of Turin, the cardinals assembled at the Sicilian's table find themselves wondering just what sort of leadership could be offered to the Church by the African, who has consorted with demons. Most of Rabuiti's dining companions — not just the Italians, but other Europeans as well — do not believe that even the horror of the disappearance of Michelangelo's fresco justified Ugamwa's use of his powers of exorcism.

The presence at the table of Paul Linn, the cardinal of Westminster, who had collaborated with Ugamwa in the years before he attained the rank of cardinal, generates even more curiosity. "Yes, it's true. Even in London, a city far removed from such customs, Monsignor Ugamwa did not scorn the use of magic. Many people sought him out, and I often had to intervene to help liberate him . . . to liberate us, that is."

Three of his colleagues immediately launch a vehement interrogation, but the English cardinal maintains his poise. "It is only proper," he continues, "that we recognize Ugamwa's many merits. That man once managed to save countless lives through his psychic powers. I have a memory of him that bears repeating here, as he once averted a collision between two trains that were headed toward one another at full speed in the outskirts of London. Were it not for Ugamwa's timely intervention by calling the Minister of the Railways, hundreds of deaths would have occurred. As he was celebrating Mass one morning, I saw him rush from his private chapel in the middle of the service. That man had in fact been hearing the continuous, piercing blast of a whistle. In spite of his urgent, repeated inquiries, he could find no one else in the entire Curia who heard it. Finally, he realized that the whistling was intended only for him, and that something, or someone, was sending him a message from that faraway train. Everything became suddenly clear to him: he had seen the train and the green signal that an hour from then would beckon it from Liverpool, instead of stopping it, allowing the express train from Cornwall to pass. There was no calming him. He forced me, with my authority as a Catholic primate, to telephone the minister in person. He immediately intervened, verifying the accuracy of the warning, and preventing a devastating accident."

At that point, the archbishop of Esztergom-Budapest, Vilmos Apponij, begins to speak, while the nuns arrive from the palace kitchens, carrying a sumptuous *brodetto di pesce* to the table. A man such as that at the apex of the Church would doubtless inflict a grave wound on Christian spirituality. People would no longer believe in faith; they would believe instead in the power of portents and the force of miracles, which would no longer be the fruit of infinite faith in the Lord, but the prerequisite test for having faith in Him. It would be necessary to stem the pernicious tendency of repressing the true sources of Revelation — the Sacred Scriptures, the Bible, the Gospel — that was being caused by a growing reliance on indirect texts — the secrets of Fatima, the letters of soothsayers, the revelations at Medjugorye, the visions of Val Corva. The fundaments of the Christian faith would be undermined, replacing the Word of God with the offerings of some of his creatures . . .

As the Hungarian prelate is expounding on those gifts granted by God's creatures, an African friar, who had begun serving forth the meal prepared by the nuns, stumbles amid the cats that have gathered about his feet, drawn by the scent of the fish stew, in hopes of obtaining a savory morsel. The steaming bowls shatter into pieces, spilling their contents across the floor, and a fury of cats descends on the fish. An enormous orange cat, the first to the scene, sinks its teeth into a piece of sole. It then leaps back, spits out the fish, and begins to hiss and meow furiously. The other cats immediately heed the warning and retreat from the spill, and a chorus of squawks from the chickens rises above the cardinals' voices.

Their Eminences must truly have thought it a comical spectacle, because the African friar watches them break into laughter, ever more uncontrollable laughter, as they bring the stew to their lips, and he will come to learn that the same thing is happening among the cardinals in the other rooms as well.

After a full quarter of an hour, the cardinals, who had initially been so absorbed in the speech of the Hungarian primate, still show no signs of stopping, while the animals, following an instinct even more basic than hunger, claw at the door to escape, as if driven by fear. Adam Mandumi, the friar from the Sahel, opens the door to let them out, hoping his gesture will help restore an air of propriety to the cardinals' meal. But by now the cardinals, who have all eaten of the *brodetto*, can control themselves no longer. They break into peals of laughter, pausing only to catch their breath before bursting forth again into a shrill, warbling fit.

Adam Mandumi is the first to suspect that the fish stew, prepared by the nuns in the papal kitchens, must have something to do with the epidemic of laughter. He does not disclose his thoughts, however, until he leaves the room and encounters his colleagues from the other chambers, whose cardinals have succumbed to similar paroxysms. He asks if they had received the same *brodetto di pesce* that had been delivered to his room by dumbwaiter from the kitchen.

"Yes, the same *brodetto*."

"Did you taste it?"

"Not on your life. Do you think we would ever eat the food prepared for the cardinals?"

"Well, for heaven's sake, make sure you don't taste it, not even a drop! And don't let them serve it to the others!"

After a few faint protests revealing their annoyance, they obey, but it is already too late. The stew has been served, and it has been consumed down to the last fishbone. The sound of laughter now reverberates throughout the palace; the cardinals can no longer speak, and their faces are purple from giving vent to such hilarity.

What should be done? Nothing, except rush down to the kitchens to find out who in the world could have prepared such an evil concoction. The cats are vomiting, the chickens are seized by an insatiable thirst, while the cardinals continue to carry on in an impious and uproarious manner.

Adam finds the nuns busy preparing the main course: sole *alla mugnaia*, accompanied by boiled potatoes with homemade mayonnaise. The three nuns are singing, and don't notice him right away.

"What did you make for the cardinals?" the friar asks brusquely.

"What do you mean? We made fish. Today is Friday. We observe this day of abstinence as per the sumptuary orders of the Prefect of the Pontifical House," one of the nuns answers in surprise.

"I understand. I know all too well that you prepared fish! But what in the Devil did you put in it?"

"What did we put in it? It couldn't be fresher, straight from the sea at Ostia this morning. Look, there is skate, sea bream, turbot, sole . . . would you like to taste the sole?"

"No, I wouldn't! Ever since the cardinals tasted your soup, they've been laughing hysterically. What in God's name did you put in it?"

On hearing that the cardinals can't stop laughing, Sister Elizabeth turns off the flame under the pot she is tending. "I'm the one who made the *brodetto*," she says with a surprised air. She thinks back to the songs she sang while she cleaned and cooked the fish. They were songs from her village in the Sahel, songs they sang when they needed rain, but also songs to chase away the evil eye and songs that were sung around the fire at night, to conquer the fear that the sun would never return. But the most beautiful of all, her favorite, was one that the village healer had only the children sing. It made the elders laugh, those who refused to eat and wished to be left to die, and they began to laugh and to eat, as soon as they heard it, to eat and to laugh until they could take no more. So that is what happened: she must have been singing that song while she was preparing the *brodetto* for those old cardinals!

Tears streaming down her cheeks, the petite nun from the Sahel tries to recall how the healer broke the enchantment, but she can't remember. Then it comes to her in a flash, and she turns back to her cooking. "No need to worry. All we have to do is serve them a nice piece of avocado after the sole; that will stop their laughter. Naturally, I hope everyone likes avocados. Now that I know what I have to do, you must leave me alone. I can't cook in front of people I don't know."

"Just make sure you don't make any mistakes this time; I'll be waiting outside to help load the plates into the dumbwaiter," says the friar.

The nun succeeds in her task, either singing another tune that cancels out the original song, or perhaps retrieving from memory whatever incantation the healer had used to bring the laughing villagers back to silence.

The avocados are served at every table to cardinals exhausted by a laughter that has eliminated their inhibitions, but not their awareness of their actions. Only a few refuse to taste the exotic fruit, so foreign to their usual diet. But at the sight of the placating effect it immediately has on their colleagues in that Dionysian fury, they realize its value and accept some as well. And after even the most uproarious have eaten the fruit, an unnatural calm falls over the entire Apostolic Palace.

They had laughed for three hours straight. Though the archbishops of Vienna, Warsaw, and Prague had laughed even longer, commented Ettore Malvezzi from his room, where he had enjoyed a cold meal prepared for him by Contarini.

23

*T*HE CHAMBERLAIN ENTERS the archbishop of Turin's quarters at the end of another fruitless day of voting. Visiting the sick is one of the seven corporal works of mercy, but it is not with this spirit of piety that the chamberlain crosses Malvezzi's threshold, for the cardinal has continued to receive votes during the recent elections: Thirty-seven votes, two days earlier, on the eve of the latest supernatural events caused by the absentminded chanting of the nun. And another thirty-seven during the following round.

Like a fever, the elections have overtaken the collective body of the Sacred College, with each vote marking another degree on the graduated scale of a thermometer. The fever does not fall, and Veronelli can't envision an expedient way to eliminate the threat of Malvezzi's elevation to the papacy, unless he himself chooses to withdraw his candidacy.

But it is no easy task to talk to a man who has been conversing with the dead, foretelling events, and spending his days in solitude, reading, ever since he summoned Cardinal Ugamwa from the Turkish bath. Veronelli has heard that Malvezzi only stops reading

to eat his frugal dinners, and to see personally that the animals residing in his chambers are fed. He was one of the few to remain
unaffected by the plague of laughter, as he had been served food
that had not been cooked by the enchantress from the Sahel. Even
in his frugality, he demonstrated his power of foresight.

Earlier that day, the chamberlain received a phone call that
complicated things even further. Upon learning that it was from
the Quirinal, he was tempted not to take it, but then a sense of
duty prevailed.

He was forced to subject himself to the president's painful admonishments. On behalf of the Italian people, the president expressed the most profound concern regarding what was by now an
inexcusable delay in selecting the new bishop of Rome. Although
Veronelli felt heartened at receiving attention from such a high
level, as compared to the noticeable disinterest among the press
over the events of the conclave, the telephone call annoyed him
greatly for its intrusiveness. He chose not to reveal his irritation,
though, alluding instead to difficult issues of balance that were impeding the elections, but which were close to being resolved, rest
assured. It was a masterpiece of diplomatic falsehoods, that phone
call, and he allowed himself a slight revenge as an added bonus:

At the end of their conversation the president passed the telephone to his wife, Gina. The palatine chaplain from the Quirinal
had recently informed Veronelli that the president's wife intended to wear a white dress upon meeting the new pope, a gesture that had for centuries been the exclusive privilege of the
Catholic queens of Spain and Belgium, as well as the grand
duchess of Luxemburg and the princess of Monaco. So when Signora Gina Slaviati née Tarallo offered her most sincere wishes for
an inspired choice by Their Eminences, the cold, curt "thank
you" she received in reply unnerved her immensely. She rambled
on for a few more minutes, perhaps in hopes of charming the
chamberlain, even adding that she would like to invite all the
Italian members of the Sacred College to dine as soon as the conclave had concluded, although the cooking in the Quirinal perhaps left a bit to be desired.

At this, the mischievous Tuscan in Veronelli was reawakened. His voice took on a mellifluous tone, and he asked permission to lend out some of the Vatican's non-Italian cooks, who had performed genuine miracles during the long days of the conclave. Signora Gina accepted his offer immediately, thanking him for such an exquisite gesture.

"Do send them to us soon, Your Eminence. Where are they from?"

"They're African nuns, Signora, from the Sahel."

If only everything were as easy as duping that vain woman! But how did one go about persuading a madman?

Accompanied by Contarini, whose appearance had grown haggard, his clothes reeking more than ever of tobacco smoke, the chamberlain meets with Ettore Malvezzi in his study. From his seraphic expression, it is not clear whether the cardinal's health has truly suffered. Seated in his armchair, his face in the light, the man looks like a philosopher of the Church, absorbed in profound reflection. Like Saint Jerome with his lion on the floor next to him — except Malvezzi has chickens, cats, and owls. Or like Saint Charles Borromeo, with his dinner of a piece of dry bread and a glass of water by his side, reflecting on the homily he will soon give in the cathedral. Malvezzi no longer has the stunned and unsettled expression on his face that had so often distressed Veronelli. He slowly gets to his feet when he realizes the chamberlain has entered the room, and he gently places his book on the table. He smiles, inviting Veronelli to sit down with him in front of the fire, in one of the two armchairs. He asks if he can offer the chamberlain something to drink, telling him he has only water.

"Water would be fine, Ettore."

"It's mineral water, of course."

"It's nice here. Your fireplace draws better than mine. By the way, I just received a call from someone in a very high position, who complained about how long we are taking to elect the pope. He says it will damage the relationship between the Church and state. What do you think?"

"Why don't you just tell me the president of the republic called? Are you testing me? Have you come here to test me?"

"Testing you? With all the worries that I already have? My dear Ettore, you've given me your share of worries, too. You really frightened us. Actually, you could probably lend me a hand."

"I know only as much as you do."

"Well, you give the impression of knowing more. The other day, for example, you knew that you would obtain thirty-seven votes, and not a single more. What does that tell us?"

"It was revealed to me only in order to appease my request."

"What request?"

"To have people vote for someone else."

"Everyone knew you felt that way, but they took it as a sign of exemplary modesty, and indeed, as another reason for voting for you."

"You can't blame me for that."

"Are you still thinking of withdrawing?"

"More than ever."

The chamberlain gives a deep sigh of relief. He has at least managed to wrest an initial promise from him. Passing to a request for a formal agreement will require a certain amount of tact and diplomacy. In the meantime he takes a drink from the glass of water given to him by Contarini and watches the various animals in the room, whose noxious scent offended his nose immediately upon entering. Oddly, that henhouse stench is now barely noticeable throughout the other rooms in the palace, but here the fetor is almost unbearable. He marvels that Malvezzi doesn't even seem aware of it.

He drinks slowly, as slowly as he can, without shifting his gaze from the animals. The cats and hens have positioned themselves in a semicircle around their master, their eyes fixed on him. Their perfect stillness is deceiving. As soon as they see Malvezzi move or make a sudden gesture, they stir as if wanting to accompany him in his motions. The owls are even more striking. They keep a safe distance from the cats, while remaining as close to Malvezzi as possible, perching over his head on the molding that runs between the ceiling and the walls. Their absolute loyalty to their

master is uncanny. When Veronelli brushes against Malvezzi's
arm as they speak, the hens peck at his shoes and the owls beat
their wings.

"What do you think of the other candidates?"

"They're very different from one another."

"I noticed that, too."

"I don't believe any of them will be elected, if that's what you
wanted to ask."

"But how will this ever get resolved?"

"I don't know. Mascheroni and Contardi couldn't see the results, either. They made every effort."

"Is that so? Were they the ones who told you about the thirty-
seven votes?"

"I don't remember."

"Naturally. Even visions have a River Lethe."

"And yet, judging from what happened to poor Mascheroni,
there is one truth that seems to have emerged with clarity."

"We can talk about what happened to him later; tell me about
this truth."

"That we are not far from seeing the day when a woman will
be elected to the papacy."

Veronelli shifts uncomfortably on his chair, his eyes opened
wide in amazement. The cats, noticing his movements, are
poised to pounce on him, but Malvezzi calms them.

"That tragic mask he was wearing on his deathbed — the one
you had removed — meant this as well."

"I certainly couldn't have left him like that, Ettore."

"No, but his final moments must be interpreted with extreme
care. One of the greatest tragedies for humankind — and something that produces more victims than war itself — is the slow
pace of history. How many men have been killed or condemned
or rejected in the name of religion, in deference to laws that were
considered absolute, yet were recognized as obsolete with the
passing of time? And we, the ministers of the Roman Catholic
Church, how wise we have been in making history move as slowly
as it can. Zelindo Mascheroni paid with his life for his desperate

awareness of playing a role in this slow machine, because as a man, he experienced a natural desire that, as the Prefect of the Congregation for the Doctrine of the Faith, he was forced to label as a sin."

"I'm not sure I follow you."

"That's because I'm talking about a poor victim who still belongs to our life and times. You would understand if I were talking about Huss or Galileo, about Campanella, or Giordano Bruno, or the Jews who were condemned for deicide, or the Albigenses, or all the witches and wizards who were tortured and burned."

"I understand what you mean when you refer to certain episodes that were our responsibility, and for which we've asked forgiveness, but not when you try to convince me that one day we'll elect a woman pontiff. Don't you see? It goes against the laws of Christ! God Himself never elevated a woman to the level of apostle."

"To this I can reply by saying that even Christ, as a man, was subject to the torpidity and opacity of history. In the society of his day, among the Jews, it never would have been tolerated. It was against the custom of the age."

"And who are we to abolish a two-thousand-year-old practice?"

"We're the ones who haven't been able to elect a pope because we don't know how to look into the distance."

"Why — because we're not courageous enough to admit women to the priesthood or to the papacy?"

"You said it, not me."

The chamberlain is astonished. He had come in search of a glimpse at the future, to extract a ray of light out of that odd man. He had come to hear Malvezzi renounce his claims on the papacy, and he hears instead that one of the keys to the future could lie in choosing a woman to ascend Peter's throne.

The poor man is truly insane. Now the chamberlain is no longer afraid of refusing him entry into the conclave. For that matter, it is his duty to isolate him, to prevent the ingenuous among the other 123 cardinals from remaining captivated by him.

"I agree with you, Vladimiro. It would be better if I stayed in my room and didn't take part in the elections anymore," he says, smiling radiantly and staring intently at Vladimiro, infuriating him. His piercing gaze makes the chamberlain feel like an executioner standing before a victim who is in favor of capital punishment. "Don't torment yourself, Vladimiro. I know it's difficult. At any rate, you can relax, it is too soon to elect a woman. Millions of women must still endure the horrors of female circumcision because of superstitions and religious taboos; millions of women will be unable to accept their masculine tendencies, just as millions of men will be forced to suppress their feminine inclinations in deference to our condemnations. Myriad victims have yet to pass through that slow mill of history, victims that we will create, along with the ayatollahs and the rabbis and any witch doctors remaining on earth."

"I don't recognize you anymore, Ettore. You never used to talk like this. Not only can I not understand you, but I'm afraid that I will have to condemn you."

"I know. In the past, you would have been forced to consign me to the Holy See, initiating a trial that would have seen me burned at the stake."

"Ettore, please stop! Don't you remember who you are?"

"It's where I am that I just can't seem to forget. It is the only agony that keeps me here, otherwise —" Malvezzi interrupts himself, unable to complete his sentence.

"Otherwise what?"

"Otherwise I would be where Contardi and Mascheroni are now. But certain memories, a handful of people who are waiting for me, a few friends, who knows, maybe even you, keep me here." Tears are running down Malvezzi's face. Veronelli, too, can no longer hide his grief. The animals in the room, as if intuiting their master's state of mind, draw closer to his armchair, a few even jumping into his lap. "Forgive their intrusiveness. Let me explain: suspended between those who have preceded me, and those who honestly love me, I find myself here, as uncertain and skeptical as ever, the same man whom you have never liked."

"But we want you to live, Ettore. Don't do me the disservice of not believing me."

"I do believe you. But what can be done with a man like me? Do you know that I can see your mother, now, as we speak? She's standing beside you, caressing your head, smoothing down your hair. I can see your two brothers, too. They're here in Rome: one of them is intent on walking along the Appian Way, while the other one is ill in bed, being cared for by his daughter. Do you know that the day after tomorrow a violent storm will strike, here in Rome, causing serious damage? You came for this, too, admit it. You wanted to see if it's true that Malvezzi can see into the future."

The mention of his mother has left Veronelli speechless. He is struck by an acute awareness of how tormenting life must be for people commonly deemed as crazy. For a single moment, he witnessed what this man has been given, and because of this gift, it has become impossible for him to anchor Good and Evil in the present. In Malvezzi's eyes, the present slides into the future in the same way that this room opens up to receive the city. It is better to be silent, to proceed no further in an increasingly painful conversation.

24

ISTER ELIZABETH and the other cooks from the Sahel were offered as sacrificial victims to the Quirinal to satisfy the ambitions of the president's wife. Almost all of the young chaplains and secretaries, whose hallucinations so devastated the conclave, have been replaced by older personnel, sent to Rome from throughout the dioceses. Cardinal Ettore Malvezzi promised his formal withdrawal from candidacy. The archbishop of Dar es Salaam agreed to be held accountable for his activities as an exorcist, both privately, in a meeting with the chamberlain, and publicly, in front of the Sacred College.

Cardinal Vladimiro Veronelli is beginning to draw some comfort from his tireless efforts in governing the longest conclave in the history of the Church. Of great comfort too, is the news from Count Nasalli Rocca that the war against the rats, scorpions, and bats can be considered won, even though it remains a good idea to keep some of the cats, hens, and owls circulating as a precautionary measure.

Even the phone call from the Quirinal gives him a modicum

of relief, as it shows that attention is being paid to the events oc-
curring within the Leonine Walls. But it is just one ray from a very
weak sun. The truth of the matter is that the teletypists in the
pressroom remain silent, while fewer and fewer Internet naviga-
tors are connecting to the Vatican website each day. And the
newspapers, a bitter chalice from which they must drink each
morning, are snubbing the cardinals and their boring conclave.
One thing is certain, though: no news has been leaked about the
lunacies that have rendered their assize anything but boring.

Still, the conclavists are proving themselves incapable of
choosing a pontiff. They follow a tired script, with voting sessions
that continue to generate the same results, albeit an improvement
over the dispersion during the early days.

Malvezzi's hold on the electors has weakened; he now regu-
larly receives only about twenty votes. The cardinals are aware of
his desire to withdraw his candidacy, and his constant absence is
no longer considered an act of modesty. Ugamwa and Resende
Costa are still the favorites; Cerini and Stelipyn follow behind,
with five and four votes, respectively. Veronelli senses that just a
single gust will allow them to tack, freeing Saint Peter's boat from
the doldrums. The wind need only pick up suddenly, and they
would be blown toward port, toward the result that the Holy Father has known all along.

The chamberlain never imagined that the metaphor he had
used to express his optimism would manifest itself so literally. Because two days after his meeting with Malvezzi, a wind whips
through Rome and the surrounding countryside with gales so furious as to uproot trees and overturn automobiles, injuring numerous people. Torrential rains follow, strong and angry as a lash,
and darkness descends, made worse by continual electrical outages, causing countless problems for the communal authorities,
and generating a stream of emergency calls from all parts of the
Eternal City. Everywhere are signs of collapse, mudslides, even
the ominous rumblings of entire buildings in ruins, the products
of the rampant construction speculation throughout the city. The
cupola of Sant'Andrea della Valle, the church where Puccini's

Tosca was set, has been severely damaged. Villa Borghese looks like the terrestrial garden after the Deluge, and the tower of the Casino Borghese that houses its namesake gallery has collapsed from the wind, ruining a number of works of art.

But where the fury of nature, foreseen by Cardinal Malvezzi during the chamberlain's visit, appears to rage with an arrogant will for destruction is in Vatican City. The wind, rain, and ice seem to have paralyzed all relief efforts, there at the site where centuries earlier Saint Peter had offered himself in martyrdom, and where now his heirs have been debating for months in search of his successor.

At Saint John's Tower the violent rainstorms back up the sewers and pipes, clogging all of the installations in the Turkish bath. The kitchens are not in operation because of the flooding brought on by the failed plumbing, and the palace is filled with a stream of chaplains and prelates coming and going with electric hot plates to scrape together meals for the illustrious electors.

The wind howls endlessly through the palace, frightening the elderly guests and often shattering the antiquated windows, which are as ancient and fragile as the people whom they had previously protected. Several statues in the Bernini Colonnade in the piazza of Saint Peter's Basilica are blown to the ground in ruins. The tambour of Michelangelo's cupola, the majestic symbol of Rome and of Catholicism, threatens to lose the golden globe surmounted by the cross, one of the most photographed and painted monuments on earth. Were it to fall, the resulting damage would be incalculable.

After the first day of the storm, the most serious malfunctions begin to occur in that strained machine that the Apostolic Palace has become during the course of the conclave. The elevators halt in their shafts, forcing several cardinals into a lengthy wait while the cabs are returned to the floor, lowered by a hand-operated crank. The furnaces suffer considerable damage, limiting their ability to produce heat. To a certain extent, candles offer illumination where the electrical outages have left the rooms in darkness. Count Nasalli Rocca, the chief engineer of Vatican City,

along with Princes Orsini and Colonna, the two prince assistants
to the throne, send out their own storm of phone calls, faxes, and
e-mail messages from the offices of the vicar general to the mayor
of Rome and the minister of the interior. But the urban center has
been besieged by too many requests; it is impossible to satisfy
them all.

"With all respect to Your Excellency, the Italian citizens take
precedence over those of the Vatican, orphaned though they are
from their sovereign." The anticlerical undertones in the mayor's
reply, which Prince Amilcare Colonna, the blackest Guelph in
Rome, grasped immediately, only render the insistence from the
Vatican offices all the more furious. As a result, the Italian city authorities, even the most religious among them, join forces to oppose them in a single united front.

Nasalli Rocca can no longer control himself as he yells at the
minister of the interior, a Catholic who always kneels to kiss the
pope's ring in front of the television cameras. He informs him that
there, inside those rooms, in the dark, the successor to Saint Peter
is being elected. Unperturbed, the minister assumes a falsetto
voice and replies that he had no idea, certainly it didn't seem as
though they had any such intentions. So they really must wait just
a bit longer. Without waiting for a response from Count Nasalli
Rocca and Prince Colonna, the minister begins to run through the
list of emergencies that are springing up across the city: the plane
trees in Via Merulana that have fallen onto nearby houses. The
Russian embassy, Villa Amabelek, that was struck by lightning and
has caught fire. Palazzo Farnese, the seat of French diplomacy,
that lost its roof. The rising Tiber that is threatening to flood the
Farnesina. The residence of the grand master of the Freemasons,
on Via Aventino, that has been damaged by a landslide. The tower
on the Capitoline Hill that threatens to collapse at any moment.
The six apartment buildings in Testaccio that were evacuated as a
safety measure. The home for the elderly in San Lorenzo that was
partially destroyed, leaving sixty residents without shelter. "You
must realize, Your Excellencies," the minister says in conclusion,
"this is just the beginning of my priority list!"

At the dry click of the telephone receiver following the minister's words, Nasalli Rocca, Colonna, and Orsini can no longer mount any protests. They could invoke certain regulations in the Concordat that make provisions for assistance by the Italian government in the case of natural disasters, but they recognize the futility in doing so, given their political weakness due to the vacant throne. Without a pope, the Vatican's powers are cut in half, thinks Prince Colonna, and no doubt there are a few government officials who would like to see it stay that way.

One person who sees that extraordinary act of nature as a blessing is Cardinal Ettore Malvezzi, for it indicates that events are conspiring to bring an end to the unbearable waiting that is consuming the members of the conclave. Seated near the window, which is still intact despite the raging storm, he believes the fury of destruction that has befallen the city is the final insult by the Prince of Darkness before conceding defeat.

"*Non praevalebunt, non praevalebunt,*" he murmurs, staring out through the heavy curtain of rain that is pelting his window, and hearing the occasional lament of the dog in the courtyard below his room.

Not far away from Malvezzi's window, in the neighborhood of Gianicolo, two young lovers gaze out their own window at the devastation in the streets. The dark brought on by the blackouts, which come and go, had taken them by surprise in the most intimate of moments, when not even the fury of the storm could pull them from their embrace. The house, near Sant'Onofrio, is no less exposed than the others in the neighborhood, but in their intimacy, the impact of the storm has been reduced.

"My God, look how hard it's raining, Lorenzo. How will you ever get home on your moped?"

"I'll stay here still it stops, and I hope it never does." A student in his final year of medical school, he holds her in his arms, and she closes her eyes, disappearing underneath the comforter, far from the sound of the wind and the rain.

The apartment on Via Marguta belongs to Anna's uncle, an

antiquarian, and it is hers to use only until the following morning at eight o'clock. But there is still time, plenty of time. For the storm stretches out the hours, allowing routines and obligations to be deferred, a gift from nature to the two of them, she and Lorenzo, who have no desire to be separated. It is so comforting to listen to the sound of the rain falling on the roof and to feel Lorenzo's warmth next to her.

From the apartment beneath them comes the barely audible sound of the television news, distracting Lorenzo. "Do you want to turn on the television, Anna?"

"No, why would I want to do that?"

"It seems like something's happened."

"So?"

"I guess you're right." Lorenzo turns back toward her, tuning out the noise from the television, and within half an hour he is asleep in her arms.

Anna doesn't move. She is never more content than when he is asleep in her embrace. She feels simultaneously like mother, sister, and wife to him as he surrenders himself to her entirely. Such complete trust does not come from making love; it is love. He has given his life over to her care, she can do with it as she pleases, and she lets herself envision their future life together.

Without a doubt, marriage will allow them to sleep together like this forever. That "forever" deeply moves her, because she has seen it realized in her parents, who have been together for more than thirty years and desire each other still. She can tell by the tender caresses they give one another when they think no one is looking. They kiss each other surreptitiously, without realizing that their furtive acts of love render them all the more endearing in her eyes.

Maybe she and Lorenzo could start by living there, if her uncle can be persuaded to rent it to them, as soon as Lorenzo finds a job. The rain lashes against the French doors that lead to the small balcony. A large pot must have been knocked over because the fronds of an oleander are flattened up against the glass. What a catastrophe this storm is, even though the lights have come back on. Lorenzo no longer seems to want to get up; she moves slightly, and instead of rousing, he turns onto his left side, stretches, and then curls up tightly, like a baby in the fetal position. Anna makes sure that he's well covered by the comforter, as the heater in the apartment is not strong enough to diminish the morning chill. She gets out of the bed carefully, so as not to wake him, and puts a hand over the radiator, which barely feels warm. The portable electric heater is working now, but it gives off little heat.

To settle her nerves, she turns on the TV, but with the sound off. The image appears, and her eyes are opened to the destruction wrought not by a disaster far away in Mexico City or Manila, but in her own city of Rome, where she finds herself at that very moment, with Lorenzo in bed beside her, oblivious. Collapsed houses, land-slides, flooding, uprooted trees flung through the air onto rooftops, the statues of the Bernini Collonade on the ground . . . what on earth has happened?

Suddenly, the image on the television switches to the piazza at Saint Peter's Basilica, awaiting the smoke to billow from the Sis-tine Chapel chimney for the umpteenth time.

The conclave? Still? Who could possibly be watching any-more? Who could still be interested in that smoke that never an-nounces a new pope? But maybe the conclave really has concluded. She holds the remote control in her hand, unable to decide whether to change the channel or to watch for the new pope. She looks over at Lorenzo, who seems unaffected by the rain, much less by the unfolding of history, which could be de-claring a new pontiff in total silence.

She sees the Sistine Chapel with its famous chimney. They'll have to take their time, because they are probably no longer ca-pable of lighting the fire; it must be difficult to make white smoke after so much black. Here comes a tentative wisp of something; it looks ash gray. Without the commentary who can tell what color it is? And besides, the television is hardly new, and the image is blurred. No, no doubt about it, the smoke is definitely dark. Burning black, once again.

How annoying! To think she even stopped to watch it. She im-mediately changes the channel, returning to the unsettling scenes of destruction throughout her city. She feels cold, even colder than before. She touches the radiator again, and this time it is as cold as ice. Slowly, she crawls back under the cover and slides up against Lorenzo's warm body. He turns toward her, still asleep, yet aware of her presence, and drapes his arm across her waist. But something begins to disturb her. She can no longer remain still, as she had before. The building feels like an enormous wounded animal, struggling to breathe. Doors slam, she hears footsteps on the staircase, a few voices, and the echo of a name being called out by a woman: "Roberto! Roberto!"

If she hadn't been feeling so depressed, she would have yelled out from the balcony to quiet the woman down.

A persistent and irritating sound from televisions on other floors grows louder. She hears broadcasts from several channels on what she is witnessing from her own bed: the rainstorm that seems bent on washing away the eternal city. And Lorenzo continues to sleep.

Looking up at the ceiling she sees a large, dark stain forming, which doubtless means that the water is not flowing through the rain-gutters along the roof. The stain is right above the bed, and soon it will come dripping down on them. Should she call someone? But why bother alarming her parents? It would only embarrass her if she had to tell them where she was.

She thinks back to what she has just seen, all that black smoke issuing from the Sistine Chapel. What a joke! Why did they even bother showing it on TV? For a while now she has noticed that no one bothered to talk about the conclave anymore, and only a few late-night news programs aired shots of the chapel's chimney. What could be happening now? At her house, only her grandmother continued to buy *Il Messaggero* every morning to read the latest news on the conclave. But whenever the subject came up, no one would listen to her predictions, she who had once been in charge of an important prelate's wardrobe.

One day she had been so upset at the news of another futile round of voting that she visited her parish priest to pour out her worries, saying that this was a tragedy for the world and for Rome, a terrible sign. For *urbis et orbis*, she said, never having forgotten the parlance of her prelate, whose solemn vestment she once stored in an armoire.

Later, while waiting for the tram at the stop below their apartment, the priest recounted the incident to Anna and her mother. He then invited them to San Clemente for the Sunday morning concert. "Most people no longer have your mother's sense of faith. A faith that knows how to read the signs of providence and heed its admonishments. These days, dear Signora Ceroni, we have to organize concerts to fill the churches," he commented as he departed.

And now, in the wake of the storm, her grandmother Cesira's words return.

Meanwhile, the first drops of water begin to fall from the ceiling directly onto Lorenzo's eyelids, waking him up. He opens his eyes and smiles.

25

ANY MILES AWAY, in a small hospital near Bologna, another young couple is enjoying an intimacy brought on by the unfavorable weather. It is a most felicitous opportunity for both of them, providing Francesco with a relief from forced immobility, as he is still encumbered by his cast and unable to take advantage of lovely days outdoors; and it has offered Caterina a relief from boredom, for with the renewed tenderness fostered by the inclement weather, she has transformed Francesco's tedium at being bound to his room into the fear that someone will come to disturb them. It is hardly a deluge, but it shows little promise of stopping any time soon. There is more mist than rain, accompanied by a sultriness that is almost summerlike, strange for December. But the forecast is calling for dreary weather for the rest of the week, until Christmas.

In the hospital room where the cardinal of Turin's nephew, Francesco Cariati, has for more than two weeks been bedridden by the fractures he incurred during his auto accident, a mild state of disorder prevails. All attempts at straightening up after him — by Caterina, by his mother, and by the nurses in the ward — have been in vain. Strewn about the room are assorted magazines on sailing, automobiles, and home furnishings. There are travel brochures, newspapers, stacks of cards, a laptop computer, pens, and stationery, free weights and exercise devices to attend to the belly he has developed during his convalescence. Adding to the chaos are a wide-screen television, piles of shirts and sweaters heaped on the bed and dresser, and a bedside table cluttered with multicolored bottles of water and wine, only partially emptied. Among them is a bottle of Veuve Clicquot, Caterina's favorite champagne, which makes the blood run fiery in her veins. She brought it to him to lift his spirits when the doctors told him he wouldn't be able to go home that Sunday, as he had hoped.

"If things go on like this, we'll spend Christmas in here."

"So we'll spend it here, Francesco. What difference does it make?"

"I can't take it any more. For years we've gone to Turin for the holidays, to my uncle's house. And you were invited, too."

"'You can't raise a fist to the heavens,' my mother always says. And I'll add, 'not even if your uncle is a cardinal.'"

Francesco had dreamed that night, and in his dreams an image of Caterina entering the room was commingled with other female images. Once it was his mother, waving his university transcripts and scolding him for being a year behind in school. Another time it was the severe but beautiful face of the head nurse, the one his father had nicknamed Greta Garbo, who was ordering him to stay in bed and not use his barbells anymore if he wanted to leave the clinic some day. Still another time it was the girl he had left for Caterina, brandishing an enormous syringe to give him an injection. From one worry to the next, he dreamed until dawn, when the hostile images finally disappeared, leaving only one figure, tender but sad, whom he had not seen in several months. It was his Uncle Ettore. He had spoken to him at length, but Francesco could make no sense of what he was hearing, because his uncle talked in a barely perceptible whisper, a stammer that came only with great effort, as if he were struggling to articulate something terribly important, yet he could not find the words out of some strange aphasia. So Francesco began offering up words, the words that were escaping his uncle, the great orator who captivated audiences with the finesse of his homilies in the cathedral of Turin, and who used the Socratic method to unparalleled effect in the confessional, where he could be met one on one. Francesco found himself saying, "Rain. Rome. Home. Turin. Return." And then, "Wind. Sail. Window. Sky. Wings."

And as he was speaking, Francesco had the satisfaction of seeing his beloved uncle's face relax, break into a smile, until finally he reclaimed his voice and began repeating the words back to his nephew.

With the rain growing heavier and the evening shadows darkening the room, Caterina decides to turn on the overhead light. Seeing her reach for the switch, Francesco stops her, pulling her closer to him on the bed. As she lies down next to him, the memory of his dream comes flooding back. He sees the faces that had visited him one by one, concluding with that of his uncle. The phone rings.

"Should we answer?" he asks.

"You decide," she says.

"It's probably my mother. It's better if I answer."

"All right. I'm going to straighten myself up, in case the nurse comes in."

The phone keeps ringing, with the accelerated, rather annoying rhythm characteristic of internal phone lines. What if it isn't his mother? He doesn't want to hear from any of his friends, calling him up as a courtesy to make him feel less like a prisoner, or making promises about what they will all do together as soon as he gets out of the hospital. They are on the outside, living their lives, while he remains . . . but at the thought of Caterina he no longer envies them. He reaches out his hand to lift up the receiver. It is his mother.

"Turn on the television right away. Channel One."

"Why, what's going on?"

"Turn it on! I think they've decided on a pope."

"What? Really?"

He hears the click of the television, and it seems never to have taken so long for the audio and video to appear. A male voice announces a direct connection with Saint Peter's Square, from where they will soon see the smoke emanating from the famous chimney. Voices speaking with great authority announce the strong probability that finally the cardinals have reached an accord, and that the smoke will be white.

The face of the journalist appears on the screen, followed by an image of Saint Peter's Square, disrupted by static. The correspondent apologizes for the poor quality of the images, explaining that Rome has been hit by an exceptionally violent storm that has caused significant damage, with landslides and collapsed buildings that have injured numerous people. The catastrophe has prompted the mayor to declare the city a disaster area.

"Are you there, Francesco? Can you hear me?" his mother says.

He holds the phone closer to his ear, but his mind supplants the image of the Sistine Chapel, its smokeless chimney rising up through the dark clouds and rain, with the vision that came to him in his dream: the face of his uncle, mumbling incomprehensible phrases until he had offered his help, repeating the words. "It's strange. I dreamed about him last night."

"You did what?"

"I dreamed about Uncle Ettore last night."

"Can you imagine if he comes out on the balcony of Saint Peter's?"

"You always said he doesn't stand a chance, that there never existed a man with less ambition to be pope."

"It's true, but the last time I spoke to him, which was more than a week ago, he seemed reticent, argumentative. You know how expansive he is by nature, how readily he usually opens up about things. It was as if he wanted to silence something that was weighing on him."

"Or is it just that your hopes of becoming the sister of the pope make you remember it that way? When I spoke to him he seemed in good spirits, and he was very kind. Actually, I'd never heard him joke that way before."

"How was he in your dream?"

"In the dream? Wait, listen: they're talking about the smoke. Can you hear?"

"Yes."

Caterina reenters the room. She sees Francesco watching the television with the phone up to his ear. It must be his mother; the image on the television confirms it. That uncle in the conclave has forged such a tight bond between them that at times it makes her jealous. She has never met him, but now she is trembling like a leaf at the possibility of seeing him appear on the screen. She knows this is precisely what Francesco and his mother are waiting for. And she disappears; for the moment she no longer exists.

She sits silently and waits for the smoke to rise, hoping with all her heart that it will be black, that an unknown figure dressed in the white robe will not appear. The first plume of smoke wafts indistinguishably from the chimney, giving the correspondent the opportunity to keep millions of viewers waiting with bated breath. It is an age-old theatrical trick that really does draw an audience.

Then the black smoke appears and the correspondent assumes the role of a director apologizing to his spectators for a failed production. Within seconds, everything returns to normal. That the world still has no pope is immediately apparent in the advertisement for canned dog food that is aired immediately following the broadcast. Francesco, meanwhile, has become absorbed in a whispered conversation with his mother, the deluded sister of a cardinal, further excluding Caterina. But this time she feels no pain at being excluded, as it gives her time to conceal her emotions, and recover from the state of mind that has overtaken her.

"You didn't even let me say hello," she says once he hangs up.

"I'm sorry, she gives you her regards, but she was in a hurry. She had to go out with my dad."

"Make sure you stay warm. It's chilly in here."

"Did you see that? They didn't manage to do it this time either. I wonder why they even put it on the air. It makes the cardinals look so bad."

"Why? Do you think it would have been better not to see an-other wasted opportunity for your uncle?"

"That's a terrible thing to say."

"Sorry. Excuse me, really. Listen, tomorrow I have to go to Maria's for her birthday. I'll come see you the day after that, all right?"

"Come here. What's wrong, Anna?"

"Nothing, why?"

"Because you've changed. I must have said something to annoy you. What was it?"

She decides to let it drop. It is worth it just to see him be affectionate again. There is no longer the shadow of the conclave looming overhead. His uncle the cardinal has now been defeated twice: once by the television, and again by her.

They say good-bye and promise to call each other as soon as they wake up the next day. At the door she turns to look at him. She studies his profile, noting that he needs to cut his hair; it is limp and flattened against his head from spending so much time in bed. She loved the way he wore his hair when they first met, at Cinzia's house for a birthday party. It cascaded luxuriously to his shoulders, so soft and inviting she immediately wanted to run her fingers through it. The two of them made love with their hair, Francesco had once said.

Francesco had just turned off the light when his mother called again. "I'm sorry dear, you were probably asleep. I'm a little worried. On the news they were talking about the terrible storm in Rome. They say there has been nothing like it in years; a real disaster. The Vatican is one of the places hardest hit. Statues and walls have been ruined, and they are without power, just like the rest of the city."

"You think Uncle Ettore is in the dark?"

"I called him, but the lines are down."

"That's normal, with weather like that. Try again later."

"All right darling, sorry. Tell me, what was your dream about?"

"In the beginning Uncle Ettore was tired, and it was hard for him to talk. I couldn't understand what he was saying, but then he got over it. I think that I helped him to speak. But anyway, it was just a dream."

"I also called you back because I knew Caterina was there before, and I didn't want to talk about these things in front of her."

"Why not?"

"Because it's better if some things remain in the family. Good night, Francesco."

"Good night."

His mother and Caterina don't like each other yet. It's the only thing that bothers him, besides his exams. But ensuring that the two women are fond of each other is beyond his power.

So his uncle was in the dark, just as he was. And just as he was locked in the hospital, so was his uncle locked in the conclave. His mother worries too much; still he should watch the news to find out what is happening at the capital. He turns on the TV and sees immediately what caused his mother's alarm. She wasn't wrong; it's not just a bit of bad weather. The faces of the people interviewed, after the collapse of a house, or after the landslides that have occurred in parts of the city, are disturbing to him. They seem to have seen something that they are afraid to describe. Not even the television can fully capture the sense of fear, for certain emotions are beyond representation. The mind, yes, the mind can experience and accept them, at least until it snaps.

He turns off the light with a slight sense of guilt, as if he had violated the privacy of those victims as they lay bandaged in their hospital beds, suffering through the interrogations of some thoughtless journalist: "What did it feel like when your home collapsed around you?"

The television is dreadful. Dreams have far more empathy than men do.

26

*I*T WAS NEVER discovered who called for the live television broadcast that was such an embarrassment to the Sacred College on that December evening while the Eternal City was straining under the forces of the storm. In the Vatican pressroom, where the chamberlain himself made the first inquiries, there was a reciprocal exchange, both in placing the blame and denying responsibility. Some said that a phone call revealing the imminent proclamation of the new pontiff had come from the chaplain of one of the three frontrunners in the recent rounds of voting; others maintained that one of the cardinals had notified the producer of a television news program in order to alert the RAI and other private channels. Still another claimed that the call had come from the RAI itself, hoping to confirm the forthcoming selection, as if the news had been leaked to them by one of the conclave's participants.

But the incriminating press release was never found, nor the indiscrete chaplain, nor the television executive: nothing to reveal who was responsible for the breach of secrecy. The chamberlain was furious with Count Nasalli Rocca, with Princes Colonna and Orsini, and with the authorities in the press office, threatening to propose to the new pontiff that they be dismissed from their duties. The sanctity of that segregation, unique in its ability to grant the cardinals autonomy of choice, had been subjected to a blow no less damaging than any of the other wounds suffered during those three long months of misfortune. Because the harm had been inflicted in front of the eyes of the entire world, a world that was already clearly demonstrating its indifference. At least the other misadventures had taken place behind closed doors, without the public's knowledge.

The chamberlain must settle for the removal of a few of the prelates from the press office, and the severe reprimand of those working in public relations. The next morning's papers only complete the negative picture with their irreverent headlines above photos of the black smoke. It is an image easily linked to the depressed mood pervading Rome, a city devastated by a storm of unparalleled violence, which after twenty-four hours still shows no signs of loosening its hold.

The elections of the next day are held in a climate of suspicion, bitterness, and guilt that provides a clear measure of the estrangement between the cardinals and the city whose bishop they are electing. It occurs to many of the conclavists that this latest abuse must somehow be related to their disjuncture, as though Rome, like an ailing body, is suffering without its pastor.

Monsignor Giorgio Contarini has just asked Cardinal Malvezzi what time he would like dinner that evening. The gusts of wind that continue to beat against the windows in the lodgings of the Turinese cardinal are sometimes so fierce as to drown out their voices. Drafts blow through the ancient window frames, rustling the curtains, tablecloth, and bedspread. It seems to the cardinal as though the entire room is being shaken incessantly by an earth tremor, impeding his concentration and keeping him from his reading.

He is reading *The Confessions of Saint Augustine*, which he has been promising himself to reread for a long time. *Pondus meum amor mei*. My prison is self-love. Over the past few days he had often discussed the African saint's phrase with his invisible interlocutors. It was a lapidary definition of a most pervasive modern illness. Both Contardi and Mascheroni expressed considerable doubts that the malady was exclusively a modern one. Throughout the ages, egoism and the cult of selfhood have concealed themselves in the propensity to care for others. At times even sanctity has experienced the metastasis of that cancer, as Augustine of Hippo demonstrated. The alibi of practicing a universal ministry in the name of the Lord has frequently masked that pride. For the ego receives not only the fruits of goodness from the direct relationship with God that is inherent in the priesthood, but also fruits of vanity and pride, fueled by self-esteem, which have often become powers of destruction in the name of God. In the three sister religions, the alibi of the revelations of Moses, of Christ, and of Mohammed has often brought on such consequences, reopening the wounds of fundamentalism.

Malvezzi concluded that the corruption of power at any level, even in the name of a spiritual authority, is implicit in the very exercise of that power. Only the innocence of youth can offer a cure for such an illness.

The advanced age of the cardinals and the pope subjects them to a natural human tendency as death draws near: the desire to compensate for a sense of fragility by taking firmer possession of the authority they already hold. To age is to feel life slip away, suffering the fear of the great leap; the fear, as Shakespeare writes, of leaving known ills for those we know not of. It is all the more true for ministers of God, who must offer their flocks a sense of certainty and comfort during that grand passage to the other side.

The sound of the howling dog kept on a chain in the courtyard rouses Malvezzi from his reflections.

Shortly, the yellow-paned window in the room across from him would be illuminated. Time for his mysterious neighbors to make their return for the evening. His immobility during those long days, in isolation far from the Sistine Chapel and the other cardinals, has rendered him as sensitive as his animals — the cats, the hens, and the owls — to any movement or change in his rooms, in the courtyard, in that wing of the palace. The hours that tick away, kept in time by his reading, and by the light of the sun, from dawn until dusk, have a few fixed points of reference, which he allows himself the pleasure of observing.

One of these, perhaps the most anticipated, is that window, when the lights come on in the morning at dawn, and later when they are turned off. Then, in the evening, they are turned on again, like now, until they are turned off a second time for the rest of the night. The shadows in motion behind the window keep him company.

Now, however, the wind has strengthened its hold on the palace. As much as he knows that these gusts are the final efforts of a blind fury that is nearing its defeat, the pounding at the windows frightens him. The dog can no longer be heard down in the courtyard. Even his animals have moved away from the window, retreating under the bed or the wardrobe to hide.

The lights in the room across from him come on again. He sees shadows moving around the room. The resurgence of the wind reminds him of a hand knocking at the window; it is no longer wind that he hears, but someone attempting to come in. Who would dare enter the house of the Lord's vicar?

In the shadows moving behind the yellow window, he now catches sight of a larger figure. Whoever is behind that glass must also be struck by the same fear that has unnerved him. He rises to his feet. Something dispels the fear caused by the shutters rattling in the wind, calling to him. It is coming from that window where others are experiencing his own uncertainty, where they are responding to the same call. More than three months have passed since he noticed the presence in front of him, but it is manifesting itself only now. He must listen to it.

As he reaches for the handle on the window to undo the latch, a strong gust rips open the window, shattering the glass.

At the same moment, the window across the way also comes crashing open. The figures who for so long have appeared to him only as shadows now stand before him. They are twins, two young men so similar in appearance as to make him rub his eyes, certain he is seeing double. They can't seem to decide whether they should close the shutters over the broken window, or leave things as they are, or begin to pick up the shards of glass. Then they realize that he is staring at them. They are definitely twins; he can see them clearly.

Their eyes meet, while the wind whistles around them and the rain comes sweeping into the room. He can tell from their white collars and cassocks that they are men of the cloth. Who are those two young priests? He has never met them, but surely he must have seen them somewhere before.

A bolt of lightning illuminates the walls, the windows, terrorizing the animals in the cardinal's room as well as the dog in the courtyard. For an instant, the light flashes on the faces at the two windows. Their eyes meet once again, and they recognize one another.

Malvezzi now remembers who those twins resemble, and he kneels down to pray, thanking the Lord for the illumination. The two young priests look at each other without moving, receiving the lashes of the wind and the rain. They remain motionless in their positions for a seemingly incalculable time, while the thunder and lightning, the low clouds, and the rain appear to be announcing the return of the Great Flood.

Now it's sure to pass, it's sure to pass, the cardinal repeats to himself, in tears. It's finished. All finished.

Contarini enters the room, out of breath. He is paralyzed by the sight of His Eminence on his knees, drenched with rain, amid the broken glass. He stares at the open window and the papers scattered throughout the room by the wind, at the rain that has soaked the curtains and furniture, advancing as far as the base of the bed, where the animals have taken cover. He arrives in time to see the window closing across from them, with its broken glass, but the lights are turned off before he can determine who shut it.

He rushes forward to close the windows, although only the glass in the upper panes affords any protection. Then he turns to Malvezzi, whose face, hair, and clothes are soaked, and helps him to his feet.

An hour later, after the glass from the window has been re-placed, Malvezzi has changed into a dry cassock and is seated at his desk. He asks Contarini to deliver a message to the chamberlain in person.

"May I read it, Your Eminence?"

"Go ahead."

Malvezzi has written to tell the chamberlain to expect his presence at the elections on the following day. It is a succinct communiqué, offering no explanations, indicative of a singular determination. Contarini agrees to execute the order, pleased with his cardinal's firm intentions. He puts the note in an envelope and brings it to the chamberlain, who is still awake.

Veronelli reads it in front of him, furrowing his brow. What does it mean? Is Malvezzi back in the running? Has he changed his mind and started to nurture his hopes again? Or is this a figment of his imagination, instigated by the spirits who keep visiting him?

"How does His Eminence feel?" the chamberlain asks.

"Quite well, I think."

"Well? But in what way, Monsignor? Does he have some sort of new ambition? Could this just be another fit of disturbance, some mental agitation that is symptomatic of his condition? Wouldn't it be better to advise him to stay in his room, or at least to call in a doctor?"

"If I may point out, Your Eminence, no one has ever declared Cardinal Ettore Malvezzi infirm of mind. His demeanor up to this point has reflected the utmost in moderation and comprehension of the requirements that Your Eminence has placed on him."

"That's precisely what stuns and alarms me about this message. What happened to him that changed his mood? You do understand, don't you, that I have the duty to protect the conclave from any further embarrassment? We have been subjected to enough already, and you are aware that only yesterday the prestige of this assembly sustained yet another injury, this time from the television."

"Your Eminence, I can't read the cardinal's mind, but I can guarantee that he is calm and in complete control of himself."

"Fine, but if he wants to come to the elections tomorrow it must mean that he has something to say or to propose, do you understand? That's what worries me most."

"Then you should ask him what his intentions are."

"You're right, thank you for the advice. You can leave now. Tell him I'll call him immediately; it's too late to visit him in person."

Contarini returns to the cardinal's room and finds Malvezzi already on the phone with the chamberlain. He retreats immediately, but can tell that the phone call is not going smoothly.

In fact, it lasts a long time.

Although the calm, relaxed, and conciliatory tone in Malvezzi's voice restores Veronelli's longstanding impression of the cardinal, suggesting that he has returned to normal, it also makes the chamberlain nervous. Because accompanying Malvezzi's mild manner are a sense of resolve and a firm refusal to divulge the reasons behind his return to the conclave that do not bode well.

Malvezzi has something planned that he does not want to reveal. He might be reinstating his candidacy from a more solid position. But who at this late stage would put any faith in a man who has been so long in isolation, spending more time with his visions than with other human beings? The chamberlain has been kept informed daily of the cardinal's every movement and his mental state. After his own visit, Malvezzi has received no visitors. Now this? Where is all this self-assuredness coming from? Could it be that his own candidacy is not the goal, but someone else's? Who then? Who in the Sacred College could have communicated to him the need for an alliance? And what kind of alliance can Malvezzi offer?

Veronelli asks Malvezzi innumerable questions in hopes of coaxing his intentions out of him, but the cardinal of Turin does not budge. He remains firm as a rock in his insistence on his rights and duties "to vote for the pope tomorrow."

There is no reading him. Ettore Malvezzi has joined in secrecy with God and his conscience. The two men end their conversation on rather cool terms, bidding each other an icy farewell after a few words on the disaster that has struck Rome, which only serves to heighten Veronelli's anxiety. He had been the one to mention the storm, and the damage that had not spared the Vatican. Malvezzi replied that their lengthy trials were almost over, and that peace would soon be restored to Rome and the rest of the world.

27

*T*HE APPEARANCE OF the cardinal of Turin in the conclave on the morning of Christmas Eve is heralded by many as an encouraging sign, restoring a sense of normalcy that had been lost during the extraordinary trials they had endured.

Even the weather seems to have improved over the course of the night. The news from Rome, though still dire in many neighborhoods, has reported no new disasters. After the recent spate of events, each one worse than the next, this is at least something positive. Several of the cardinals in the Curia are residents of Rome, and their inability to return to the places most damaged by the storm, often their own neighborhoods or the areas where their loved ones reside, has only added to their anguish at being sequestered.

Almost four months have passed, and the next day is Christmas. Rome and all of Christianity will most certainly celebrate the holiday as orphans, without a supreme pastor. But the world doesn't seem too upset by this eventuality; the recently televised false alarm has even further distanced the people from the Sistine Chapel, as if also in that debacle was manifested the malicious will of someone who did not want to see the election of a new pontiff.

As he draws close to the marble gate that divides the chapel in two, Malvezzi is stopped by several cardinals. He is complimented on his healthy appearance and teased about the time he has spent bedridden during his imaginary illness. He is asked point blank if he is still a candidate, while others more suspicious inquire whether he has come up with a new solution during his absence. Still others request with an air of mystery to speak with him that evening, alone, in his chambers.

Ettore Malvezzi's enigmatic smile, coupled with the polite evasiveness of his replies, results only in confusing his interrogators. He hasn't seen them in days. Exhausted in their appearance, their expressions pained and quick to surface, the uncertainty that still seems to govern them after so much elapsed time fills him with pity. Many had suffered during that prolonged wait. Selim, his Maronite friend, can stand only with the help of two assistants. Youssef, the Palestinian cardinal, has lost several pounds and seems a shadow of his former self. Rabuiti, the stocky cardinal from Palermo, has been suffering frequent attacks of asthma that force him to carry oxygen at all times. The archbishop of Nairobi, plagued by congestive heart failure, has grown pale, his voice reduced to a whisper. He asks to vote immediately so that he can return to his room, given his ill health. The archbishop of Lviv is only the first in a long list of cardinals who must make his entrance into the Sistine Chapel in a wheelchair, pushed by his secretary.

Surely they can bear no more. In a corner, already seated in their thrones, he sees the cardinals of New York and Philadelphia, the two men who had attempted to escape. They too, seem to have dwindled to nothing. Who could ever believe that, only a few weeks ago, they had been able to lower themselves into the void from a rope made of bed linens as they tried to flee? He senses that a single thought is unifying every cardinal in the room: the desire to leave, to succeed in returning home, putting an end to that cloistered life.

The crowd of cardinals blocks his entrance to the chapel. The preliminaries before the roll call proceed exceedingly slowly, as doctors shuttle from one entrance to the next, attending to the needy. What a demoralizing scene, what defeated old men they are, this congress of the distinguished electors of Christ!

Christ, who lived to the age of thirty-three, consummated all of his adventures in his final three years, and then disappeared into the heavens with his glorious body, at an age promised to all of his sons through the resurrection of the flesh. Malvezzi looks up above the balding heads, above the red skullcaps, and sees Christ the Judge in the splendor of his immortal youth.

Just then, he notices them. The twin priests are up there, too! They are carrying out their humble duties as chaplains, probably in the service of a cardinal. They raise long rods to light the six tall altar candles behind the chamberlain's throne, the only source of illumination after the power failure. They stand apart from the perplexed body of the Sacred College, apart from those heads, that sea of white hair. Their own hair is blond, and their faces are raised upward to oversee their movements as they reach toward the six silver candlesticks, which soon send up flickers of light in front of Christ the Judge and the Holy Mother. Malvezzi looks up at the Christ figure and then back down at the twins. His memory has not betrayed him; they resemble each other in a most striking way. The twins are the perfect copy of Michelangelo's representation of Christ. No one else seems to have noticed. They are as invisible as two angels. Perhaps the rest of those old men are unable to see them. Otherwise, how else could the similarity have escaped them?

"What are you looking at, Ettore?" a heavily accented voice asks.

He turns, lowering his eyes to find the Estonian cardinal, Matis Paide. Without saying a word he points to the twins lighting the candles. Once he sees that Paide has spotted them, he touches him on the shoulder, inviting him to look higher up, at the center of Michelangelo's fresco.

"Where should I look? At Saint Bartholomew?"

"No, farther up, at Christ."

The Estonian cardinal fixes his deep blue eyes on Christ.

Then he lowers his gaze back to the two young priests. He checks again, up and down, with growing stupor. "Incredible. Absolutely incredible," he murmers, incapable of taking his eyes off them.

They are forced to stop looking when an assistant to one of the scrutineers asks them to take their places. The chamberlain of the Holy Roman Church is about to enter the chapel, preceded by the choir, whose younger members have been replaced by older men, as have many of the young chaplains in service to the cardinals.

"Promise me that you will help them, and that you'll help me in what I'm about to do," Malvezzi whispers to Paide, who is still speechless at the incredible resemblance between the twins and the figure of Christ.

"But where are they? They're gone . . ."

"They had to leave after the *extra omnes*. Don't worry, we didn't dream them. They're probably in the sacristy."

The choir of older men begins to sing the *Veni Creator Spiritus*. Their deep, quavering voices impart a more solemn gravity to the hymn than that created by the sweet sound of the younger voices. Where before there had been a sense of angelic lightness, there is now a hint of tragic supplication, addressed to a Lord who does not deign to appear.

The chamberlain arrives, late and out of breath, and after asking his fellow electors to pardon the delay, he commences with the roll call. He declares the elections open, and concedes the floor to whomever wishes to talk.

For the rest of their lives, the cardinals will retain a profound impression of what was said after Ettore Malvezzi, the archbishop of Turin, rose to his feet and started to speak, his voice initially cracking with emotion, but gaining confidence with every word. And yet each time they will be asked to recount the particulars of his speech, their memories will fail as they try to recall the exact succession of his observations, his transitions, his summations and closing arguments. It appears that a veil of secrecy, binding on all of them before God and the rest of mankind, had truly fallen across their collective memory, protecting the man who had received enlightenment from the Holy Spirit, and those who had acquiesced to that enlightenment, in one of the most difficult decisions in the history of the Church.

How long did he speak? No one can say for sure. It seemed impossible to measure that stream of words, or rather, that inspired delirium, issuing from a cardinal who had been deemed crazy, yet was still respected even as an idiot of God.

He spoke of humanity's need for faith, guidance, and love, as well as for joy, happiness, and strength. He spoke of a weary Church, depleted by the two-thousand-year-old mission that had rendered it exhausted by guilt, by sins, and by errors; and of a Church too quick to brand new products of the times as evil; a Church which had subsequently been forced to acknowledge its haste, asking forgiveness from humanity. He spoke of the Sacred, which does not know where it will rain down, but rains down anyway, over the heads of all mankind, who cannot withstand the emptiness of an existence without God. He spoke of the great hope that opens up to those who are tormented by that void, which is God Himself. He spoke of the hunger for a new Christ, who will be revitalized by their choice, yet who could die in their choice at the same time — if dying signifies to them, the cardinals, reaching beyond themselves, outside of their consecrated circle where Christ is calling them to follow, replenishing the ranks in the Christian field. He spoke of the humbling effects of self-questioning, in light of the horrifying events they had experienced over those past few months, when in their weakness Evil had discovered an open door through which to stage its most ruinous attack. He spoke about their sorrowful old age, of the egoism accompanying it, and of the fear of their imminent demise, often the only point they could all agree on in the frenetic meetings that were finding them incapable of making a decision. The Holy Spirit, the Paraclete, had presented himself to them in the extent of their desire to leave the conclave, in their readiness to settle on any name whatsoever, any solution that would allow them to enjoy their last remaining privileges before dying. He spoke of the evil they had been bearing without knowing it, of their hearts, deaf to the invitations of solitude and silence during those four months of conclave. They had not known how to appreciate the cloistered experience because their hearts had been burdened by the compulsion of doing, and doing, and doing again, without even stopping to ask themselves the purpose of their actions. He spoke of the arrogance of their pastoral letters, which no longer resounded with charity, but with cold doctrine, using terminology by now far removed from life itself, repeating on holy days what for Christ and his apostles had indeed been life. Christmas, celebrated with pomp in the ancient cathedrals of Europe as well as in the most modern churches across the world, no longer evoked the trepidation that the angels and shepherds had felt on the night Christ was born.

Malvezzi interrupted himself for a moment, upset perhaps by the thought of finding themselves alone that Christmas, far from everyone, busy seeking a successor to the One who had been born on that day more than two thousand years ago. Then he began again, without attempting to conceal his emotions.

How many times had he lifted up the host as he celebrated Mass and asked himself, as he was sure they all had, if he weren't a Don Quixote seeing giants in windmills! How many times had he cried out in despair for the help of God! How many times had the Gospels seemed to be locked in a strongbox, to which he had lost the key, refusing to use his intellect to recreate them, as they had been recreated by the saints who were their heirs.

Because, and they should not doubt it for a minute, he was reproaching them now for faults of which he, too, was guilty; he who was the weakest and most irresolute, the most weary, confused, and selfish, and the most terrified to die of any cardinal seated there in the conclave. He begged their forgiveness for having offended them, but only after having said those things could he request that which he was about to ask in the name of the Lord. He implored them to contemplate the youthfulness of Jesus Christ, Lord of the present and of eternity, who had been immortalized in the fresco of Michelangelo at the resplendent age of thirty-three. Surely they would understand the meaning of that splendor in the age that God would grant to them, too, through resurrection. He urged them to comprehend fully the importance of the choice that they were about to make in selecting Christ's new heir, because for the first time Christ could literally relive the destiny of a young shepherd guiding an aging humanity. Perhaps all of humanity, even those who had not recognized the Church, would bow their heads in front of the new pontiff, in recognition of the symbolism and hope in his rebirth.

At about this point during his speech, the surviving witnesses recount, the cardinal of Turin makes a sweeping gesture with his hand, pointing at Christ the Judge in the upper part of the fresco. Then, as the cardinals begin whispering among themselves in response to his rebuke, as well as in anticipation of his proposal, Malvezzi quickly descends his throne, and he rushes toward the sacristy as the chamberlain rings his bell in a furious call for order.

There is no stopping him as he exits the chapel, and he is not seen until a few minutes later, when he reappears at the door with the twins on either side of him, dressed in their sacerdotal robes, and so identical as to seem an illusion.

Silence begins to settle over the great hall. Malvezzi nudges the two handsome blond priests, embarrassed and intimidated, toward the center of the Sistine Chapel. As the murmurings in the audience cease, and even the chamberlain becomes calm, Malvezzi invites the twins to turn and look, along with him and the rest of the assembly, at the face of Christ as conceived by Michelangelo, the face of the Lord, to whom Peter had been the first successor.

"Now, my beloved brothers, I call on you to elect the priests Lino and Stefano as the heirs of Saint Peter, whom I submit to you now in your wisdom, illuminated by the Holy Spirit!"

There are shouts of offense, denunciations of anathema, gestures of outrage, accompanied by ironic calls not to turn the conclave into the Roman Senate with its two elected consuls, or the palace of Sparta with its diarchy. Someone even attempts to strike the archbishop, only to be blocked by the Swiss Guards, who are forced to intervene to protect him. All of this passes over Malvezzi's head without affecting him in the slightest.

But the cardinals soon become aware of the stunning resemblance between Michelangelo's Christ and the two young priests, Lino and Stefano, whom some say are in the service of Cardinal Lo Cascio. No one can deny it: they have the same nose and forehead, the same arched eyebrows, the same blond hair, even the same expression in their eyes.

At one point, the twins motion simultaneously, either by design or unintentionally, brandishing their arms in an attempt to calm the crowd and to defend Malvezzi by shielding him from the most impertinent cardinals. Gasps of awe echo throughout the hall, for it is the gesture being made by Christ the Judge, and it has been etched too deeply in their minds not to create tremendous excitement.

Matis Paide seizes the opportunity to rise and address the cardinals, who are slow to return to order. Only after several minutes do they allow him to speak. He proceeds cautiously, respectful of the all too justifiable reactions of the Sacred College, and with great sensitivity toward the chamberlain, as well as empathy for Malvezzi and indulgence toward the twins Lino and Stefano, who remain at Malvezzi's side, ready to defend him. He concludes his brief statement by affirming that, indeed, the cardinal of Turin's comments had been distressing, as they required the eminent cardinals to consider their important task from a perspective so foreign that not one, nor even a thousand nights would be sufficient to contemplate it adequately.

Nature has offered them a single night instead, but it was an extraordinary night, marking the birth of the Lord, and they could spend it in the silence and solitude that, as Cardinal Malvezzi so rightly observed, many of them had perhaps not truly appreciated, exhausted as they were by the prolonged trials of the conclave.

Paide then asks Chamberlain Vladimiro Veronelli to adjourn the elections, and suggests that they be reconvened with the new candidates the following morning, when their minds would be more at ease.

The chamberlain, in need of time himself to formulate a strategy for confronting such an unprecedented situation, takes

advantage of the general state of confusion and grants Paide's request. He will use the additional hours to meet, first of all, with
the two young priests, whose presence he suspects must somehow
be linked to the misfortunes that have besieged the conclave.

The first person to leave the Sistine Chapel is Cardinal Ettore
Malvezzi, escorted by the Swiss Guards. The other cardinals
follow after him, braced to spend the night of Christ's birth in
contemplation of this latest travail.

28

THE HOLY SPIRIT has pity on His suffering sons that night, lifting the fog that has clouded their thoughts, and opening their minds to the truth by means of a shared dream. They see themselves reunited again in the Sistine Chapel, just as the cardinal of Turin is entering the hall, appearing beneath the fresco of the *Last Judgment*. Escorting him on either side, as in the last round of voting, are the priests Lino and Stefano, each with an impressive pair of wings on his shoulders, and eyes so radiant as to force the cardinals to lower their own, though not before glimpsing the divine splendor of their nude bodies, the same bodies as those of the angels depicted in the *Last Judgment*, the same body as Christ the Judge.

Cardinal Malvezzi continues to defend the cause of the twin priests' candidacy, unaware of the knowing smiles they bear on their beautiful faces. Through those smiles, the young priests communicate to the cardinals that Malvezzi is likewise unaware of their wings, as if shielded by some kind of blindness. And then they suddenly disappear, just as Malvezzi finishes speaking, bringing the dream to an end.

❖

On Christmas morning the news quickly spreads among the cardinals as they make their way to the Sistine Chapel that there is no sign of the two priests, and that their apartment, piled with discarded furniture and full of dust, seems to have been uninhabited for years. Gradually, they begin to understand the meaning of their dream, acknowledging in their hearts the sign of a supernatural event, performed this time as an act of mercy.

In fact, as soon as the chamberlain declares the floor open for discussion after the singing of the *Veni Creator Spiritus*, Cardinal Matis Paide, Prefect of the Congregation for the Evangelization of the People, stands up to speak. The serene, yet serious expression on his face immediately commands the attention of the entire assembly.

He knows he need not talk at length about the dream they all had on the holiest night of the year, the anniversary of the birth of Christ, he merely declares that if the Holy Spirit has deigned to indicate His choice to them in the person who was escorted by the angels to the conclave, it would be a sin of pride not to submit to His will. Thus, he believes in full conscience in his obligation to nominate as Sovereign Pontiff of the Roman Catholic Church and the Bishop of Rome His Eminence the Archbishop of Turin, Cardinal Ettore Malvezzi.

The commotion that rises up from the assembly as soon as he has finished speaking appears to the chamberlain to be the reaction of people who are preparing to concede with dignity, and who feel great joy in doing so. The chamberlain looks around the room slowly, allowing the opinions and comments, the confidences and emotions to unfold freely, as is the privilege of a sovereign assembly when preparing to make a decision so important and so long in coming. But after more than forty years of consistories, capitular sessions, councils, synods, and assemblies, he has grown adept at measuring the pulse of his assembly. He has no doubts, for the first time, after so many months of uncertainty. He knows that finally, a unanimous decision has been reached. And as the supreme notary of the conclave, he is glad to see it; as a witness and instrument of the supreme will of God, it moves him to tears.

"*Fiat voluntas tua. Fiat voluntas tua,*" he says in a whisper, thinking that the man who will soon be proclaimed as pontiff will be his last pope. And his joy is heightened by a touch of the melancholy that stems from an awareness of the finiteness of all things. Even the conclave, which had seemed interminable, is now drawing to a close. Certainly, he will not live to see another.

Ettore Malvezzi, seated motionless in his room, staring at the yellow window that is no longer illuminated, has benefited by his absence from the elections. To no one else has the night's dream more clearly confirmed the destiny that is already unfolding for him.

Malvezzi's absence has exposed his terror at having to accept the candidacy to almost all of his colleagues, who view it not as an evasion of responsibility, but as a sign of genuine humility. The reason for his behavior has now been explained, and the providential design behind his malady, behind the obscure words mistaken for the ramblings of an idiot of God, has now been made clear in the minds of all the cardinals.

So when the chamberlain rises to propose the elevation to pope of Cardinal Ettore Malvezzi by acclamation, without the need for a vote, a shudder wends its way through the Sacred College in sudden recognition of what has just happened.

Soon after, everyone rises to his feet in confirmation of their unanimous consent. Cardinal Dean Antonio Leporati begins to sing the *Tu es Petrus* and is quickly joined by the rest of the cardinals. In accordance with the rituals of the conclave, all of the baldachins are lowered, with the exception of the one covering the cardinal of Turin's empty throne. Meanwhile, the chamberlain, anxious to acknowledge the new pope, is escorted by the cardinal scrutineers and the chaplain crucifer to Malvezzi's quarters to convey the news.

Veronelli enters Malvezzi's apartment and walks over to his study, finding the cardinal sitting in his chair, his eyes still fixed on the dark window across from him. Were it not for his deep breathing, making his chest rise and fall with increasing rapidity, it would seem as though he hadn't noticed that anyone had entered. Finally, a trembling Monsignor Contarini announces the chamberlain and his entourage.

"Most Eminent and Reverend Cardinal Ettore Malvezzi, in the name of Christ I hereby announce your election as Supreme Pontiff of the Universal Church and Bishop of Rome as inspired by the Holy Spirit and the Sacred College of cardinals."

A long silence ensues, followed by a nervous cough from the chamberlain, who must proceed with the formalities. His timorous, quavering voice is barely audible as he continues with the rite. "Do you accept?"

Cardinal Ettore Malvezzi rises to his feet. He seems taller, the cardinal dean thinks.

He turns with painstaking slowness toward the chamberlain, and stares at him with his large green eyes. His hands grip his pectoral cross tightly to conceal his nervousness. He moistens his lips and clears his throat several times, as if struggling to find his voice. "*Fiat,*" he says in a whisper, bowing his head and letting his arms fall to his sides.

"What name do you wish to bear?" Veronelli asks, almost shouting, unable to conceal his relief at Malvezzi's reply, which for a second he had feared wouldn't come.

"Lino Stefano."

There is a tremendous rustling of robes as everyone but the chamberlain and the crucifer kneels before him, and Ettore Malvezzi glances one last time to his left, toward the darkened window that had illuminated him until that day.

"So shall you be then. Lino Stefano I. Linus Stephen I." Veronelli replies, recalling that there had been popes in the past who had gone by the name Linus and others who had chosen the name Stephen, but never a pope who had used both names. When he kneels to kiss the right hand of the new pope after slipping the fisherman's ring on his finger, he sees once again the two angels who had appeared in his dream.

After orders have been given to open the balcony of Saint Peter's for the imminent *Habemus Papam*, and while the white smoke from the chimney in the Sistine Chapel is announcing the news to the world on Christmas Day, the chamberlain guides the new pontiff and his cortege toward the chapel, where the cardinals are waiting by his throne to proclaim their vows of obedience, once he has donned the white robe.

VENICE REVEALED
An Intimate Portrait
by Paolo Barbaro

ROME AND A VILLA
Memoir
by Eleanor Clark

The Adventures of
PINOCCHIO
Story of a Puppet
by Carlo Collodi

TORREGRECA
Life, Death, and Miracles
in a Southern Italian Village
by Ann Cornelisen

WOMEN OF THE SHADOWS
Wives and Mothers of Southern Italy
by Ann Cornelisen

THE TWENTY-THREE DAYS
OF THE CITY OF ALBA
by Beppe Fenoglio

ARTURO'S ISLAND
by Elsa Morante

HISTORY
by Elsa Morante

THE WATCH
by Carlo Levi

DARKNESS
Fiction
by Dacia Maraini

THE CONFORMIST
by Alberto Moravia

THE TIME OF INDIFFERENCE
by Alberto Moravia

TWO WOMEN
by Alberto Moravia

THE WOMAN OF ROME
by Alberto Moravia

LIFE OF MORAVIA
by Alberto Moravia and Alain Elkann

Claudia Roden's
THE FOOD OF ITALY
Region by Region

CUCINA DI MAGRO
Cooking Lean the Traditional Italian Way
by G. Franco Romagnoli

A THOUSAND BELLS AT NOON
A Roman's Guide to the Secrets and
Pleasures of His Native City
by G. Franco Romagnoli

THE ABRUZZO TRILOGY
by Ignazio Silone

MY NAME, A LIVING MEMORY
by Giorgio van Straten
(available in Fall 2003)

LITTLE NOVELS OF SICILY
by Giovanni Verga

OPEN CITY
Seven Writers in Postwar Rome
edited by William Weaver